NO ESCAPE

ALSO BY CASEY KELLEHER

THE LUCY MURPHY SERIES
No Escape

THE BYRNE FAMILY TRILOGY
The Betrayed
The Broken
The Forgotten

OTHER BOOKS BY CASEY KELLEHER
The Taken
The Promise
Rotten to the Core
Rise and Fall
Heartless
Bad Blood

NO ESCAPE

CASEY KELLEHER

bookouture

Published by Bookouture in 2020

An imprint of Storyfire Ltd.
Carmelite House
50 Victoria Embankment
London EC4Y 0DZ

www.bookouture.com

ISBN: 978-1-83888-698-1
eBook ISBN: 978-1-83888-697-4

No Escape *is dedicated to Heather Fitt*

Thank you so much for taking part in the Beyond the Pages online auction to win a signed copy of *Mine*, and to help raise money for the rural firefighters of QLD and NSW in Australia.

In loving memory of Irene Doyle

PROLOGUE

2000

'Get in the wardrobe.'

Ignoring her mother's instructions, the little girl shakes her head, wrapping her small fingers around the material of her mother's soft dressing gown instead. She clings on tightly, petrified to leave her mother's side.

'Do as you are told.' Jennifer Murphy's tone is urgent now and laced with panic. 'Get in there right now and stay quiet, don't make a sound. Do you hear me? And don't you dare come out! No matter what!'

Thud. Thud. Thud. The banging is louder, as if the walls around them are physically shaking. Any minute the front door is going to come crashing in.

'Now!' Jennifer commands.

Finally, the little girl does as she's told, her body trembling as she climbs inside, sinking down into the pile of clothing that adorns the wardrobe's floor, aware that something very bad is about to happen, as she stares up at her mother's stricken face.

Pale and sickly looking, Jennifer grabs at her large woollen coat before wrapping it over her daughter. Without saying another word, she slams the wardrobe door shut, plummeting the little girl into complete darkness.

She is scared of the dark. But all she can think about is her mother. So she takes a deep breath and peeks out from behind the thick material that she's hiding behind, immediately grateful as her eyes fix on the tiny slither of light that shines in through the small gap in the door.

She sees her mother dragging her dressing table across the bedroom with all of her might, struggling against the weight of it as all the expensive make-up and fancy bottles of perfumes that the little girl is forbidden to touch, that sit on the top, tip over and roll to the floor with each movement. Her mother doesn't care about them now.

Having wedged the dresser up against the bedroom door, in an attempt to keep the man out, Jennifer pauses. She stands deadly still, as if frozen to the spot.

The little girl notices it then too. How the flat has been plunged into a deathly silence. The banging stops. Which is far more terrifying than the loud noise before.

Because it means that whoever had been trying to get in must now be inside.

Footsteps. Her mother can hear them too, the child notes, seeing the look of sheer terror spread across her face as she stares over towards the wardrobe and places her finger in the middle of her lips, telling the little girl to stay quiet.

Obediently, the little girl nods, even though her mummy can't see her now.

'Get in the wardrobe with me, Mummy,' she tries to whisper in a last-ditch attempt to try and keep her mummy safe.

But the sound that lingers in the back of her throat is sucked back down inside her as the bedroom door crashes open, sending the dresser flying across the room. The little girl sees the man now, his whole body taking up the entire doorway. Her mother is talking, pleading and begging him to leave her alone. Only he doesn't leave her alone. He grabs her mummy by her hair and yanks her hard across the room as she claws desperately at his hands, trying to break free of his hold. But he is too big, too strong. She can't fight him off. He throws her down on the bed with terrifying force and starts punching her. Over and over and over again. And the little girl can't bear to look.

She is crying now, squeezing her eyes shut and sending silent tears running down her cheeks as she sinks further down, underneath the coat, welcoming the feel of it around her as it cocoons her small body. She is helpless. And she just wants to make it all go away. She wants to make the bad man go away. She wants him to leave her mummy alone.

Trying her hardest to do as her mummy told her, and stop her own screams, she forces the corner of her mother's coat sleeve inside her mouth to muffle any sound that might escape.

Biting down as her mummy's screams fill the room.

CHAPTER ONE

Trying to keep her balance, Michelle Winters hoisted herself up from the front room floor, gulping down the burning bile that rose in the back of her throat as she moved. She could barely stay upright.

The room was spinning violently now, as if uneven on its axis and she didn't stand a chance. Nauseous and dizzy, she plummeted back down to the floor with a thud, pressing her forehead against the carpet to steady herself, as a stringy trail of dribble dangled down from her mouth. The laughter behind her erupted even louder then. The men hysterical, revelling in her humiliation. Gary and his arsehole mates all taking great pleasure at the state she'd managed to get herself in. The state that Gary had purposely got her in more like. He'd drugged her.

She could hear him boasting proudly as the men all continued laughing at her expense, while she lay in the middle of the lounge floor, convinced that she was going to die.

'I slipped a little something in your drink, Shell. Didn't realise you were a lightweight, girl.' His tone was mocking, and his rowdy mates all thought it was hilarious. To them, she was nothing more than a joke. She needed to get away from them.

Dragging herself up on to her knees, she stared over towards her bedroom door. It was blurry and out of focus now, as if she were looking through a tinted lens. She was done with being Gary's entertainment for the night, she needed the solitude and the safety of her bed. She could make it. It wasn't far. She'd be okay after a sleep; she was sure of it.

She started crawling, ploughing her fingers into the carpet to gain momentum as she went, ignoring the chorus of chants and jeers behind her, willing their voices to melt into the background as she moved. She was at her lowest ebb. He'd done that to her. Gary. Making her way along the hallway on her hands and knees she cursed him now. Deep down she knew that he was no good for her. That he used her at every opportunity. And for the most part, it suited her that way. Because she used him right back. All she really wanted these days was the drink and the gear. She had no use for a man. She just wanted to feel better for a short while, to block out some of the pain inside of her, and Gary supplied that to her in abundance. The numbness that she'd so badly craved. The much-needed oblivion.

At first she'd mistaken his generosity for kindness, convincing herself that he wouldn't be like the other leeches and the hangers-on that she was used to. But he was just like the rest of them. And Michelle had no real leverage over him, not really. Gary wasn't really interested in her, not like that. They'd slept together a few times, at the start, when they'd both played the obligatory cat and mouse game of reeling each other in, pretending they were different people to what they really were. These days there was no pretence: Gary had only ever wanted a place to stay. He told her now that she disgusted him. That she was old and haggard, a useless drunk.

He couldn't bear to look at her, he'd said one night and admitted to her that that was why he fed her with drink and drugs, so that she'd pass out and go to bed. He'd have free rein of the flat that way too.

Reaching her bedroom, she stopped still on all fours, her face pressing hard against the wooden panel of the bedroom door, as she reached up for the handle. She pushed the door open with more force than she realised she could muster and groaned loudly as it slammed off the wall, bouncing back and hitting her hard in the face. Immediately her head started pounding. She'd have a bruise there tomorrow. For now, she just needed to get into her bed.

Slowly she made her way across the bare floorboards, the coarse wood pressing hard against her knees. She wondered when she'd become like this. Because she'd been 'normal' once, years ago, when Shannon and Kian had been small.

She'd done everything the right way, determined to do right by her kids and to prove everyone wrong who had doubted her or chastised her for being a single mother: all the people who had whispered behind her back about how she'd ruined her life by getting pregnant so young, or those who had said she'd never become anything more now. And for a while she'd done a good job, working every hour that God sent so that she could pay all her bills on time and put food on the table. She'd done whatever she'd had to do, to bring in the money, cleaning the local school's toilets by day and working behind a grotty bar at night. But there always seemed to be more money going out than she could bring back in. And soon she'd started begging money off Peter to pay back Paul.

Patting the duvet that dangled down from the mattress, Michelle wrapped the blanket around her wrist and used it to pull herself up onto the bed, before throwing herself down on the mattress and staring up at the ceiling. Fresh tears welled in her eyes as she thought about Shaun Riley and his sick, twisted ways. She'd been warned about taking money from his type.

He was a loan shark, notorious for getting his money back, any way he pleased. He'd charmed her, and she'd always intended to pay him back, so she stupidly hadn't listened to the warnings and found out to her cost that men like Shaun Riley were a law unto themselves. Because when she didn't have the money for him, and she couldn't pay him back, he had made her pay in other ways.

Preying on the desperate, vulnerable mother that he'd seen in her back then, Shaun Riley had taken full advantage of her, showing up at her flat whenever he got the urge, twice, sometimes three times a week. And he never cared if Michelle hadn't yet put her kids to bed, or whether she was sick or too tired. It had all been on his terms. It had taken her two years to clear that debt and by then the damage had been well and truly done. There had been nothing much left of the old Michelle by then.

She'd given up on everything after that, resigning herself to her flat, unable to step outside without suffering the onslaught of debilitating panic attacks. She'd had to learn to survive in other ways. First depending on the social for benefits so that she could pay her bills, then later, knowing how easy men could be manipulated, how eager they were for sex, deciding to use them right back. And for a while it had worked, going from man to man and promising them the world, in return for them giving her some money here and there to pay for things.

Drink mainly, and sometimes something more medicinal to help take the edge off. And as the years had passed, Michelle had become more and more bitter as she poured more and more drink down her throat, allowing it to ruin her. And the men that she kept company with could all see it too. Her raw desperation. Her need of them. She'd been forced to lower her standards, and accept whatever dregs had come her way. Only Gary might be the worst of the lot as it turned out.

Squeezing her eyes shut then, as if to try and shut out the truth, Michelle thought of Shannon. She'd seen the way that Gary looked at her daughter. The way he couldn't stop his gaze from sweeping every inch of her perfect little figure. Linger for just those few seconds longer than he should each time. Deep down Michelle knew that made her a much more disgusting person than Gary would ever be. Because she knew he lusted after her young daughter and yet she'd never once asked him to leave. She felt sick then. The hot bile burned at the back of her throat as the room continued spinning. Michelle stared up at the light shade, praying that the feeling would pass, while wondering what the bastard had given her this time.

Because he was getting worse. More lethal, more daring, mixing things up a bit and adding more to the potent concoctions that he fed her. She closed her eyes, feeling herself slipping into the oblivion that she'd been willing to come. Her last thought was that one day he might go too far. Maybe it would be an accident, or maybe he'd do it on purpose. But one day, Gary Miller might just kill her.

CHAPTER TWO

'The walk-in's all done, Benny! Though, to be fair, we only did a deep clean on the fridge on Wednesday. You could eat your chips off the floor in there now!' Shannon quipped, taking her rubber gloves off and throwing them in the bin.

'Well, you never know when the old Food and Standards Agency will rear their ugly heads, do you? Springing one of their surprise inspections on me when I'm least expecting it. Better to be safe than sorry!' Benny Lynch reasoned as he finished cashing up the till, before handing Shannon the envelope he'd put by for her.

'There you go. There's a few quid extra in there, too. The customers obviously like you. I never get this many tips when I'm here on my own.' Benny winked, closing the till, before untying his overalls and slipping his hat off, glad that the shift was over and they could both go home. He decided to keep the fact that they'd actually made a loss tonight to himself.

It was to be expected really. Sunday evenings were for good intentions. Most people didn't gorge on fish and chips, after spending the entire weekend eating their body weight in junk food. But there was normally just enough business to justify him opening the place for a few hours. Only the truth was, he couldn't justify paying Shannon's wages too. Now, with the shop's overheads on top, Benny hadn't made a penny tonight. He'd have been better off staying at home with Anita and the girls. Not that Benny would ever admit that to Shannon, of course.

'Well, you know, Benny,' Shannon smiled, taking the money gratefully and shoving it into her bag, 'customers just can't resist my obvious beauty and charm.' She gestured sarcastically down to her stained overalls, well aware of the greasy mess she must look right now after spending the evening divided between working over the hot, oily fryers and scrubbing the fridge floor on her hands and knees.

'That must be it!' Benny said with a shrug, shaking his head at Shannon's humour. He decided that he wouldn't even tell Anita that he'd let Shannon work tonight. His wife would skin him alive after the last conversation they'd had about it. Because as much as Anita was in favour of him helping Shannon out from time to time, she also felt that Benny needed reminding that they weren't a charity either. But how could he refuse the girl, especially when he'd heard the desperation in her voice when Shannon had asked him for any extra shifts that might be going over the next few weeks?

She'd tried to hide it, of course – Shannon was too proud to beg for help – but Benny knew that the girl was struggling and that she needed help. She didn't want to earn cash for the usual crap that teenage girls spent their money on, make-up and magazines and the odd cheeky bottle of cider that they could take down the park with their friends at the weekend. Shannon wanted the money so that she could help her mum out. And by God, that woman needed all the help she could get.

Benny knew Michelle Winters from his school days. Michelle had seemed nice enough back then, but he guessed that life had found a way to grind the woman down. Benny had almost not recognised the woman on the few occasions he'd clocked her making her way past the chippy late at night on her way back home from the pub, staggering uneasily on her feet, hanging around with all the no-marks that frequented the Red Fox at the end of the parade. The usual suspects that sat around propping up the bar all week, or at least until their benefits money ran out.

'Same time tomorrow?' Shannon asked as she pulled her jacket on and looked at Benny expectantly, interrupting his thoughts. He knew that he should say no. Mondays were even quieter than they had been tonight.

He should just be honest with Shannon and tell her that he couldn't afford to give her anymore shifts until business picked up a bit. But he just couldn't bring himself to let her down.

'Yeah. Same time tomorrow, Shan,' he said, smiling back at her and nodding, unable to help but admire the young girl's work ethic. Wherever she got it from, it certainly wasn't from her mother, that was for sure.

'Here, you might as well take this lot home with you, too. It will only go to waste otherwise. And you know I can't bear throwing food out,' Benny said, casually, holding out the food that he'd deliberately kept back for Shannon to take home tonight for her and her brother.

'Are you sure, Benny?' Shannon said gratefully, peeping inside the bag and spotting her brother's favourites, sausage in batter and a steak pie.

Benny nodded. 'Yeah, course. Otherwise it will only end up in the bin. Or worse still, I'll end up eating it and, trust me, you'll be doing me a favour, because I could really do without the extra calories. Kian's favourites too, ain't they?' Shannon nodded gratefully, suspecting that Benny had cooked the food especially for her. He always gave her a few extra pounds in her wages, or loaded her up with a big bag of food to take home with her at the end of the shift.

'That's if he even bothers to come home tonight,' Shannon said, letting on what had been on her mind all evening.

Benny had sensed something was up. 'Is everything okay with the kid?' he asked raising his eyebrows questioningly, knowing not to pry.

'I guess…' Shannon shrugged. 'He's been staying out till all hours lately and he's started being secretive with me about stuff.'

'And how old is he again?' Benny grinned, knowingly.

'Thirteen.'

'Yeah that sounds about right. I bet I know exactly what he's up to then…'

'You do?' Shannon said, seeing the smirk plastered across Benny's face.

She was worried that Kian was up to no good. That he might have got caught up with people who would get him into trouble. There were so many gangs knocking around the estate these days, and Kian had started acting so out of character the past few weeks. He wasn't normally so secretive about where he'd been or who he'd been with, and whenever Shannon questioned him, it more often than not turned into an argument.

'Sounds to me like he's got himself a girlfriend,' Benny said, tapping his nose as if he'd just let Shannon in on the world's biggest secret. 'I mean, that's about when it starts, isn't it? About that age. I remember my first girlfriend. Samantha Jones. God, I was only twelve and I was completely besotted with her. Always late home for my tea and never wanting to spend time with my family anymore. My whole world revolved around only her. Drove my mother mad it did. Luckily for my mum, it didn't last very long, as I caught her snogging my mate, Jimmy, behind the bike sheds at school. The girl had been playing us off against each other the whole time. Jeez, I almost got in a punch-up because of her. My mother said I had a lucky escape at the time, but the truth was she'd broken my heart.'

'A girlfriend? Kian? Do you think?' The thought of Kian having a girlfriend hadn't even crossed Shannon's mind. Maybe this was the age that Kian would start showing more of an interest in girls. And it would certainly explain a lot. Like where he'd been sneaking off to most evenings, and why he was always so late home and never wanted to tell Shannon where he'd been or who he'd been with. 'I hope you're right, Benny,' Shannon said, sounding more hopeful. 'I was starting to worry that he'd got in with a bad lot.' She grinned then too. 'Who'd have thought, my little brother is all loved-up, huh!'

'I'd put money on it.' He winked then. 'And your Uncle Benny is always right, you remember that!' Then throwing Shannon the bag of food he added, 'And don't forget to take this lot home for Romeo. He'll be needing all his energy from now on too.'

'Eww, Benny! That's gross!' Shannon laughed. Grabbing the package of food tightly with one hand she blew Benny a kiss with the other as the man held the door open for her and saw her out.

'See you tomorrow night,' Shannon called out just before Benny shut the door behind her.

Hurrying off to get home before the food went cold, Shannon felt a lot happier now that she'd spoken to Benny about her brother. She hoped that he was right. A girlfriend would be a much better distraction than the alternatives that Shannon had been imagining.

CHAPTER THREE

'Mum?' Peering into her mother's darkened bedroom, Shannon instantly recoiled as the potent, sour stench of sick hit her with its full force. Covering her nose, she reluctantly stepped inside, hoping that her mother had at least managed to aim into a bucket, and not covered herself and the entire bed in sick like she had last time Shannon had found her.

'Are you okay, Mum?' she said again through the darkness, her voice louder this time, hoping that the sound of her voice would wake her mother, because at least then she'd know if she was all right. Knowing how badly her mother suffered with frequent migraines, Shannon knew better than to turn the light on and startle her when she was already feeling sick. Though Shannon was old enough and wise enough these days to know that 'migraines' were really code for her mother drinking herself into a stupor once again. And the chances that her mother had been in any right mind to even think about taking a bucket to bed with her were slim to none, going by the state she usually got herself into.

'I just finished my shift at the chippy, Mum. Benny gave me a few extra hours this week,' Shannon said, holding her breath as she spoke so that she wouldn't gag as she stepped carefully around the edge of the bed, praying that she didn't step in anything disgusting. She could just about make out her mother's silhouette through the darkness. Shannon was pleased her mother had at least made it to the bed this time. She normally found her sprawled out somewhere on the floor downstairs.

'Mum? Can you hear me? It's me, Shan.' Her mother didn't move. Shannon stared for a few minutes, too scared to even reach out a hand and touch the woman, as the familiar sensation of anxiety rippled away inside of her as she wondered if this was it. If this was the moment that she'd find her mother dead. She leant in closer, her heart pounding inside her chest. She could feel the tears forming in her eyes. Her hand trembled as she forced herself to reach out and touch her mother's arm. Her skin still warm.

The sudden movement made her mother almost waken. Letting out a low murmur, the woman turned her head, her eyes flickering open as she took in the sight of her daughter at her bedside.

'Oh, thank God!' Shannon breathed a huge sigh of relief, just as her mother let out a strangled gurgle from the back of her throat. Her body was suddenly convulsing.

'Shit!' Too comatose to move, she was choking on her own vomit, Shannon realised as she rapidly pulled her mother onto her side, placing her into the recovery position, before expertly inserting two fingers inside her mouth to clear her airways, just before her mother projectile vomited all over both her and the floor at the side of the bed.

'It's okay, Mum, you're going to be okay.' Shannon tried to keep the panic from her voice as she tried to soothe her mother, who continued to retch violently until there was nothing left inside of her. It was over quickly. Incoherent, Michelle slumped back down on the mattress and closed her eyes as if nothing had happened. Shannon sat down next to her, exhausted now, and relieved that she'd paid attention at school when they'd been taught first aid.

She'd been right to take note that day, when all of her eight- and nine-year-old classmates had been messing about and laughing at the ridiculous-looking plastic dummy that the school had provided for them to practise CPR on, the boys all refusing to put their lips on Resusci Annie, because their fellow classmates had kissed her before them. Only Shannon had listened intently to the instructions. Because even at that young age she had known first-hand how scary it was to find someone you loved unconscious. And she'd used the techniques often since.

She dreaded to think what would have happened if she hadn't been here tonight. She could hear Gary and his mates out in the lounge, their loud, jovial voices floating up the stairs as if they didn't have so much as a care in the world. And they probably didn't. Gary wouldn't have given two shits about the state that her mother had been left in. In fact, Shannon would be willing to bet her life on the fact that the man wouldn't even have bothered to check on her, not once tonight. Too busy entertaining his mates and acting the big I am. The man was such a selfish bastard.

Scraping back the long dark strands of hair away from her mother's face, Shannon tried to picture how she used to look. When she was little, Shannon had always said that she'd looked like an angel. She meant it, too. Shannon had never seen anyone prettier. Her mother always had poker-straight dark brown hair, so long that it went all the way down to her bottom. Her eyes were a bright sparkly blue and always kind. These days her mother's eyes always seemed vacant and bloodshot. The drink had destroyed her over time, turning her into a shadow of her former self. Her once beautiful hair was now lank and greasy and stuck to her head. And it stank. Just like she did and this bedroom, of sick and body odour.

Shannon stroked her mother's hair as she sat at Michelle's side and fretted about things that a fifteen-year-old girl shouldn't have to worry herself about. No matter how much she pretended that she'd become immune to finding her mother in such states, the truth was, she could never switch off the fear. One day, her mother wouldn't be so lucky, and Shannon might find her dead. That scared her more than anything. Holding back the tears that threatened to fall, Shannon was annoyed with herself for being so weak. She was angry too, not just for herself, but for Kian.

This drunken mess of a mother was all that her brother had ever known. He was too young to ever remember a time when she had been normal. It was the mess, the chaos, the destruction that were the norm to him. Shannon had had to grow up. She was the one who had to look out for him. Shaking her head sadly, Shannon saw her mother shiver and a spray of raised goose bumps prickle on her skin. Pulling the bed sheet up around her to shield her from the cold, she doubted her mother would even feel it really. She doubted her mother felt much at all these days.

But then, that was the point of all of this, wasn't it? The reason why she got herself in such a state in the first place was so that she wouldn't have to feel anything anymore. And she had been getting worse lately. Ever since her mother had met Gary, it was as if she had been sucked down inside some deep, dark vortex and she had no way of clawing her way back out again. It was as if she was completely lost.

'You're going to be okay, Mum, I'm here. I'll look after you,' Shannon whispered softly, before eyeing the trail of vomit that dripped down the side of the mattress and formed a pool all over the floor next to her. The acrid liquid was already seeping its way down into the bare floorboards. Shannon needed to clean it, otherwise the smell would linger for weeks, and the whole flat would stink of regurgitated cheap cider mixed with what little amount of food her mother had bothered to consume the last few days. And let's face it, she thought, as she hauled herself up onto her feet, mentally preparing for the clean-up job, no one else was going to volunteer to do it.

CHAPTER FOUR

'Here she is, my little Shan-Shan!' Standing purposely in Shannon's way, blocking the doorway to the kitchen, Gary Miller chuckled to himself triumphantly as Shannon was forced to brush up against him as she made her way towards the sink.

'Oh, steady on, darling! Are you making a pass at me?' Gary laughed purposely, knowing full well he was pushing his luck now that Michelle had taken herself off to bed. He loved nothing more than winding Shannon up. And the girl didn't disappoint. Going by her stony expression and the way she was pretending to ignore him, Gary knew that he was getting to her.

'You got the hump or something?' Gary continued, not bothering to hide the lust from his face as his eyes roamed Shannon's figure. Catching her eye, he blatantly licked his lips, then smirked again when he saw the disgust spread across her face.

'I'm fifteen,' Shannon reminded him sternly. 'And you're a dirty *old* man. God knows what my mother sees in you.' She fought to keep the tremor from her voice. Gary was drunk, too. And he was well aware that her mum must be in a bad way, because he'd never be so blatant otherwise. As much of the man's shit as her mother put up with, she'd never stand for him talking to Shannon like this.

'You want to be careful my mum doesn't hear you talking to me like that!' Shannon said, refusing to let Gary get the better of her. She hoped that the mention of her mother would pull him back down to reality. It was even worse when she came home in her school uniform when Gary and his pervy mates were here because they always made lewd comments about her. Deliberately trying to intimidate and belittle her was all part of Gary's twisted mentality. And tonight it was working.

'You need to chill out, Shan, and get a sense of humour. I was just messing with you. Jeez, you're far too serious for a girl your age, you know. Why don't you come and have a drink with us?' Gary said, holding out his can of beer as if it was some kind of peace offering.

Shannon rolled her eyes. 'I'd rather drink my own piss than share a can with you, Gary,' she muttered, turning her back on the man and busying herself filling up a bucket of hot water and bleach. It didn't matter how many times she tried to fend off Gary, nothing seemed to deter the man. Not even the threats of her telling her mother, because the last time she'd tried to talk to her mother about Gary's unwanted advances, she hadn't received the response she'd hoped for.

He's got bloody eyes in his head, Shan! What do you want me to do about it? Pluck them out? If it bothers you that much that he's gawping at you, maybe you should cover yourself up a bit more. He is a man, after all.

Shannon didn't know why she had expected any different. Since then, she'd learned to keep her mouth shut, because she knew her mother had repeated their conversation to Gary and Gary had lapped it up. He'd got worse after that, as if he'd been given free rein to say and do as he pleased. Relishing in causing her untold misery, Gary was constantly at her now: purposely blocking her way when she was trying to leave the bathroom in the mornings, his eyes lingering on her towelled body just those few seconds longer than they should have. Or, like tonight, he'd 'accidentally' rub himself up against her, as he passed her in the flat's narrow galley kitchen. Or he'd force her to push past him, which was even worse.

'I take it you've seen the state my mum's in?'

'Now, that's a bit bitchy, Shan! I mean, I know she's getting on a bit, sure. But she tries, bless her!' Gary cackled at his own wit as his friends joined in with the laughter. Shannon shook her head, clenching her fists tightly to her sides so that she didn't pick up the bucket of bleach and launch it at the man, as he and his mates all laughed at her mother's expense.

'She could have died tonight. She was choking on her own vomit when I went in to check on her!' Shannon's tone was sharp, her glare loaded with hate. 'Don't you care about her at all?'

'Course I care!' Gary's body language contradicted his words as he shrugged nonchalantly before making his way to the fridge and helping himself to another can of beer. Which only confirmed what she was already well aware of, that Gary didn't care about her mother one bit.

'What did you give her?'

'Oi, don't go blaming me if your mother can't handle her drink! She's a big girl, Shan, and I ain't her babysitter. Your mother ain't exactly picky these days; she'd probably give that bleach a go if she thought it would help her lose her head for a bit,' Gary said with a smirk, nodding over at his mates, who all chuckled as if they'd just been let in on a private joke. He'd given her something he shouldn't have. Shannon was certain of it.

'She could have died, Gary. She could be in there now, dead on that bed. She was choking on her vomit!' Shannon reiterated, raising her voice now as she shook visibly with anger, though she knew it was no good. Even if Gary did realise the severity of the situation, he didn't care. And nothing Shannon said would make him.

'Well, shit then, Shan, it's lucky you came home when you did, huh! Like fate or something. An angel.' His tone was loaded with sarcasm. 'Just in time to clean it all up, too! I was wondering what that stink was!'

Placing the bucket down on the kitchen side, Shannon turned the tap off, before allowing her gaze to rest on the knife holder that sat next to the draining board. How easy it would be to grab a knife and plunge it into Gary's chest. To shut him up once and for all. To wipe him off the planet. Blinking back her tears, she cursed herself silently for not having the guts to actually do it.

'You brought back some grub from the chippy, did you? I'm bloody starving,' Gary said then, making a grab for the bag of chips that Shannon had left on the kitchen side.

'Oi, I got them for Kian!' Shannon protested, trying to grab the bag from him, but Gary was too quick. Tearing his way into the wrappings, he scooped a large handful of hot chips into his mouth before continuing speaking with his mouth full.

'Well, Kian ain't home, so it would be a shame to see this lot go to waste.'

'Did he say where he was going?' Shannon asked, distracted from the food. She looked up at the clock and saw that it had gone eleven now. So much for Kian sticking to the agreed curfew of ten p.m. Shannon should have known he wouldn't keep his promise. And what made it worse was that he knew how she worried about him if he was late home.

'How the fuck should I know where the kid is? I ain't his keeper! Fucking hell. You lot really need to start communicating better with each other,' Gary sneered sarcastically, before picking up the sausage in batter and mimicking a lewd act with it as his mates all laughed in unison, licking it slowly with his tongue before stuffing it down his throat, enjoying the obvious disgust written all over Shannon's face as she glared at him. He finally bit into the sausage like a hungry animal and ate with his mouth open, the food sticking to his yellowing teeth.

'I hope you choke!' Shannon muttered to herself, grabbing the bucket of bleach and cleaning rags and stomping past the man before she said or did something she really regretted.

'Well, if I do, at least I'll be in safe hands with you here, eh Mother-fucking-Teresa! Maybe you could give me mouth-to-mouth or something. The kiss of life, that's what they call it, isn't it, Shan?' Gary called out, as Shannon made her way back into her mother's bedroom, screwing up her nose at the rancid sickly stench that seemed to have got worse since she'd left the room.

Now, it was so acrid, so overpowering that it made her eyes water. Kneeling down next to her mother's body, Shannon pulled on a pair of rubber gloves and dipped both hands into the bleach and water, before making a start on mopping up all the sick, vowing to herself as she cleaned that she'd never become anything like this woman sprawled out on the bed in front of her.

Shannon Winters wanted more for herself. She wanted better than this, and she'd have it, too. One day she'd take her brother out of this life and away from this estate. Away from the likes of Gary and his mates. If it was the very last thing she did.

CHAPTER FIVE

Stepping on to the train at Clapham Junction, Kian Winters slumped down in the seat before glancing behind him and spotting the two lads from earlier, both taking a seat further down the carriage. They were looking directly at him, neither of them bothering to divert their gaze when Kian's eye caught theirs. They were doing it on purpose. Watching him. Following him.

And they wanted him to know it, too. It was all part of their game. They were trying to intimidate him, and as much as Kian was trying to play it cool, it was working. Turning back around to face the other way, Kian squeezed his eyes shut and swore under his breath. *Shit!*

Pushing the envelope full of money deeper down into the inside pocket of his jacket, Kian pulled the zip up tightly and glanced at the train doors, debating whether or not to make a run for it before the train started moving. Only he wasn't quick enough. The train doors closed and it pulled away from the platform. He was almost home now anyway. Wandsworth Common was the next stop; he'd do a runner then.

Glancing out of the corner of his eyes he guessed both boys were a couple of years older than him, around fifteen or so. They were dressed in tracksuits and baseball caps, with their hoods pulled up to conceal their faces. He'd spotted them both earlier, at Horsham station, where he'd met with the contact and made the drop. But Kian hadn't thought anything of it then; instead, he'd been too busy watching out for the Old Bill and making sure that no one clocked him. He'd felt smug with himself that his first drop had gone so well. In fact, he'd almost convinced himself that working for Jax Priestly and his gang, the Griffin Boys, was turning out to be easy money.

The worst part had been meeting the contact at Horsham station. Fronting it out, Kian had acted as if he'd done drops like this a thousand times before, when really, inside he'd been shitting himself. But he knew that this was all part of his initiation. Today was a test. Jax had sent him out on his own for the very first time so that Kian could prove himself worthy.

If he wanted an in, then he needed to earn his place and his keep, Jax had said. Just like the rest of the Griffin Boys had. And it felt good being referred to as one of the Griffin Boys. It made Kian feel as if he belonged somewhere, as if he was part of something so much bigger than himself. Dangerous and scary and exciting all at once.

And Kian had seen the wealth of goods that Jax's boys all raked in. He knew how much money they made from doing the regular runs for Jax. 'Going Country' as Jax referred to it when he sent them all out on drops at stations just outside of London. It was hardly a difficult task, sitting on a train for most of the day before dropping off one envelope and picking up another. The other boys had all been reaping the benefits for months now. Flashing the newest iPhones and the latest designer trainers, and Kian wanted a bit of that for himself.

Not just for himself, but for his mother and his sister, too. Shannon was doing her best to hold everything together by working extra shifts at the chippy on the estate, but she was hardly breaking the bank with the few quid she managed to bring in, and they couldn't pay the rent with leftover battered sausages. The bills were mounting up. It was only a matter of time before they cut off the electricity and gas again, or worse still, they got kicked out of the flat for not keeping up with the rent. This was Kian's time to step up and show his family that he could look after them. That he was the man of the house. Then maybe his mother wouldn't feel the need to depend on leeches like Gary. There was a lot hanging on today, and Kian was sure that he'd proved his worth so far. He'd done good.

Jax had been right. The police wouldn't suspect that a thirteen-year-old boy would be making a drug's deal. They hadn't even looked at him twice as he'd walked past a couple of coppers hanging around outside the front of the station. They were too busy looking out for older, more suspicious-looking passengers or groups of lads. And Jax had warned him that even if the worst happened and he did get caught with a package on him, he was a minor. The police wouldn't be able to do jack shit to him. Jax had boasted that police didn't have a clue what they were dealing with. That they didn't have the resources and they had no idea how high up these enterprises went. Or who the really bad men were at the top of the food chain. That was the genius of it all.

They were calling it County Lines on the news. A pandemic of knife crime and drug dealing. Every time Kian turned the TV on lately there was some news piece about young kids from the boroughs being used by gangs as drug mules. They were saying that boys and girls, like him, were being tricked into a murky life of crime. That they were often manipulated and threatened. Forced to do these jobs against their own wills. But it wasn't like that at all. Kian had wanted in. He'd purposely chosen this life. And all Jax had done was given him the golden opportunity to become one of the boys who went out of London to do their drops in the quieter, more rural locations, cashing in on the rich, bored teenagers who lived in sleepy villages on the outskirts of London, with too much money and nothing better to kill their time with but getting high. It was easy. A few hours on a train, you kept your mouth shut and your head down and after a quick exchange of packages, it was job done. All Kian had to do now was get the money back to Jax.

But suddenly that didn't seem as if it was going to be as easy as he'd first thought. Not if these two lads were tailing him like he was beginning to suspect. Pulling the burner phone that Jax had given him earlier from his pocket, Kian dialled the number. At least he had a backup plan. If Jax and his boys got a move on, they could meet him at the station. The Griffin Boys would sort these two lads out, no problem. Jax had said that they were all family now, as good as blood. They'd look out for each other. Only he wasn't answering the phone.

Come on, come on! Kian pleaded silently as the phone rang out without giving him any option of leaving a voice message. He bit his lip. Jax had instructed him to only use the phone if there was an emergency, so why the fuck wasn't he answering it? Rubbing his head, he placed the phone back inside his pocket and stared out of the window. These lads must be after the money. They must have seen him doing the drop at the earlier station and fancied their chances at trying their luck. Why else would they be following him? Wracking his brain to try and think back to the drop, Kian was sure that he'd been discreet. That he'd kept his head, doing everything exactly like Jax had told him to do, executing their plan to perfection despite the hammering inside his chest and his sweaty palms as he swapped the package full of gear for an envelope full of money. The actual exchange had taken all of five seconds and neither Kian nor Jax's dealer had even spoken to each other. Unless Kian was just being paranoid and the whole thing was in his head.

Seeing the platform approach as the train slowed down, Kian turned his head to check, flinching as he saw the boys still staring in his direction. Then an elderly lady dragged her shopping trolley past the two boys' seats, blocking the aisle between them and him. Kian psyched himself, knowing that if he ran as soon as the doors opened, he'd buy himself a few seconds' head start. Jumping from his seat as soon as the train pulled in at the station, Kian sprinted out of the doors and along the platform at record speed.

He leapt down the station's steps two at a time, grateful that despite being a Sunday evening there were still plenty of people all milling about the busy station, hopeful then that he could lose the boys amongst the crowds. Seeing the ticket barrier just ahead, and the ticket collector standing close by, Kian didn't bother getting his ticket out of his pocket. He'd bought one after Jax had explained that they had to do everything by the book. That he wasn't to draw any unwanted attention to himself. *Pay your fare, and keep your head down.* Only now Kian had no other choice.

Jumping the barrier, he continued to run for his life, ignoring the irate voice that bellowed after him. The second bellow sent a jolt of fear right through him, because he knew, even without turning back to look, that the two lads must be hot on his heels. Reaching the station exit, Kian welcomed the cool rush of air that hit him as he made it outside and raced across the busy Wandsworth road towards the entrance of the common opposite. He didn't see the car as it plummeted towards him. Slamming its brakes hard, it screeched to a halt in the middle of the road, just inches from Kian. He stumbled, placing his hands down on the car's bonnet to steady himself. Quickly mouthing sorry to the elderly female driver, he continued running onto the common. The Griffin Estate loomed above him just across the back of the field, lit up now in all its glory under the blanket of darkness. The towers stood twinkling with a thousand lights that masked the poverty, rot and decay that the harsh daylight couldn't. He was almost home.

Only, he was running out of steam. He had been sprinting so fast that his sides burned as a stitch seared through him. His lungs were gasping for air, feeling so tight that they might explode. He forced himself not to look back. If he turned now, even for just a few seconds, it would only slow him down and he needed every second that he had to outrun these lads.

Staring up at the row of windows as he pelted towards the tower block, he tried to work out which flat was Philip's. Maybe one of the boys would be looking out for him? They'd see he was in trouble. Only it was dark now, and the chances of one of the boys clocking him from up there didn't seem likely.

'Shit!' Kian yelped, just as his foot hit a loose clump of mud, and sent his body sailing forward and slamming down to the ground. He tried to drag himself back up quickly onto his feet. But it was too late.

The boys were on him. A rock-hard fist slammed into the back of his head, sending him plummeting back down again before he winced at the punt of a trainer. The two boys were attacking him. Punching and kicking repeatedly, showing him no mercy as he screamed out in pain. Kian had no way of fighting back. Jax had offered him a knife, but Kian had refused to take it. And even now he was glad about that, because he would never have had the guts to actually use it. And the chances were, if these lads had clocked it, they would have taken it from him and used it on him first. A kicking would have been the least of his worries then.

Curling into a ball on the ground as the blows kept coming, he cradled his head in his hands in order to try and protect himself. He could taste the metallic tang of blood at the back of his throat. He felt as if he were going to pass out. In fact, part of him hoped that he would. Because then he wouldn't be able to feel the pain anymore. Squeezing his eyes shut as one of the boys leant over him, Kian flinched as he felt the zip of his jacket get tugged down.

The older boy reached inside and made a grab for the envelope of money and the burner phone. And then as quickly as it started, the attack stopped. Both boys made a run for it.

Staring up at the dark night sky above him, Kian let out a loud groan of pain and fought back his tears. He'd thought that he was going to die. Taking a few minutes to get his breath back properly Kian carefully started dragging himself back onto his feet, wincing in pain with every movement as he began to make the rest of the journey across the common. His body felt as if it were on fire but, worse than that, they'd taken the money. Jax was going to be fuming when he found out. Kian just hoped that once he saw the state he was in, he'd take his anger out on the two lads who attacked him and not him.

CHAPTER SIX

As she drummed her bitten-down fingernails against the worn grain of the kitchen table and stared up at the kitchen clock, Shannon didn't care if she woke Gary up from where he lay, currently passed out on the sofa. In fact, she hoped that she did. Because the sight of him lying there with his mouth wide open, a deep rattling snore filling the room, as if he didn't have a care in the world, made her so angry that she felt capable of smothering him. Gary had become a permanent fixture these days, managing to weld his feet firmly under the table. He stayed here most nights, regardless of the state her mother was in, as tonight had only proved.

It had taken ages for Shannon to get rid of his freeloading mates too, all lounging around in the front room, drinking the rest of Gary's cider and helping themselves to all his fags whilst he lay unconscious on the sofa beside them. They'd only left after Shannon literally had to spell it out to them that Gary had passed out drunk and it was time for them all to bugger off to their own homes. And even then one of the men had still had the cheek to try his luck with her, telling her that she was very pretty and that if she wanted to make a bit of extra money, he had much quicker and more lucrative ways for her to do so than by working every night in the local chippy. Following Gary's example, no doubt. Shannon had cringed as the man had winked at her before licking the spittle from his crooked, twisted mouth. She couldn't shut the front door quickly enough behind them all, and had pulled the chain across for good measure, just in case he got any funny ideas and decided to come back.

So now she was forced to sit up and wait for Kian to get home so she could let him in, and, truth be told, even if she hadn't put the chain on the door, she still wouldn't have been able to sleep until she knew that he'd got home safely. It had gone midnight now and there was still no sign of him, and Shannon was genuinely worried because as much as her brother had been pushing his luck lately, coming home a little later every night, he'd never stayed out this late. Not when he had school tomorrow. She thought about calling the police, but quickly banished that fleeting thought from her head. Getting the police involved would only make things worse. She couldn't risk having that lot poking their noses around the flat and finding their mum in the state that she was in. And no doubt Gary would have some gear stashed about the place too. The Old Bill would love that, wouldn't they? They'd say that her and Kian were at risk again. They'd threaten to take them both away like they did last time. Knowing that she didn't have anyone else she could ask for help, Shannon decided that she'd have to go out and search for her brother herself. Grabbing her jumper and her trainers, she was just about to leave when she heard his key in the lock.

'For fuck's sake!' Kian muttered, attempting to push the door open as it bounced off the chain.

'Oh, I'm sorry! Bit of an inconvenience, is it? Me locking the front door before I go to bed?' Shannon said sarcastically, rushing over to unlock the door and let her brother in, her initial concern about her brother instantly turning to anger now that Kian was home safe and sound.

'It's almost half past midnight, Kian. I've been waiting up for you. You know you're supposed to be home by ten. We agreed.

You're taking the piss, Kian…' Pulling the door open, Shannon faltered, losing her words mid-sentence as she caught sight of the state her brother was in. She stared in horror at the blood smeared across his battered, swollen face.

'I'm fine. It looks worse than it is,' Kian said unconvincingly as he hobbled into the flat, clutching his side, doubled over in pain.

'You're not fine at all! What happened to you, Kian?' Shannon cried, unable to stop the tears springing to her eyes at the shock of seeing her brother in such a state. She hated seeing him in so much pain.

'I was jumped by some kids. It's no biggy,' Kian said, leaning on the kitchen table to steady himself before sinking down into the chair, trying and failing to suppress the groan of pain that escaped his mouth.

'Jumped? By who? Did you get a look at them? Do you know who they are?' Shannon said quickly, her brain whirling. She felt physically sick at the thought of someone attacking her younger brother.

The estate had been getting worse recently. There were rumours of new gangs hanging about and recruiting younger kids. Kids Kian's age. And Shannon was petrified that Kian might get caught up in something that would get him into some serious trouble. All she could do was pray that Kian would be smarter than that. That he'd listened to all her warnings over the years about getting in with the wrong crowd and he'd kept his head down and stayed out of trouble.

Only lately he didn't seem interested in listening to anything Shannon had to say. She felt as if she was talking to the wall.

'I didn't see jack. It all happened too quickly. They were just kids. It's nothing. Just leave it, yeah, Shan?'

'Leave it?' Shannon said incredulously. 'Are you joking, Kian? Look at the state of you. You need to go to the hospital. You're hurt.' She picked up her mobile phone and started tapping in the phone number for the local taxi firm.

'I'm not going to the hospital, Shan. I said leave it.' Kian raised his voice, standing back up. His face twisted with pain at the sudden movement as he made a grab for Shannon's phone. 'I mean it, Shan. Don't get involved. You'll only make it worse.'

'Worse?' Shannon said suspiciously. Kian was adamant about not going to the hospital and despite his claims he seemed shaken. 'How will I make it worse?' she asked slowly, staring at her brother now. She left the loaded question hanging in the air between them for a moment. 'This wasn't just some random kids, was it?' she said quietly, suddenly consumed by an awful feeling that Kian had been up to no good. Why else would he be so defensive?

'Kian, please? Tell me who did this?'

'I said leave it, Shan. The less you know the better. Trust me on this one.' Lowering his voice, Kian held his ribs as he sat back down again. Seeing the thunderous look on her brother's face, Shannon knew not to push her luck. Kian would only clam up if she continued to question him. He could be stubborn like that.

'Well, at least let me have a look at you then and check that nothing's broken and that you don't need any stitches. That cut above your eye looks bad,' Shannon said. She went to the kitchen and came back a few minutes later with a bowl of warm water, a flannel and a bag of frozen peas.

'What the hell? I ain't eating no peas, Shannon! You know I hate peas,' Kian said, recoiling as she placed the bag down on the table next to him. Shannon couldn't help but smile at that.

'They are for your eye, stupid! For the swelling. You hold the bag against your skin, you don't eat them! Here, let me clean your face up a bit first.' She pressed the wet flannel to Kian's skin as lightly as she could so as not to hurt him anymore than he was already clearly suffering and wiped as much of the dry blood away as possible.

'Your face doesn't look as bad now that I've wiped some of the blood off…' Shannon lied, wrapping the bag of peas in a tea towel and placing it against Kian's swollen eye. 'Put your hand on here and press gently for a few minutes if you can. It will help.' Watching as Kian flinched before the numbness of the ice took over, Shannon added, 'You're lucky. I thought you'd broken your nose but it looks as if it's just a bad nose bleed. I can't be so sure about your ribs, though.' She watched her brother wince in agony every time he moved. 'I'd say you might have broken a couple?' Kian nodded in agreement. He'd never known pain like it.

'Kian, please tell me what really happened? Are you in trouble with someone? You know you can tell me. I won't be angry with you. I just want to help,' Shannon said then, feeling tears threaten once more. Though she held them back, not wanting Kian to see her cry. She was his big sister. She needed to be strong for him. But she couldn't bear the thought of anything happening to her little brother.

'Honestly, Shannon, it's nothing for you to worry about. I was just in the wrong place at the wrong time. Forget it, okay. I'm going to bed.'

'Well, take this first, yeah…' Shannon got up, fetched Kian some paracetamol from the kitchen drawer and poured him a glass of water. 'You won't get much sleep otherwise.'

She watched him take the tablets, but she doubted he'd get much sleep anyway, the state he was in.

'Try and get some rest. I doubt you'll be going to school tomorrow though. Not in this state. If you're still bad in the morning, you're going to A&E okay?' Shannon said, vowing to try and talk to Kian again in the morning after he'd got some rest. She watched as her brother hobbled from the room, before sitting back down at the kitchen table.

The Griffin Estate was rife with older gangs, with nowhere better to go, hanging around the communal gardens and stairwells at night. And if it wasn't the teenagers causing trouble, half the residents that lived here were at it too. Late-night domestics. Booze and drugs. There were dealers at every corner waiting to prey on their next new customer. Loud music and shouting blared through every wall.

Kian had always been such a good kid. He was soft by nature. The kind of soft that the wrong kind of people would take advantage of, and Shannon had a bad feeling about all of this.

She knew Kian better than anyone and she knew when he was lying about not knowing who attacked him tonight, she was certain of it. And as much as he tried to play it down, he looked genuinely shaken up. Shannon had no intention of just leaving it alone. If someone was out to get her brother, then she wanted to know who and why. Kian was involved with something; he was clearly out of his depth. Shannon would be keeping tabs on that brother of hers from now on. Whether Kian liked it or not.

CHAPTER SEVEN

'Okay everyone, grab your coffee and gather round,' DS Morgan called out, leaning against his desk at the front of the room as his team gathered for their usual morning ritual.

'Let me start by introducing you to the newest member of the team. This is Trainee Detective Constable Lucy Murphy.' Morgan shot Lucy a confident smile to reassure her on her first day. 'DC Murphy joins us after a commendable eighteen months working over in uniform, and she will be joining the team directly under my mentorship for the next six months, in order to gain her DC's.'

Lucy smiled warmly at the dozens of officers that made up Wandsworth station's CID team, suddenly feeling self-conscious under their scrutiny as they stared back at her. Eyeing her up as they made their own assumptions of whether or not she was fit for the job, their expressions gave nothing away.

Though DS Morgan had warned her prior to this morning's briefing.

News of a new young police officer being fast-tracked to a Trainee Detective Constable position after such a short amount of time working in the force might put certain officers' noses well and truly out of joint, and there might be an element of bad feeling amongst some of the uniformed officers who had spent years trying to claw their way up the ranks in order to make it to DC or DS, without success as yet.

'Thanks, Sarge!' Lucy beamed back at her boss. She was grateful that Sergeant Morgan had handed her the opportunity of a lifetime by offering this position, but the last thing she wanted to do was come across as the teacher's pet on her first day. She took her cue to address the room, which felt smaller suddenly than when she'd first walked in, claustrophobic almost. The space was crammed with large white desks, all housing individual computers. The smell of coffee lingered in the air from the cafetière that sat in the compact kitchen area that took up the far corner of the room. And judging by the fact that everyone here was already on their second mug, she guessed the place ran on its caffeine dependency in order to get through the day's brief and the heavy workload that followed.

'I'm really looking forward to working alongside you all. If there's anything I can help any of you with, please let me know.' Smiling at DC Ben Holder, the officer standing in front of her, Lucy faltered as she saw the flicker of disgruntlement spread across his face, before he sarcastically rolled his eyes, muttering something under his breath about yet another officer getting the gold star special treatment.

'This isn't a pissing contest, Holder,' Morgan said, shooting the officer down instantly. He'd known that it would be Holder who'd have his nose put out of joint. The man was old sweats, he'd spent ten years working for the force, doing endless hours of over-time in the hope that his commitment and dedication to the job would one day get him noticed and earn him the much sought after Detective Sergeant status that he so desperately wanted. Holder was always easily rankled by anyone who might appear as direct competition, standing in his way of a future promotion.

Lucy shuffled awkwardly, glad that DS Morgan had her back. Her boss had been right to warn her that news of her recruitment at CID might not go down well with some of her fellow DCs. DC

Holder being one of them clearly. Sensing his animosity towards her, Lucy couldn't help but feel vulnerable, which wasn't helped by the fact that she didn't even have her uniform to hide behind. Today, for the first time. she was dressed as a plain-clothes officer, which in a weird way made her feel as if she'd lost some of her identity. She'd taken hours shopping, painstakingly searching for the perfect outfit to wear to help her give the right impression on her first day. Scouring the shops for most of the weekend prior for something smart and professional looking, she'd finally opted for a simple white blouse and pin-striped grey fitted suit. Her black leather boots had just a small lip of a heel so that they didn't appear too casual nor too dressy. Her initial impression on the team needed to be a positive one. Now, Lucy forced herself to hold Holder's aggrieved gaze, her stare unwavering until finally Holder looked away. She knew the drill well enough by now after working on the beat for the past eighteen months. Never, ever back down, and never show any fear. As a female officer, that rule went as much for the officers that she'd worked with as the suspects she'd detained.

'Some of you may or may not be aware, but our Trainee Detective Constable here has made some fantastic arrests while working in uniform. Her hard work and dedication to the job has helped to put away one of Wandsworth's most prolific burglars, who has been plaguing homes in the borough and the surrounding areas this past year. The suspect somehow managed to stay off our radar, until DC Murphy here, caught him in the act whilst on duty and made the arrest. DC Murphy also played a big part in detaining several suspects behind a very high profile money laundering scam, which I'm pleased to say, has since been completely shut down. Her presence here at CID is not only welcomed, it's much needed. She's more than earned her place here on the team and I believe she'll be an asset. So I'd like each and every one of you to make sure she's welcomed on board.'

DS Morgan looked to DC Holder then, his eyes flashing the man a warning, as the officer had the good grace to stare down at the floor, well aware that that little rollicking had been mainly for his benefit.

'Which brings us to today's tasks. Holder, I want you to take Murphy with you when you go and secure the witness statements from the GBH assault yesterday over at the Griffin Estate.' Pairing Murphy up with Holder on her very first day wasn't ideal for her, but DS Morgan figured that at least if the officers were forced to spend time together in close proximity, the chances were they'd resolve any petty differences, and the sooner that happened the better. 'Following a manic weekend, I've got a meeting with the CPS this morning about the backlog of cases that have been building up, and I think it would be far more productive if Murphy partners up with you on this one. You're familiar with the Griffin Estate I take it?' DS Morgan asked Lucy, who nodded.

'Throwing her to the wolves on the first day?' Holder smirked. 'Don't worry, Sarge, I'll keep an eye on her. Make sure she doesn't get into any bother.' The patronising tone was clear to everyone in the room.

'Thanks, Sarge, and yes, I'm more than familiar with the Griffin Estate,' Lucy quickly interrupted the DC. 'I'd have to be living on another planet not to be. Uniform are called out there on the daily.' Then, directing her words at Holder, she added, 'And I don't need babysitting, thanks for the offer. I'm more than capable of keeping myself out of bother.'

A couple of the other officers close by sniggered, and Lucy felt as if she'd just gained her power back. Men like Holder always tried to talk down to her or belittle her, and she knew from experience that if you didn't stand up for yourself in this job, people would walk all over you. And Lucy had no intention of being anyone's doormat.

DS Morgan gave a tight smile, trying to hide the fact that he was impressed by Lucy's ability to quietly stand up for herself. She'd go far in this game, he thought to himself as he cleared his throat, before getting back to giving out his instructions.

'Okay, DC Murphy, to get you up to speed, we are conducting a formal investigation following a brutal unprovoked assault on one of our community support officers over at the Griffin Estate yesterday. He was hospitalised and suffered a broken nose and slight concussion. The suspects, we believe, are part of an organised gang on the estate. They kicked our PCSO to the floor, and one of the boys stamped on his head. Of course, when we opened the investigation, there were apparently no witnesses, which we all know is bullshit. We believe that people on the estate are being intimidated and threatened not to talk to us.'

'Bunch of Jeremy Kyle referrals, the lot of them,' Holder chimed in again, shaking his head angrily at the state of affairs, and looking for an excuse to redeem himself in the room again after DC Murphy spoke down to him so blatantly. Then, seeing the puzzled look on Lucy's face at his turn of phrase, he muttered, 'You know, the type of kids with mothers all too busy organising DNA tests instead of dental treatment for their offspring.'

'While that may be so,' DS Morgan interrupted, his tone clipped, not wanting to indulge Holder further with his speculation on the type of people they were dealing with here, 'it's the first attack of its kind, unprovoked and aimed directly at a member of the force. Relations with the PCSOs on the estate have always, until now, been very positive. This changes everything. So, to say that tension is high right now between us and the residents of the estate would be a major understatement. We've had a hard time getting anyone to come forward and make an official statement, but apparently we had a lead come in this morning from a resident willing to go on the record for us. Holder, you might want to let Lucy read through the files on the case before you make the visit. And it goes without saying that you'll both need to keep your wits about you at all times when you're on the estate.'

DS Morgan glanced at the team. 'The rest of you can finish your coffee, you're going to need it. We need to get through all of these case files today. We've got a shit load of work to get through in order to play catch up and, as per, not enough hours in the day to get it all done.' Morgan nodded to the stacks of files mounted up on the desks. 'It's getting to the stage where they're holding the office walls up!'

Once they were dismissed, Holder quickly downed the rest of his coffee. He had no intention of letting Lucy finish hers. 'You don't need to read the file; I'll get you up to speed on our way over to the estate. The sooner we get this witness statement, the better. You never know who might get to them before us, especially with the scrotes involved in this case.' Holder grabbed the keys as Lucy placed her cup down on her desk.

'You driven one of our cars from CID's luxury fleet yet?'

'No, I've only driven the patrol cars…' she said cautiously, seeing the flash of amusement in Holder's eyes as he tossed her the keys.

'Well, that's your first task then. To try and get us to the Griffin Estate in one piece.'

'Excuse me?' Lucy said, taking offence at the man's subtle dig about her being a female driver. 'I'm more than capable of driving a car.'

'Easy, Murphy! Bit touchy, aren't you?' Holder laughed, glad that Lucy had taken the bait, though he knew better than to always be so blatant with his comments. 'I meant, good luck getting us through the rush hour traffic! Especially when you see the car we've got too. It's a right beast of a motor.' Holder grinned to himself as he made his way out of the office, Lucy trailing behind him with a look of trepidation.

Though unknown to Holder it had nothing to do with the fact that he'd made a snarky comment about women drivers, and everything to do with having to go back to the Griffin Estate today. As she'd said in the briefing, calls out to incidents on the estate were all part of the job. In fact, they were a daily occurrence more often than not, but Lucy had hoped that now she was working in CID her time there would be far less frequent. She could concentrate on catching the real criminals now and working on much more complex, serious cases. Yet here she was, her first day on a new job and she was back there again. Shaking her head to herself as she followed Holder out to the car, Lucy Murphy braced herself to face her demons once more.

CHAPTER EIGHT

'All right, you fat fucker!' Jax Priestly sneered as he caught sight
of Philip Penfold peering back at him through the crack in the
door; the scared expression on the older man's face made Jax
want to laugh.

'The element of surprise, eh?' Jax loved having that effect
on people. That just the sight of him turning up unannounced
could turn some people into a trembling wreck. It made him feel
powerful. Especially as he knew that he was the last person Philip
expected to see today, on a Monday. He and his boys had only
just left Philip's flat late last night and Philip wasn't expecting to
see them again until the following weekend.

'Are you going to let us in then, or what? Only that poxy chain
of yours ain't going to help ya if you don't, Penfold!' Jax said with
a wry grin, tapping the newly fitted security chain before jerking
his head at one of the boys standing behind him, who, taking their
cue, held up a pair of bolt cutters they'd come armed with. Jax
was enjoying the look of terror on Penfold's face at the realisation
that, yet again, Jax was one step ahead of the bloke.

'Not today, Jax. Please. I'm not feeling very well. I've got a
dicky tummy,' Philip pleaded with a trembling voice. His eyes
darted nervously from Jax to the other lads behind him, all eagerly
waiting to get inside.

He'd been practising what he was going to say to Jax ever
since he woke up this morning, vowing to himself that the next

time Jax and his mates turned up at the front door, he'd tell him straight that he couldn't come in. He'd stand his ground.

Now, though, faced with Jax standing just feet away from him with that horrible smug look on his face, all Philip's earlier bravado had vanished. He'd completely lost his bottle.

'Ahh, well that's a real shame that you're not feeling well, Philip! But to be honest with you, I don't actually give a fuck. So stop being a bellend and open the door, yeah? Or we'll use the bolt cutters on the chain and then we'll all have a go at using them on you too, you get me?'

Knowing when he was well and truly beaten – there was no arguing with the likes of Jax – Philip reluctantly did as he was told and unhooked the chain from the door, stepping aside as the boys all stormed in. Philip had barely shut the door behind them all when Jax was on him, grabbing him by his throat and slamming him hard up against the wall.

'You try any of that shit with me again, Penfold, and I'll show you exactly where it will get you, understand?'

Philip nodded compliantly, not wanting to rile Jax up anymore than he already had. It seemed to work.

Jax laughed again; the fear on Philip's face was priceless, the bloke was such a fucking plank.

'And who put the chain up? You better not have been telling tales on us, Philip?' Jax said now. His steely eyes bored into Philip's as he purposely tightened his grip around the older man's windpipe. Unable to speak, Philip tried to shake his head, wincing in pain until Jax finally loosened his hold on him and let him talk.

'I didn't tell anyone. I haven't, I swear to you, Jax. I didn't mention you!'

'Bullshit! Why would you have a chain fitted then, huh?' Jax said, his face so close to Philip's now that their foreheads were touching.

'I just told my care worker that sometimes I felt a bit scared sleeping here on my own. With all the noise in the flats at night time. That's all I said. I promise. She got a handyman to come over and install it for me. They've only just left.' Tearful now, Philip prayed that Jax believed him because technically it wasn't a lie. He didn't feel safe in his flat. He wanted a chain on the door for extra security. To make sure that no one could get in. Specifically, to make sure that Jax couldn't get in. Though he hadn't relayed that to his care worker. He realised now that the whole idea had been a stupid one. As if a flimsy door chain would keep Jax and his boys out. He'd just made things worse.

'Yeah, well, you better not bloody blab either. Or you know what will happen.' Jax nodded in the direction of Philip's overfed furball of a cat, lying strewn across the sofa, oblivious to the tension in the room, licking its fur. The cat was Philip's pride and joy. The sad fucker's only companion, which meant that it made great leverage when it came to Jax making Philip do stuff that he didn't want to do. It was amazing what someone would agree to when their beloved pet was being dangled from a twelfth-floor balcony by the scruff of its neck. Like him taking over Philip's flat every weekend.

'I swear. I didn't say anything. I promise.'

Jax released his grip on the man, laughing then at the snivelling wreck before him as Philip slid down the wall, his hands clutching at his raw throat.

'Don't worry, I know you haven't got the bollocks to start telling tales about me. Not if you know what's good for you!' Jax threatened before adding, 'Don't forget, I see and hear everything. One word out of your mouth, and I'll know about it!' Jax tapped at his temple, pretending to Philip as if he had some kind of magical power. He enjoyed playing up to this dumb fucker's stupidity. Jax had managed to convince Philip that he was watching him night and day. That he could see Philip even when he wasn't here. Philip believed him too, because Jax always knew everything.

He knew what food Philip had eaten when he wasn't here, what TV shows Philip watched in the evenings. And even today, turning up with some bolt cutters – how did he know that Philip had just had a security chain fitted to the front door just a few hours earlier? Philip had tried a few times to search his flat for Jax's secret cameras and microphones under the guise of spring cleaning, convinced that Jax must have bugged the place and be watching him on some kind of device.

Yet, so far, Philip hadn't managed to find anything. So he continued to live in constant fear, scared to even tell his carer what was going on, in case Jax heard him.

'Oi, lads, remember your manners. Give the fat bastard his payment then.' Jax grinned, nodding to one of the boys, who, after waiting for Philip to get up from the floor, handed him a huge box of cream cakes.

'Now, go on. You know the drill, make yourself scarce, and take that mangy furball with you,' Jax said, roughly shoving the cat off of the chair before picking up the remote control and switching off whatever shit Philip had been watching before they'd arrived. Some boring animal documentary or something equally as mind-numbing. Jax put MTV on instead, turning it up loud and blasting out some music, while another of the boys went about setting up the Xbox.

'But my carer, Karen. She'll be back soon…'

'No she won't, mate! She's not due back here until Wednesday,' Jax said with a certainty that made Philip waver. 'And I tell you when I'm coming over, not the other way round. So, go on! Off you fuck!' Jax said again, sitting down in the sofa and rolling himself a joint.

Philip didn't need asking twice, glad to leave the boys to it, and get as far away from the lot of them as possible. He picked up his beloved Bobcat from where he'd landed on the floor and quickly retreated into the sanctuary of his bedroom, shutting the bedroom door behind him. He placed the cakes down on the bookshelf next to his bed, his hands shaking. He knew full well that his peace would be short-lived. This was all part of Jax's sick and twisted games. He would bring him twelve of the biggest, fattest cakes from the bakery as a gift to Philip for letting them all use the flat – as if he had any real say in the matter – and Philip had to eat every single cake by the end of the day, so that they could taunt him about how fat and disgusting he was. Or worse, they would force-feed him until he was sick.

Picking up one of the cakes, he crammed it into his mouth, knowing that Jax would be sending the boys in to check on him soon. Tears ran down his cheeks as he chewed, the memory of the last fiasco still lingering freshly in his mind. How he'd doubled over, crippled with pain after finishing the box of cakes at Jax's insistence, trying his hardest not to throw up. But he was so bloated and the taste of the whipped cream had lingered in his throat, igniting that awful watery nausea feeling. Unable to stop himself, he'd puked up all over the bedroom floor, and when Jax had come in and seen the mess, instead of being sympathetic, he'd ordered Philip to get down on his hands and knees and eat that too. In front of them all, while they all laughed and jeered at him. And Philip had known that if he hadn't done as he was told, the consequences would have been much worse. They'd have all taken it in turns to beat him. And they'd have hurt Bobcat.

Picking up the second cake now, Philip forced himself to swallow it down, all the while cursing himself for being so pathetic and not being able to stand up for himself. He wished he was braver instead of cowering away inside his bedroom all alone, as the music blared through the walls. The neighbours didn't bother to complain anymore, because if they tried, Jax would force Philip to go to the door and tell whoever it was to fuck off. They'd all turned against him now, too. Even Mrs Wilson next door, who had always been nice to Philip, didn't give him so much as the time of day anymore. Instead she kept her head down if she spotted him on the balcony or in the stairwell, just so she wouldn't have to talk to him.

Flopping down on top of his duvet, he hugged his little Bobcat close to him as he listened to the loud laughter and chatter floating in from the next room. They'd start drinking soon. And doing drugs. That was the bit he dreaded most. When they all started acting even crazier than they normally were. He'd had nightmares all week about what these boys were capable of. Which was why he'd asked for the door chain in the first place.

'I won't let anything happen to you, Bobcat. Not ever. I promise you, boy,' he said putting the cat down and forcing himself to eat another of the cakes, all the while praying that that Jax was wrong, and Karen would come back soon. And more importantly that no harm would come to him and his beloved Bobcat.

CHAPTER NINE

2000

The room looks nicer than the other rooms in the police station, the child thinks as her eyes sweep the surroundings. A big comfy sofa to the side of the room, and a bookshelf overflowing with colourful children's books. But the real gem is the huge dolls' house that sits in the centre of the room.

'I thought we could play with the dolls' house again. We had so much fun with it last time,' Doctor Mary George, the child psychiatrist, says with a smile.

The child nods, not needing to be asked twice, before crouching down on the coarse, hard-wearing carpet and picking up the dolls nearest to her. She likes Mary George, she decides. She's nice. Nicer than all the other police officers who keep looking at her all funny, and talking to her in their silly voices as if she's some sort of a baby. But she's not a baby. She's five now. She's a big girl. Her mummy had said so.

'I thought that today, we could try something new with the dolls' house,' Mary George suggests, sitting down cross-legged on the floor next to the child. 'I thought that it might be really helpful for us both, if we do some role play. A bit like acting.'

The child looks up at the woman, narrowing her eyes, unsure if she'd be any good at it. But she is willing to try if it means that she can play with the dolls' house again.

'You'll be just fine. It's just you and me. Just talking. We can stop at any time.'

The child nods. They've already spoken about a lot of things. She's told Mary what food she likes to eat the best. Fish finger sandwiches smothered in ketchup. But not with the crust, she hates crusts, they're yucky and her mummy always cut them off for her. And she's told Mary that her favourite TV programme is *Pingu*. Because that little penguin is so funny and he makes her laugh a lot. She'd said that her favourite colour is blue. Even though her bedroom at home was bright pink, and Mummy said that when they had some more money, she'd paint it blue for her. And Mary had said that her favourite colour was blue too.

'So what I thought we'd do today, was set the dolls' house up just like your house. We can put all the furniture in there and make it all nice for the two dolls,' Mary suggests.

'But I don't live in a house, I live in a flat,' the child says, disappointed, then, that they won't be able to play Mary's game today.

'That's okay, because we're just pretending, aren't we?' Mary nods at the pieces, encouraging the child to start putting the furniture into each room. 'You'll have to be in charge of where everything goes, though. Because I don't know what your house looks like, do I? So you'll have to show me.' Mary George passes the child pieces of furniture, doing her best to make the game sound exciting.

The child takes the lead, in her element for a while, caught up in her own little world of make-believe, as she makes everything just so. She sets up each room just like her home.

'Our TV is near the sofa,' she says, placing a sofa by the wall and the TV in the corner by the window. 'The dining table is in the kitchen and we have four chairs, but we only need three. One for me and Mummy, and one for Nanny when she comes over for her tea.'

Mary nods, passing the child some kitchen appliances to add now. A small shiny kettle and a matching toaster.

'This kitchen is much bigger than our kitchen,' the girl says, taking the pieces and arranging them on the kitchen worktops, just so.

'That's okay! We're just using our imaginations today, aren't we?' She passes her more furniture until the house is nearly full up. Apart from one room that the child deliberately avoided. Until now. Her eyes are frequently flickering to the empty space, her anticipation building as she runs out of other furniture to place inside.

'Where does this bed go?' Mary George says, passing the child a double bed with the purple blanket, prompting her to continue their game.

The child pauses, moving her gaze and her hand back down to the kitchen again, pretending to be busy moving the furniture there. She concentrates on the two dolls sitting at the kitchen table eating their dinner.

'Do you want to come back to the bedroom in a minute?' Mary says softly, not wanting to push the child too much, too soon. 'I tell you what, why don't you tell me what you and your mummy are doing?' she asks brightly, taking in the scene that the child is acting out. 'It looks like you are having a lovely afternoon.'

The child nods, relieved that she doesn't have to go to the bedroom just yet. Instead she focuses on arranging the tiny plates of food on the dining table. Two little plates. Two little cups. Some pretty flowers in a vase. Mary George smiles, not doubting that the child had come from an extremely loving home. A safe home, until recently.

'We're eating our dinner,' the child says proudly, enthralled in the moment, as she re-enacts the meal. Bending her doll's head down to the plate as if to eat. 'Spaghetti hoops and fish fingers. Yum yum. But Mummy is saying that she wishes we had something better. But I don't know what's better than that though, cos it's my favourite dinner in the whole wide world.'

'Even better than fish finger sandwiches?' Mary laughs. The child nods before enacting the mummy doll getting up from the table.

'And where is Mummy going now?' the doctor asks, secretly hoping that she'll get more from the child today, aware that this scene has got longer each time they've re-enacted it. That it's slowly becoming more detailed.

'My mummy's going to get a cloth cos I spilled my hoops all down my mermaid top.'

Moving the dolls around the kitchen, the girl brings the mummy doll close to the child doll and pretends to clear up the mess.

'Oh, you mucky-little-pup!' the child says, mimicking her mother's sing-song voice.

'Sorry, Mummy!' the child replies with a giggle. It's a delaying tactic. The child is purposely refusing to move past this point. Mary notes that the mood is playful. The parent is a good role model, the home environment stable. The dolls are back to eating their dinner again, and Mary needs to try and gently press the child forward on this.

'And do you remember what happened later? After your dinner?' The child nods reluctantly.

'Mummy said we can have ice cream later…' She falters. Her expression is thoughtful, as if she has only just remembered that. She places the dolls down, her expression sad now. 'We didn't have any ice cream though.'

'Oh no that's a shame, why not? What happened after dinner?' Mary asks, her voice soft and neutral, willing the child to take her lead and open up to her.

Only the child stops talking and simply shrugs. She stares at the dolls' house, her eyes going to the bedroom that still sits empty. Her mother's bedroom. Mary waits patiently, allowing the child to process her thoughts. She can see her expression changing. Her gaze hardens and she suddenly appears more guarded as she purses her lips tightly, keeping whatever words that might have come to her safely locked inside. Still Mary pushes forward.

'Shall we talk about what happened in Mummy's bedroom?' she asks, pointing to the room that they'd earlier established was her mother's bedroom. The room that has remained completely bare through all of these sessions. The same room that the child had point blank refused to acknowledge at all. The child doesn't move. She's gone small now, as if she's sinking into the floor that she's sitting on, her whole body rigid with terror. Picking up the mummy doll, she wraps her fingers tightly around the tiny figure, clutching it in her hand, before hovering awkwardly for a few seconds near her mother's make-believe bedroom.

Mary holds her breath, silently hoping that this will be the much-needed breakthrough that she's worked so hard to get to. That the child will be brave and finally place her doll inside the room, so that they can finally talk about the trauma that she suffered that fateful night. Mary can see the cogs turning in the girl's head, her mind deep in thought. Only at the last second, something stops her and she quickly looks down at the doll, her face twisting with doubt before she shakes her head sadly.

'This isn't my mummy,' she says then, throwing the doll down on to the floor and watching it fall. The same curly brown hair as her mum, but she didn't recognise the pink top and blue jeans. 'She wasn't wearing those clothes. It's just a stupid doll.'

Mary George nods patiently. A new detail. Progress at last.

'Can you tell me about what your mum was wearing? Was she wearing her dressing gown? Do you remember?'

The child nods. She remembers. She remembers it every time she closes her eyes. How her mother had pulled her in for a hug after she'd lifted her out of the bath that night. How she'd buried her head into the soft, fluffy gown. Breathing in her mother's familiar scent, like flowers and chocolate, she'd said, and her mother had giggled at that. She was trying to remember that smell now, breathing in through her nose as if some part of her mother might still be up inside there. Only she couldn't smell it anymore. It was gone. She was gone.

And even though she had her eyes shut tightly, she couldn't stop her tears from leaking out of the corners of them. And now she didn't want to open them, because they'd pour out of her like a waterfall and Mary George would see them and she'd think that she was a stupid crybaby.

'I know that you are really sad, darling. And it's very scary talking about what happened to your mummy. But I want you to know that you are safe now and that I'm here to help you. It might make you feel better if you tell me what you can remember…' Mary George says, gently trying to coax the child into opening up to her as she watches the silent tears cascade down her little plump cheeks. Her heart breaks for the young girl. It doesn't matter how professional she is, or how detached she tries to be, she is human and what this little girl has been through has really got to her.

'What colour was your mummy's dressing gown?'

'White. It was white and fluffy. But there was red too.' The child gulps down the sob that tried to escape her throat as she spoke, unable to say the rest out loud. How the dressing gown had been white, but afterwards it was covered all over in bright red. Blood. She opens her eyes; she is scared now. Her hands are shaking.

'I don't want to put my mummy back in that room! I don't want her to be hurted anymore.' The child speaks sternly, getting up from where she'd been sitting on the floor and walking over to the settee where she sits, her small hands resting on her lap, her gaze fixed on the floor.

'We don't have to talk about the dressing gown, not if you don't want to. We don't have to talk about Mummy. How about you show me the kitchen again?' Mary George says, trying to entice the girl back over. But she has shut down. She simply shakes her head.

'I don't want to play with that stupid dolls' house ever again.'

CHAPTER TEN

Turning off the main Wandsworth road and into the Griffin Estate, DC Holder shook his head, unwilling to admit that Murphy's driving had impressed him thus far. The new DC had balls, he'd give her that. Unfazed by the Wandsworth gridlock she had expertly weaved the Mini Cooper they'd been allocated for the job in and out of the London traffic, moving rapidly between the other vehicles on the road as if she was completely invisible.

'All right, speedy! You've proved your point,' Holder had joked at one point, guessing correctly that Murphy was only driving so erratically to teach him a lesson. Holder had now conceded to himself that, while he wouldn't say the same about all women, there was absolutely no denying that DC Murphy knew how to drive.

'Jesus Christ!' Holder shouted grabbing on to the dashboard as Lucy stamped on the brake, the Mini Cooper screeching to an emergency stop in the middle of the street. Hearing the almighty bang made by whatever it was that had just been launched at the car, Holder closed his eyes. Murphy didn't even so much as flinch. Undoing her seatbelt, she leapt from the car.

'Oi, be more careful, boys, yeah? I could have run you both over then,' Lucy warned, shouting at the two young boys who had run out in front of her. Not that they were interested in her clear concern.

'Keep your hair on, love! We were just getting our ball,' the smaller of the two boys said cockily, before reaching down to grab the football that had been launched at the car. Probably on purpose, Lucy thought to herself. The second boy stuck his tongue out at her and flipped her the middle finger before they both ran off laughing.

'Bloody kids, must have a death wish,' she said, getting back in the car and continuing to the front of the estate, where she pulled up and switched the engine off.

Only then did Holder speak. 'Jesus! I thought walking the estate and making enquiries about this gang was going to be the most terrifying part of our day!' he quipped, getting out of the unmarked car, glad to get his feet firmly back onto solid ground.

'We'll we're still alive, aren't we? So you do actually have something to be thankful for,' Lucy shot back, raising her eyes sarcastically, though she couldn't help but smile. 'Bet you'll think twice about making comments about women drivers in the future though, huh?'

'I told you, that isn't what I meant,' Holder lied before adding, 'But, from now on I shall only ever sing your praises! Ayrton Senna, eat your heart out! Here, are you all right?' he continued, looking over to where Lucy stood glued to the spot as she stared up at the depressing grey concrete tower blocks that loomed high above them.

'Look. If you are worrying about what happened to that PCSO yesterday, don't. I know the sarge thinks that it might be the start of something, but I think it was a one off,' he said, trying to reassure her. 'Wrong place, wrong time, that's all. The sarge said that relations with PCSOs are usually good, but the truth is that's only because the kids around these parts don't see PCSOs as any kind of a threat. I mean, let's face it, they are only a hi-vis jacket away from being any other Joe Bloggs member of the public, aren't they? And I think the kids just pushed their luck a bit. You know. They took the piss. And the PCSO didn't handle the situation very well, and then it just blew up. Still, don't get me wrong, I wanna catch the little bastards just as much as anyone else.'

Holder led the way towards the block of flats with Lucy following closely behind him. 'But, it's always us that have to pick up the pieces. Gone are the days of old-fashioned, friendly bobby-on-the-beat ethos. We are and always will be public enemy number one around these parts. But they'd be stupid to try anything while we're here gathering witness statements. Especially as that means they'd only be incriminating themselves further. So don't look so worried.'

'I'm not worried,' Lucy said quietly. 'This place never changes though, does it? Who's the witness?'

'An elderly lady by the name of Margaret Piper. Seventy-three years of age, bless her. Though how much we'll get from her is anyone's guess. She told the dispatcher on the radio that her cataracts are so bad that some days she can barely see further than her own hand, when she was given a crime reference number, but yet she claims she saw the attack from her balcony. Which, so far, is all we've got.' Holder pointed up to the security camera that was dangling down from the wall by its cable. 'We can't even rely on the CCTV, because some little scrote vandalised it. Probably for that exact reason. The sods rip them down quicker than the council can put them back up.'

Lucy shook her head.

'Looks like we'll be taking the stairs then,' Holder said, resigned, as he opened the main door of the block and saw the broken lift sign. He let Lucy step inside first. 'Good job it's only four floors up, eh!'

Making a grab for the stairwell door, Holder stepped back just in time as the door swung out with full force and almost hit him in the face.

'Steady on, lad!' Holder said, eyeing the boy who walked towards him with suspicion, noting how he had his hood pulled up tightly around his face as if deliberately concealing his identity. Putting his head down as soon as he clocked the two detectives, the boy made an attempt to speed up, but Holder stepped deliberately in the way of his exit.

'Hold up.' Holder stared down at the boy. 'Do you live here?'

'What's it got to do with you?' the boy said, guarded.

'We're carrying out an investigation into an assault that happened here on the estate yesterday. I'm DC Holder and this is my colleague, DC Murphy. What's your name?'

'Kian Winters,' Kian said; he'd known on first sight these two were coppers. Far too formal looking for the estate, they stood out like two sore thumbs.

'Who reported it? My sister?' he asked, clenching his fists at his side, fuming with Shannon for sticking her nose in. He'd warned her not to say anything.

'The attack on the Police Community Support Officer?' Holder said, narrowing his eyes at the boy and guessing, rightly, that wasn't what Kian was insinuating.

'An assault on a copper? Oh, nah. She wouldn't know nothing about that,' the boy said, impatient now, wanting to get away. Which only made Holder even more suspicious.

'Shouldn't you be at school?'

'I'm off sick, aren't I? I've only come out to get some medicine from the chemist.'

'If you're off school sick, you should be indoors. And someone else should be getting your medication for you.'

'Yeah? Like who? Father Christmas?' Kian said sarcastically. Then, realising that he was probably pushing his luck, he quickly added, 'Both my parents are at work.'

'Are they, now?' Holder said, not bothering to hide his expression of disbelief as he recognised yet another lie. Holder could see right through the kid. 'Take your hood down,' he instructed. The kid reluctantly yanked the material down from his face, revealing what Holder had suspected. The kid was hiding something. A split lip and swollen eye, and some bruised ribs judging by the way the boy was standing so awkwardly. Holder shook his head.

'What happened to your face?' he asked, debating whether or not to walk the boy back to his flat and have a nose at his living arrangements, so that he could make sure that the poor kid hadn't had a pasting from his old man. Only Kian wasn't giving anything away.

'I fell down the stairs, didn't I? Bloody lift's never working and I was in a hurry and slipped.'

'Good one, like we ain't heard that one before. Come on, Kian. Did someone do this to you? We might be able to help,' Lucy interrupted, hoping that she might come across as easier to speak to than Holder, who had a permanently hard edge to him.

'Yeah right! You lot can't even help yourselves,' Kian shot back at her. Bored of all the questions, he just wanted to get out of here now and away from the two coppers. He didn't have time for this. 'I fell. There's nothing else to say. It looks a lot worse than it is! Otherwise, I wouldn't be going to the chemist, would I? Now can I go or what?' The last thing Kian needed today was to be spotted talking to two Old Bill. That would do his already depleting street cred no end of good.

'You really expect us to believe that you are going to the chemist?' Officer Holder regarded the boy suspiciously, knowing full well that they'd probably never get the truth out of him anyway.

'Yeah, to get some paracetamol. Then I'm going back to bed. Honest.'

Holder recognised a lie when he heard one. He'd bet his month's wages that this kid was truanting from school and probably up to no good, just like the rest of the little shits that lived on the estate.

'What flat number are you in?'

Kian stared at the officer, wondering for a few seconds if he could get away with lying, but then thinking that the copper might call his bluff, he told the truth instead.

'I live at seventy-two, on the tenth floor. I wouldn't give you my address if I was lying, would I?'

Holder raised his eyebrows, half believing the lad. By rights, he should walk him back to his flat and check out his living conditions, make sure he was telling the truth about being off school sick. Though the last thing he could be bothered doing today was babysit some truanting stroppy teenager, especially when they had this witness statement to secure and time was, as always, of the essence.

'Five minutes, straight there and straight back. I'll be checking,' Holder said, hoping his threat was incentive enough as he glared at the kid.

'Of course!' Kian said, taking his cue and continuing past the officer and out through the main door, barely able to believe his luck that they were actually letting him go.

'Are you sure we shouldn't have taken him back to his flat?' Lucy asked, eyeing the boy through the door's glass panel, as he hobbled his way across the communal garden outside.

'Nah, he's fine. He's probably been in a fight, and he's bunking off school today. And we haven't got time to deal with bullshit sob stories. Have you seen our caseload back at the station?' Holder said, making excuses for not working to the guidelines that they were supposed to adhere to. 'We've got enough paperwork to keep us going for at least a month, we don't need to add some kid bunking off school to the ever-growing admin pile.' He held the door open for Lucy. 'Ladies first.'

'Oh, ever the gentleman!' Lucy muttered, deciding that, despite the fact that she completely disagreed with Holder, there was no point arguing with her colleague over the matter. Choose your battles wisely, as her nan used to say.

'Jesus, this place stinks of piss!' Holder said, pressing the sleeve of his shirt firmly over his mouth as they made their way up the four flights of stairs to Mrs Piper's flat. 'Makes you wanna gag, doesn't it?'

Lucy nodded in agreement as she followed her colleague, holding onto the handrail as she went. Her palms were clammy, her heart beating erratically, though she couldn't let on to Holder that she was shaken up. Flat seventy-two, the boy had said. The twelfth floor. What were the chances. *Breathe!*

'Are you sure you're okay?' Holder said, turning and catching Lucy tugging at her shirt collar as if it was too tight suddenly, and choking her.

'Yeah, it's just this place. It makes me feel sick,' Lucy said trying to act normal; though it was taking every ounce of concentration not to throw up the entire contents of her stomach.

And, unbeknownst to Holder, it had absolutely nothing to do with the smell of the place.

CHAPTER ELEVEN

'Well, well, look who it is!' Jax said, eyeing Kian as he walked into Philip Penfold's lounge. 'I was starting to think you'd done a runner with my money.' Jax glared as Kian stood in front of him, straining to hear Jax's veiled threat over the loud music. The bass pulsated through the floor, making his legs tremble even more than they were already. He'd only been to the flat a couple of times and he hadn't really had much interaction with the man who lived here, but he knew that his name was Philip and that he was mentally disabled. Jax had mentioned that the man had a carer looking after him a few hours here and there during the week. When Jax was here, he was made to stay in his bedroom out of the way, whilst Jax and his boys took over the place.

'I said, I was about to send a few of the boys out looking for you,' Jax said, nodding at one of the boys to turn down the music, before jerking his head at Kian to follow him into the kitchen. Jax leant up against the sink and folded his arms, staring menacingly at Kian for what felt like an age before he finally spoke.

'So, what happened to you last night? Why didn't you bring the cash straight to me like you were told?' He rolled up another joint before glaring back at Kian with disdain. 'And what the fuck happened to your face?' he added, as if only just noticing Kian's battered-looking face.

'I got mugged, Jax.' Kian spoke quietly then, a tremor of fear as he spoke, suddenly aware of the volatile situation he was in. Jax wasn't the easiest person to deal with on a normal day, but now when he was already half-cut, Kian knew that this conversation wasn't going to go well at all. He should have come straight here last night and let Jax and his boys see the state of him.

'Mugged? What do you mean? Mugged as in someone stole the money? My money?' Jax's expression was thunderous.

'It wasn't my fault, Jax. I swear. There were these two lads on the train. They followed me all the way back to the common and jumped me. They took everything, my phone, the money…' He was mumbling now, the words tumbling from his mouth quicker than he could physically say them, in the desperate hope that if he just explained what had happened, Jax might go easy on him. 'They gave me a real beating too, Jax,' Kian went on, lifting his shirt to show the mass of purple bruises that were spread all over his chest and stomach, determined to prove that he wasn't making this up. That he'd had no choice but to hand over the money. 'I think they broke my ribs.'

'For fuck's sake! I knew you weren't up for this,' Jax said, shaking his head disappointedly before inhaling a long pull of his joint. 'I should have listened to the boys. They said you were a liability. That you were too bloody soft. Shit! I should never have given you a chance.'

'Honestly, Jax, I did good up until then. But these boys, I think they knew about the drop; I think they followed me. Because they knew exactly what they were looking for. They went straight for the cash. I think it was a set-up,' Kian said, desperately trying to wrack his brains as to what had gone wrong. 'I did everything just like you said. No one saw me. Maybe your contact got greedy and sent them after me to get the money back, so he could keep the gear and the money?' It was the only thing that Kian could think of that made any sense. Only Jax clearly didn't agree.

'Oh, that's what you think, is it? That's your theory? You do one job. One half-arsed job that YOU completely fuck up, and then YOU have the balls to come in here and start spouting off bullshit to justify it all and try and pin the blame on my contact. Someone I've dealt with for months and never had any problems with until now.' He was trying to intimidate him. It was working. Kian felt as if he was rooted to the spot, so scared that he couldn't move.

'And what if you weren't set-up, huh? Did you think about that?' Jax said, stepping forward and poking Kian hard in the chest, not caring about his injuries, enjoying the younger boy's wince of pain. 'What if it was down to you that the job fucked up? What if you weren't as low-key as I told you to be? And those boys saw you waving that cash about and assumed, rightly, that you were an easy fucking target? Cause from where I'm standing, that sounds much more likely than one of my contacts, that I've been working with for months, that I've never had a problem with, suddenly mugging me off!' A shower of spittle left Jax's lips as he raised his voice, spraying Kian's face as he leant in close.

'You're fucked, mate!' Jax announced finally. 'That money didn't belong to me. It belonged to the bosses. And trust me, they are the sort of blokes that you don't want to piss off, Kian. Do you get me?'

Kian nodded. This was exactly the kind of thing that he was afraid he might hear.

'There's going to be big repercussions for this, let me tell you. That kicking will be the least of your worries. The boss man will be wanting his money. He won't accept any lame arse excuses. That ain't how things work around here.' Jax slapped Kian around the head to drum his point into the boy.

Kian flinched. He'd never seen Jax so angry, and he could tell by the way that the older boy was pacing the room now that this was going to create a load of shit for both of them.

More so him, though, he was starting to realise that for certain.

'I'll have to pay it,' Jax said, more to himself than anyone else as he stamped back and forth across the kitchen, his fists clenched at his sides, looking as if he was ready to explode.

'I'll have to save our arses. Otherwise one of us will end up getting stabbed up.' Jax's mood shifted then as soon as he decided what was to be done. Taking another deep toke of his joint, he inhaled the smoke deep into his lungs.

'Thanks, Jax. I appreciate it,' Kian said, believing, wrongly, that Jax had calmed down. That he understood this wasn't Kian's fault. Not really.

'Nah, Kian. You've got it wrong, mate.' Jax couldn't help but laugh, despite the bad mood he'd been in. Kian really didn't have a clue. 'I ain't bailing you out. I'm saving my own arse. Proving to the top dogs that I can run my end of this operation.' Kian's face turned pale as he listened. 'You're going to have to pay it back to me. Which means you are in debt to me now. You owe me two grand. And somehow… I don't give a flying fuck how… you're going to get it back for me. Every single penny of it.'

Jax finally flashed Kian a genuine smile then, as he stubbed out the joint in the kitchen sink.

'Yo boys, one of you get that fat prick Philip out from his bedroom and get him in here to make us all some food, yeah! I'm starving,' Jax called out as he made his way out of the kitchen to see what the boys were doing, before turning as he reached the doorway and addressing Kian one last time. 'You don't get to walk away from none of this until you've repaid your debt. Until then, Kian, you're mine.'

CHAPTER TWELVE

'Oi, what do you think you're doing?' Holder shouted, running out the main doors of the tower block on the Griffin Estate, as he spotted the two young lads from earlier who'd thrown their ball at the car, squatting down by the side of their unmarked police car.

'Just checking out your car, mate! Bit gay even for a pig, isn't it?' one of the lads shouted back, nudging his friend to get up from where he was currently crouched, slashing the car's tyres with a screwdriver. Getting closer, Holder could see that both the wing mirrors had been smashed and were hanging off too.

'You two are nicked,' he shouted, nodding to Lucy, knowing that she'd be thinking exactly what he was. That they were going to have to bring both these boys in for criminal damage. Only as he turned back to them, they'd already started running.

'You'll have to catch us first, you old bastard!' one of them shouted over his shoulder.

'Little shits!' Holder muttered to himself. 'Murphy go round the back way, in case they manage to make it out the other side.'

'Are you sure we shouldn't stay together? They've just slashed the tyres, they'll have weapons.'

'They look about seven, Murphy. I'm sure we'll cope!' Holder shouted, giving chase to the boys.

Making his way back into the grounds of the estate, Holder followed the boys as they raced across the communal gardens, ignoring the footpaths and bolting across the grass, until they

made it into a secluded courtyard at the back and both ducked
down behind a bench, clearly believing that they'd outsmarted
the officer. Holder shook his head and smirked.

'I can see you both! Come out.'

Both boys stood up.

'You giving up then?' Holder said, assuming that the lads
were surrendering, though bracing himself for another chase,
just in case.

'Are you giving up, more like?' one of them taunted.

It was only then Holder saw that they were standing next to
a pile of bricks, both of them holding one in each hand, before
seconds later launching them at the detective.

Holder dived out the way, managing to avoid most of them,
but he wasn't quick enough for the last one, which caught him
full pelt, straight in the face. An almighty pain exploded inside
his head and Holder was floored. Knocked unconscious.

'Shit! That was a right shot!' one of the boys said to the other,
not able to believe their luck that they'd not only hit their target
right between the eyes, but they'd knocked the copper onto his arse.

'He's bleeding,' the other boy said, noting the trickle of blood
running down the officer's face, as the man lay sprawled out on
the ground.

'We ain't killed him, have we?' Stepping closer, one of the
boys prodded the man with his foot, to check he wasn't just
pretending. Then, seeing that he was out cold, he bent down
and checked for a pulse. 'Nah, he's still breathing.' He sounded
almost disappointed before adding, 'Here, get your phone out,
you need to film this, it's pure gold.'

The boys were so busy laughing to themselves that they didn't
hear DC Murphy sneaking up behind them. And by the time
they'd heard her creeping close, she was already on them. Grabbing both the boys by their hoods, she yanked them backwards,

away from where DC Holder lay injured. The two boys knocked heads as they fell back on to their own arses then.

'Officer down. Get an ambulance out here now.' Standing over the boys, Lucy shouted her order to one of the officers who ran towards her from the backup unit that she'd already called. Going against Holder's earlier judgement, Lucy had made her own decision to call this in. She didn't want to take any chances on herself or Holder being the victims of an ambush. Especially after the recent attacks. Looking down at the two snotty nose, sulking kids, Lucy shook her head.

'Christ! You two barely look as if you're out of nappies! How old are you?'

'What's it got to do with you? Fuck off,' the boy who had sworn at her earlier said.

The second boy was more contrite.

'We're ten,' he said, looking teary now that they'd both been caught and were going to get into trouble.

'Well, I bet your parents are going to be proud of you both. You are under arrest for criminal damage and assaulting a police officer.'

CHAPTER THIRTEEN

'Oh, Lucy, darling! I wasn't expecting you!' Winnie Murphy flashed a huge smile at her beautiful granddaughter standing in the doorway. 'I didn't see you there watching me. Perfect timing, though, my darling. Look what I've got.' Winnie beamed, in her element. She was sitting in the middle of the lounge floor, a pile of her precious photo albums spread out all around her. 'I was just going through my old photos. Christ, there's some funny ones in this lot. The things I used to wear. I wish someone had told me how frumpy I always dressed back then. I think I look better now. Don't you, dear?'

'I do, Nan!' Stepping into the room, Lucy placed her handbag and the takeaway bag down on the table, before plastering a smile that she no longer felt to her face, in the hope of hiding the deep feeling of dread that had formed in her stomach at hearing her nan say she hadn't been expecting her. She silently reminded herself what the doctors had advised her to do. That she had to try not to react. To act normal. Although nothing around here felt anything near normal anymore.

Taking in the sight of hundreds of bright yellow Post-it notes that covered the walls, TV screen and all of the picture frames around the room, Lucy eyed the thick black writing, scrawled on each one. Her nan's handwriting was barely legible anymore. But she could read what they said. *The baby is coming! The baby is coming!* Lucy closed her eyes, not sure she even possessed the strength to summon up the energy she'd need in order to deal with all of this again, tonight. *Act normal.*

'You always look lovely, Nan. Vibrant!' Lucy said, taking in the sight of her nan's colourful, mismatched outfit. Her observation wasn't a lie. Her nan was wearing a bold, eccentric floral and leopard print outfit today. The mismatched clothing matched her outgoing personality perfectly. 'I got us a Chinese, Nan. I'll dish it up, yeah?'

'Oh, it can wait for two minutes, surely. I haven't seen you in so long. Come and sit with me, Lucy, darling,' Winnie said, patting the patch of carpet on the floor next to her enthusiastically.

Knowing how volatile her nan could be when she was in this mood, Lucy did as she was asked. She eyed the piles of photo albums and watched her nan's face light up animatedly each time she picked up a photo and looked at it.

'Look at this one, Lucy. It's you as a little girl; such a beautiful child you were! So angelic.' Winnie held up the photo for Lucy to look at, not registering the strain on her granddaughter's face that stared back at her. Because even as Lucy nodded and smiled on cue, she knew where this conversation was going ultimately. When her nan started to drag up the memories that were buried so deep from the past.

At first, reminiscing had made her nan so happy. Remembering old people and places she'd been to had perked her up a little. Each little trip she'd taken down memory lane had put a smile on her face for a short while, but it was never long until she'd see something that triggered the memories that she tried so hard to block out. That was when the confusion would set in and then her nan would quickly spiral into turmoil once more.

Though the truth was that her nan was confused about most things these days. Lucy was ashamed to admit it, but sometimes her nan's vagueness made everything a bit easier for her to deal with. She'd play make-believe, going along with all of her nan's stories, nodding and smiling and never directly answering any of her questions, simply for an easy life.

But then her nan had started to get angry and volatile, demanding answers from Lucy, suspecting that her granddaughter was keeping things from her as the old memories slowly crept back in, and things in her head didn't add up. Things that weren't familiar to Winnie.

A flicker of a recent memory, the sharp stab of pain all over again at the realisation that they weren't back there. Before. The spell would break then, and Winnie's little make-believe world crumbled around her once more. And then the tears and heartbreak would come. Only Lucy wasn't able for any of that today. Her only hope of getting her nan out of this mood was to distract her, and gently prise the woman away from the albums without her realising what she was doing.

'I went down to the Chinese, Nan, and picked up your favourite. Duck pancakes. With extra hoisin sauce, just how you like it. Come on, it's going to be getting cold,' Lucy said, getting up and holding the takeaway bag out to her nan, faking a chirpiness that she no longer felt, and hoping that the food would be a welcome distraction from her nan's trip down memory lane. For them both.

'Duck? Oh, I couldn't eat that. You know I hate duck!' Winnie said, screwing her face up in disgust before shaking her head. There was clear disappointment in her tone that Lucy hadn't remembered such a detail, which Lucy thought was ironic under the circumstances. It was her nan's favourite. Only today, she couldn't even remember that.

'I'm not hungry anyway. I made a lovely roast dinner earlier!' Winnie declared, just as Vivian stepped out of the kitchen and shook her head with a grin.

'I heard you come in, Lucy, darling. I thought you could probably do with a minute alone together,' Vivian said softly, her eyes sweeping the Post-it notes around the room. Lucy nodded gratefully, taking the woman's hint. Vivian Alton was a fantastic carer, so patient and considerate. The woman was worth her weight in gold. She'd known that Lucy would be saddened by her nan's mood tonight and that she'd want to try and talk her nan down. She hadn't been able to, though, and her nan seemed to be slipping into the dark place so often lately.

'What was that I just heard you telling Lucy, Win? That you made a lovely roast dinner, did you?' Vivian chuckled, catching the tail end of the conversation and seeing the takeaway bag, and confirming to Lucy what she had already worked out. That this was yet another of her nan's stories. 'Must have been while I wasn't looking, my love! Though, it's a nice idea, getting you out in that kitchen whipping up a feast for us all! But I think you're getting yourself mixed up, sweetheart. We had sausage and mash for lunch today, remember? You had extra gravy on yours, didn't you, love?' Vivian said, hoping to gently jog the woman's memory.

'And you love duck pancakes, Nan. They are your favourite,' Lucy chimed in too.

'Oh, do I? Oh, yes. I do remember my lunch now. I had two sausages with mine.'

'You had four sausages, Winnie. And extra mash.'

Winnie shrugged her shoulders. Her expression had changed to a look of frustration now at not being able to remember. Furrowing her brow suddenly she looked flustered as she looked back down at the photo albums. She didn't seem convinced at what Vivian was telling her, but she was going along with it for now, not wanting to bother herself in arguing with the woman. Her attention turned back to the loose photos that had slipped from one of the books.

'Come on, Nan, let's leave those for now. We can look at them again later. I'll dish this up before it goes cold,' Lucy said, placing the bag down on the table and getting some plates. 'I've got enough for all of us if you fancy joining us, Vivian?'

'I'm good, thanks,' Vivian said, busying herself taking her apron off and rolling it up in her hands, readying herself to leave for the day now that Lucy had returned home from work.

'Has she been like this all day?' Lucy said, keeping her voice down so that her nan wouldn't overhear her, and nodding over towards the wall, and TV where Post-it notes were plastered across the screen. She hoped that her nan hadn't been too much trouble today, but she could tell by how exhausted Vivian looked that she must have had her work cut out for her.

'We've had a very busy day, haven't we, Winnie?' Vivian said with a cheerful smile, as Winnie stopped what she was doing and looked at the two younger women, suspicious suddenly that she was the topic of their conversation. 'We've been looking at all the photos and making space in the photo albums for all the new ones too.' Vivian made subtle eyes at Lucy, and Lucy knew instantly what she was referring to.

'She's okay,' Vivian said, offering a small smile of reassurance to the younger woman. 'It's what I'm here for.'

'Is she telling you what I made room for, Lucy?' Winnie interrupted, her tone suddenly abrupt. 'New photos of the baby!'

Lucy bit her lip; she'd anticipated this conversation.

'Oh, well, Nan, that's lovely. Shall we eat, before it all gets cold?' Lucy didn't wait for an answer. Instead she busied herself with dishing the food up onto the plates. Her appetite was gone now, replaced instead with a familiar feeling of angst that bubbled away in the pit of her stomach. She'd have to eat something, though. Her nan wouldn't eat if Lucy didn't eat with her.

'Come on, Winnie. You must be hungry, lovely,' Vivian said, bending down and helping to pick up the photos before she left, sensing Lucy's upset and hoping that her intervention would have the desired effect and make Winnie forget all about the photo albums.

But her actions only seemed to have the opposite effect.

'You're not taking my photos from me!' Winnie said, snatching the pictures out of the woman's hands before glaring at Vivian with contempt. 'Why are you still here anyway? You can go now! Lucy has come to visit me. I don't need you here babysitting me anymore.'

'Nan!' Lucy cried, horrified at her nan's sudden change of mood. Her cheeks blushed red, just as they always did when her nan suddenly spoke out of turn. Especially when she aimed her venomous mood at Vivian. The woman really didn't deserve to be spoken to like that. Not after all she did for her nan. 'I'm so sorry, Vivian, she doesn't mean it…'

'I do bloody well mean it. She's always here. Hanging around like a bad bloody smell. Haven't you got any friends of your own?'

'You're right, Winnie. I should go,' Vivian said serenely, not wanting to antagonise the elderly woman any further as she got up from the floor and held her hands up to prevent Lucy from apologising, as she knew she would.

'Lucy, my darling, I am the very last person you need to apologise or explain to. It would take a lot more than a few comments from that little firecracker to offend me. I'm a big girl, Lucy. Besides, she's right. I do need to get off home to see to my own brood now anyway, my darling. Otherwise they'll end up sticking dried pasta in the deep fat fryer like they did last time, or microwaving frozen burgers again. Boys, huh! They'll be the death of me, or each other by giving themselves food poisoning! You have a good night, Win!' Vivian called out to Winnie as she made her way to the front door. Only Winnie didn't bother to reply; she simply waved her hand absently in the air, dismissing the woman.

'I'm so sorry, Vivian, really I am,' Lucy apologised, shaking her head as she walked Vivian out to the front door, mortified at how rude her nan could be sometimes after spending the day in the woman's care.

'Don't, Lucy!' Vivian said again. 'I know how she gets, it's fine, honestly. And to be fair, she's been a real delight today, keeping me entertained with all her little stories. And let me tell you, can that woman spin a yarn or two. She'll be exhausted tonight just from all her chatting alone.'

Vivian laughed before placing a hand on Lucy's arm and lowering her voice. 'She's been talking about it all day though… the baby.' Vivian whispered the last bit.

Lucy nodded, grateful for the warning. She'd known that this was coming the second that she'd set eyes on all of the Post-it notes that were dotted all around the house. All of her nan's little reminders. Scrawled with the same sentence on every one. *The baby is coming.* And it had been all Lucy could do not to run around the place, snatching the notes from every surface, before screwing them up and chucking them in the bin so that she didn't have to look at them anymore.

'She insisted on getting those albums out, and I tried to talk her out of it, and find things to do to distract her, because I know the state she gets herself in…' Vivian paused. Not wanting to say what they were both thinking. The state Winnie got herself in when she remembered the truth. 'But she was hell-bent on looking at them and there was nothing I could do to stop her.'

Vivian spoke honestly now. 'I think that she is getting worse, Lucy. And I know you said you don't even want to consider what we spoke about last week, about getting some extra care, but I hate to say it, darling – soon, that decision might not be yours to make anymore.'

Lucy nodded, grateful for the woman's honesty. She knew that Vivian only meant well and she wouldn't say anything that wasn't true. But Lucy couldn't even consider placing her nan in a residential home. Just the thought of it made her feel like a complete failure. But she also knew that her nan was getting worse and it would only be a matter of time before she'd need care around the clock.

'I've seen it with so many of my patients before, Lucy. Dementia is a cruel disease and it swoops in quickly and doesn't leave much behind in its wake.'

'I know…' Lucy said sadly, realising that she was learning that herself first-hand. 'I'll think about it, but I can't promise anything. And thank you for today. For being so patient with her. We'd both be lost without you!'

'Oh trust me, Patience is my middle name. It's got to be with all my lot at home all running around and almost killing each other every five seconds. You know, over real important stuff, like who ate the last biscuit, or who took the batteries out of the remote control to use in their Xbox controllers. Looking after your nan is sometimes a very welcome break.' Vivian winked, before stepping out into the cold dark night and letting Lucy close the door behind her.

She slowly made her way back into the lounge.

'Oh, Lucy, darling. Look at my hair in this one. So long. I must have been about thirty here,' Winnie said, tapping the image of her wearing a fashionable hairstyle of the time. Then, placing the photos back down on the floor, she looked up at Lucy, her face twisted with confusion.

'I wonder what the baby's name will be, Lucy? When do you think she'll be home, Lucy?' Winnie's glance lingered expectantly on the front door. As if any minute now, it would burst open and they'd both be transported back in time.

Back to before.

'I don't know, Nan,' Lucy said, her back to her as she gathered the photos up, forcing back her tears.

How many times did she have to go through this? Replaying the same painful conversation over and over again. Lucy shook her head, unable to find any words that would take away all the hurt and pain. Unable to say anything that would make any of this any better.

'Nan…' she started, taking a slow deep breath as she squeezed her eyes shut with apprehension, about to tell Winnie the truth. Only, turning to her and seeing the hope in the woman's eyes, she couldn't bring herself to say the words that would break her heart over and over again. The only choice she had was to play along.

'Let's eat our dinner, yeah? Before it gets cold.'

A lump formed deep in her throat as she gathered up the photo albums and shoved them all in the nearest cupboard before her nan could argue with her further.

'Come on, Nan, let's get you comfortable.' She helped her nan up and into her usual seat directly in front of the TV, before quickly unpeeling the sticky notes from where they decorated the screen. 'Your programme's just starting and it's supposed to be a good one tonight,' Lucy lied, switching the TV on, relieved to find one of her nan's favourite soaps starting.

'Oh yes! I like this one, Lucy,' Winnie said, gleefully.

She was immersed in the programme as soon as it started, and Lucy placed a tray of food down on her lap. The background noise of the TV show allowed her to zone out as she grabbed her own dinner and sat down in a chair opposite her nan.

Having forced a mouthful of her own food into her mouth, Lucy decided that she could no longer stomach it. Instead, she pushed her food aimlessly around the plate and stared over at her nan. The woman's expression was blank, and the eyes that were fixed to the screen were vacant. She wasn't even watching it. She was gone again. A million miles away. Off in her own dream land. Then Winnie Murphy looked down at her plate and wrinkled her nose in disgust as if she'd only just seen it for the very first time.

'Is this duck, Lucy? I don't like duck…'

CHAPTER FOURTEEN

'What the fuck is the matter with him?' Ronnie Western asked, unable to drag his gaze from where Philip Penfold sat naked and tied to a chair in the middle of the front room. He took in the sight of the bloke's rippling rolls of white flab as he slumped there as rigid as a corpse. The only signs that proved Philip wasn't dead were that he was dribbling profusely and his eyes were rolling in the back of his head.

'One of the lads thought it would be funny to get him on a bit of spice. The mad fucker went off his head on the stuff. So, we're keeping him like that until that shit wears off. The bloke's a unit; he could cause some right damage if he wanted to,' Jax explained.

The two Western brothers exchanged nervous looks. Ronnie could see by the look on Zack's face that he was thinking the same as he was. That this bloke Jax had tied up had special needs and, by the looks of it, Jax and his boys were having themselves a permanent party at this poor fucker's expense. They'd trashed the place. There were empty bottles of alcohol all over the floor and the smell of weed hung in the air. They'd been terrorising the man, judging by the puddle of piss that pooled at Philip's feet. It was a step too far over the line, even for the likes of them. Though Ronnie and Zack both knew better than to voice their opinions. Jax Priestly was a law unto himself. And Ronnie and Zack had both been working for him long enough to know that if you pissed him off, you'd pay a heavy price. Even more so now that he'd got in with some big faces who were running County Lines and wanted Jax to front this end of the operation.

Jax had landed on his feet with this set-up. Recruiting younger kids to 'go country' and do drops at quieter, more rural locations outside of London, meant Jax barely had to do any of the dirty work himself anymore, because he had an army of his boys doing his work for him. Which meant the chances of him getting caught were almost slim to none, and he was starting to believe that he was untouchable. He had connections now. He had protection. All he had to do was keep his boys on their toes and make sure they knew who was running things around here. Which was where Ronnie and Zack came into it.

Clocking the exchanged look of panic on both boys' faces, Jax couldn't help but laugh.

'Don't you worry about him, lads. Seriously. He's had the time of his life today, ain't you, Philip? The best day ever!' Jax said, getting up and giving Philip a light shove, to make sure the man was still slightly coherent. The last thing he needed was anyone snuffing it. Especially as Jax and the boys were going to have to clear back out again tonight, because Philip's carer was due to come back around tomorrow morning.

Seeing Philip's body jolt with fear at his touch, Jax shrugged his shoulders to hide his relief.

'Funniest thing I've seen in ages, though. He was proper monged-out on the stuff!'

Ronnie smiled, though the fact that it didn't meet his eyes was duly noted by Jax.

'Anyway, enough of that crap. Sit down,' Jax ordered. Done with the niceties, he nodded at the two younger lads to sit opposite him. 'The others will be back soon, and I want you both to be long gone by then. I can't risk any of them clocking you here, in case they recognise you.'

So far Ronnie and Zack were Jax's best kept secret.

'I take it by the state of the kid, you got it then?' Jax said finally, impatient now as Ronnie dutifully pulled out the envelope of cash from his inside jacket pocket.

'Two k, it's all there,' Ronnie said, almost sounding offended as Jax snatched it from his grasp and thumbed his way through the pile of notes regardless to check for himself. 'I double-checked it myself, to make sure Kian hadn't creamed any off the top before we'd gotten our hands on it. It's all there.'

This was too much of a good earner for them to mess up. Ronnie and his brother were on to a good thing here, and they both knew it. Jax paid them two hundred notes each, and all they had to do was follow Jax's newest recruit on his first job and make sure they got the money off him. To make it look like a random mugging they always dished out a decent beating in the process. That was all part of Jax's orders too. Jax wanted his runners scared and he wanted them in debt to him. It was the only way the system would work. The only way that Jax would be able to keep tabs on everyone.

And it meant that Jax doubled his money too. He got back the money he owed his bosses, but he also made sure that his boys paid him back the money that they'd thought they'd lost. So he was quids in, no matter what. And next time his boys did a drop, they'd be more astute, more alert. They'd learn the hard way to keep their wits about them, not only looking out for the Old Bill watching them, but also more aware if anyone else was tailing them. It was a no-brainer all round.

'You boys proper mashed him up,' Jax said, shaking his head and pulling out four hundred pounds in fifty pound notes and folding them neatly in the palm of his hand. 'You might have broken a couple of his ribs. I said a beating, but I didn't want the lad put out of action. He'll be fuck all use to me all battered up!'

Ronnie shrugged.

'That was Zack. I told him he went too hard. He'd had a row with our old man before we left for the station. The stupid bastard was drunk again, wasn't he? Went to clump Zack one, only Zack managed to clump him one back. Now he ain't allowed back in the house again. The old git said he's gonna make him sleep in the shed until he apologises. Only Zack won't apologise, will you, Zack?'

'I ain't fucking apologising to that twat. He can apologise to me first, for whacking me one. Doesn't know his strength when he's had a drink. You wait until one day he does it to me and I lose my rag with him and beat ten shades of shit out of him. Then he'll be sorry.'

'See!' Ronnie said, raising his eyebrows to prove his point. 'Stubborn bastard, just like the old man.'

Jax couldn't help but laugh at that.

'How did the kid do with the rest of the drop?'

'He was good,' Zack said. 'Fast, too. We watched him do the drop and take the money. There was no chat, no BS. It was done in seconds and he was back on the next train. Shit his pants when he realised that we were following him, though. He clocked us straight away! He did a bunk as soon as the train stopped. I've never seen a kid run so fast!'

Jax nodded then, secretly pleased that the kid could hold his own under a bit of scrutiny. He knew that Ronnie and Zack would be straight with him. If they thought anyone was messing Jax about, or doing anything they shouldn't on the sly, they'd tell him. Jax had thought about offering the two boys a place with the Griffin Boys. They'd be a real asset to the firm, but they'd told Jax from day one that they preferred to do their own thing and Jax got it. They weren't like some of the hood rats and wannabe gangsters that had latched onto him over time from the estate.

Mistakenly believing that just because they were on his payroll, they were now the big I am. Ronnie and Zack were a bit like him in that respect. They wanted to give out their own orders and play by their own rules. They did their job, collected their money and stayed out of all the bullshit. Jax had to respect them both for that. And in the meantime, he'd use them in another way instead.

'So he's got potential then? Apart from not being able to handle the kicking?'

Ronnie nodded.

'If he hadn't have stacked it, I reckon he would have outrun us and made it back to the flat easily!'

This pleased Jax too. He'd been dubious about letting Kian have an in. The kid wasn't like a lot of the other boys on the estate. He was quiet, and Jax had guessed that the kid had lived a sheltered life in comparison to most of them. From what he'd learned from Kian so far, he'd been brought up by his sister because his mother was a waster of an alcoholic. Kian had no idea what he was getting into. Not really. He just saw all the wealth that the boys pulled in and wanted some of it for himself. And not just so that he could waste his money on fancy trainers and expensive phones like the other kids. Kian wanted money to support his family. Which meant that the kid would be prepared to graft harder than all the others because he had a real reason to need to do well. And now that Kian had thought he'd fucked up and lost Jax his money, Jax had some real leverage over the boy. Not only that, but Ronnie and Zack were reciting word for word what Kian had already told him. Which only stood Kian in better stead, because that meant that he hadn't tried to embellish the facts or exaggerate the story of what had happened. He hadn't tried to come off better than his attackers.

'Good work, boys!' Jax said, handing the money over to Ronnie before he nodded in the direction of the front door. 'Now get the fuck out of here, before the boys come back and realise that you two are the fuckers giving them all a pasting for me.'

Casting a final look of sympathy at Philip as they passed him on the way out, Ronnie and Zack happily obliged, glad to get their money and get out of the place.

Watching them shut the door behind them on the way out, Jax sat back in his chair and lit up a spliff. Taking a slow deep breath, he inhaled the first pull of smoke. Kian Winters was clean skin – he wasn't known to the police and certainly wasn't the type to attract any attention. Not only that but the boy had passed his initiation as far as Jax was concerned, and with flying colours. The lad had well and truly earned his 'in'. He couldn't help smiling at that expression. All these stupid fuckers had no idea! Once they were in to this way of life, there was no way of ever getting back out.

CHAPTER FIFTEEN

'Just do what I do, yeah? Follow my lead,' Jax ordered Kian as they both huddled under the shelter of the newsagent's doorway just off Wandsworth High Street. The shop was in darkness. The shopkeeper had long since gone home. Kian nodded and did as he was told, mirroring what the older lad was doing and pulling his hood tightly around his face.

'For fuck's sake, Kian. I mean in a bit, when we spot our mark, not now. Jesus you gunna scratch your arse every time I scratch mine too?' Jax said sharply, het up now.

He had been trying to shield himself from the icy wind and the rain that ran down his face.

But he figured it wasn't a bad thing that they both concealed their faces; they didn't want anyone to be able to recognise them or get their descriptions. It was almost midnight, the perfect time to strike. The street was illuminated only by the streetlamps that sporadically lined the road. Half of them were not even working, so they had less chance of getting seen and even less chance of getting caught. Only their plans had been dampened by the pissing rain. The streets were pretty much deserted now.

'Everyone's getting poxy cabs,' Jax said, nodding up the road to the last crowd of pub goers, a group of lads, all piling out of the kebab shop and making a run for it to a nearby waiting taxi before the car sped off, leaving the street empty and quiet again.

'Fucking weather!' Jax said, lighting up a cigarette and taking a deep drag before blowing white smoke rings out into the black sky. Kian scanned the road, feeling grateful that the rain had messed up their plans. The longer they both stood around waiting for someone to come along, the more likely it was that they wouldn't be going through with this tonight.

'Shall we leave it then? Maybe tonight ain't the right night?' Kian said, his voice full of relief. He just wanted to go home. Every part of his body hurt and he needed to get a proper night's sleep. He hadn't slept the past two nights. Zipping up his jacket, he waited for Jax to answer. The torrential downpour that Jax was pissed off about was turning out to be Kian's saving grace. He knew even if Jax did call this off, he would only make them come back another night, but at least it would buy Kian a bit more time to get his head around what they were both going to do tonight. Because there was no way that Jax was going to let him off scot-free, not when he owed him so much money.

'Bingo!' Jax said, nodding to the movement further up the road that had caught his eye. Kian turned to look, his heart sinking at Jax's sudden gesture, and saw the man, in the distance, staggering up the road towards them. A twisted smirk spread across Jax's face.

'That's our man.'

Kian took a deep breath as he eyed the rest of the street hoping to see someone else lurking there in the shadows, watching them, so that they'd have a real excuse not to go through with it. But of course there was no one else around. It was just the two of them, and the man. Kian sized him up. An older man, in his mid-fifties, Kian guessed, with a bald head, glasses and a slight paunch displaying his love of beer. And, judging by the way that he could barely stand up, let alone walk, clearly paralytic. Soaked through to the skin from the rain, too; though he was too drunk he didn't appear to even notice the rain. Too busy steadying himself as he walked, before losing his balance as he neared them. The two boys watched as he grabbed onto the nearest lamp post for support, before falling sideways and placing his hands down onto a garden wall.

'Right, are you ready?' Jax asked.

Kian nodded. He wasn't ready at all. Chewing the inside of his mouth as the man came closer, he bit down hard on the flesh inside his mouth, a bad habit of his when he got nervous. And he was more than nervous now. He felt sick. His hands were clammy and his skin prickled with beads of perspiration. Once he did this, there would be no going back. Everything would change forever. But what choice did he have with Jax here, standing over him? He had to get Jax his money back, and Jax had insisted that this was the only way to do it. By robbing people in the street.

'Get ready…' Jax whispered.

Kian yanked his hood up around his face further to protect his identity, before peering out from the sheltered doorway, his eyes on the mark.

Jax had said he was going to start him off with an easy target. That was why they'd waited just down from the pub, hoping that their victim would leave in a drunken state at last orders so that they would have an advantage over them. So that their victim wouldn't be able to fight back. And if they were drunk enough that they weren't completely sure of their attacker's description, even better.

The man was coming closer now. Taking a step back so that he wouldn't be spotted, Kian hid among the shadows, his heart pounding inside his chest as the man's footsteps got louder. He looked at Jax for reassurance, but Jax just stared ahead, concentrating. The man was close now. Kian could hear his unsteady feet slapping against the wet pavement as he made his way towards them. Jax was staring at him then, his eyes boring into his. Nodding, he gave Kian the signal. Kian counted to three. Ready to strike. And the man was there. Right in front of the shop doorway. In direct line of the two lads. It was time. Only Kian couldn't move his legs.

It was as if they'd become suddenly weighted down by lead. As if they were stuck to the pavement.

'Move, you fucking div!' Jax shouted.

The man turned, startled by the voices as he twigged the two lads were up to no good.

Jax charged towards the man as fast as he could and punched him in the face with as much force as he could muster. Because he only wanted to do this once. And once was all it took.

The man's body plummeted to the ground in one swift movement, thudding loudly on the pavement. One punch and the man was out cold.

'Get the money,' Jax commanded loudly, forcing Kian to snap out of his trance-like state. They needed to move, and fast. Kian did as he was told.

Moving swiftly, he hunched down on the floor on his knees, ignoring the wet that seeped through his tracksuit bottoms, and rummaged through the man's pockets, pulling out a packet of cigarettes and a dirty, screwed-up tissue. Then, bingo, he found the man's wallet. And what looked like a brand-new iPhone.

'We need to move!' Jax shouted suddenly.

Kian was startled by the sudden bright yellow hue of light that shone directly at them, blinding them both as a car screeched loudly to a halt in the middle of the road in front of them.

A woman leapt out from the driver's seat, leaving the car engine running and the driver's door wide open. Her screams of terror filled the street. As her cries became hysterical, Kian followed the woman's gaze to the man on the ground, wondering why he wasn't trying to get back up. He didn't look right. His body illuminated now by the car's headlights, he lay sprawled out on the pavement. His neck was twisted at an awkward angle, his head hanging limply just off the edge of the kerb. And then Kian saw the blood, a thick pool of it seeping out from where he must have cracked open his skull as he landed.

'He's dead?' Kian said, his voice sounding far off and unrecognisable even to himself as he stared at the man's vacant, glassy eyes. Staring straight ahead. Unblinking. Not moving.

'Nah, mate! Get up! Please get up!' Kian said frantically.

'Run!' Jax shouted.

Only Kian couldn't move.

'What did you do to him? What did you do?' the woman screeched, falling to her knees and cradling the man in her arms. Her hands and clothes were quickly covered in blood. There was more noise then, as people further up the road ran towards them to offer help. Someone pulled out a phone and started calling for an ambulance. But it was too late for an ambulance now. Even Kian could see that.

Kian ran too then.

Ignoring the shouts behind him, he turned off Wandsworth High Street and legged it through all the quiet side roads and long winding alleyways that mazed their way in amongst the estate. He ran until he could barely breathe, his ribs burning in agony from the beating, his lungs struggling from the lack of air.

Crying now, Kian stopped. Doubled over in the alleyway, feeling the sharp dig of the man's wallet and phone digging into his thigh, he pulled them both out of his pocket. His eyes went immediately to the screen saver. He recognised the man in the photo as the man lying on the pavement. The woman next to him had been the woman at the scene. They were both staring back at the camera, cuddling two young children. Grandkids?

Kian frantically switched the phone off and took the SIM card out, snapping it in half before he threw it into the alley behind him. Hopefully no one would be able to trace his movements now. Then he opened the man's wallet to see how much money was inside. Fingering the tatty leather material, he noted the old worn library card. There was a single fifty pence piece in the loose change compartment. And nothing else.

Kian squeezed his eyes shut. The rest of the wallet was empty. Tonight had all been for nothing. The hysterical woman's last words were still swarming inside his ears.

What did you do to him? What did you do?

Leaning up against the fence Kian threw up the contents of his stomach. Jax had said that this was a no-brainer. He'd said that nothing could go wrong. That it would be easy money. A tatty old wallet containing only fifty pence, and an iPhone. That was all that man's life had been worth.

CHAPTER SIXTEEN

'Your breakfast's probably gone soggy now! It's been sitting there since I called you forty-five minutes ago!' Shannon sniped, nodding down at the cereal and tea that she'd placed down on the dining room table for her brother, for when he finally dragged himself out of his pit.

'I told you, I'm not hungry,' Kian said, slumping down on the seat anyway, and taking a mouthful of the cold tea. 'And I'm not going to school either. I still don't feel great.'

'Where were you last night?' Shannon asked, eyeing her brother suspiciously and noting the dark bags under his eyes which only mirrored his current mood.

'Just out.' Kian shrugged before letting out a dramatic yawn.

'Well, you look like shit, and thanks to you staying out until almost two a.m., so do I,' Shannon said tartly, making it very clear to her brother that she wasn't impressed by the previous night's antics one bit. Shannon had waited up half the night for her brother, and when he'd finally decided to show his face, he'd barely even acknowledged her, sweeping past her in a hurry to get to his room, without so much as a word of apology for coming home so late.

'It's not fair, Kian. I was at school all day yesterday, and then I had to do a shift at the chippy. I was knackered…'

'Well, that's your problem then, isn't it, Shan? I didn't ask you to wait up for me, did I?' Kian snapped back, picking up the spoon and eyeing the cereal, before deciding that he couldn't stomach anything to eat, and dropping it back down into the bowl. 'You ain't my mum!'

'When it suits.' Shannon rolled her eyes. 'I don't hear you complaining when I'm making you breakfast or washing your school uniform. Cos your mother ain't going to do it for you, is she?'

Unable to hide the tears in her eyes then, at her brother's blatant disregard towards her, Shannon scooped up the bowl and chucked it down into the sink. She'd looked out for Kian ever since she could remember. Taking on a motherly role when he was little without even realising it. She'd taken over where her mother couldn't. Bathing Kian and dressing him. Making sure that he always had something to eat, even if some nights it was just toast or cereal. How dare Kian throw everything back in her face now that it suited him?

'I'm going to school.' She grabbed her trainers from where she'd left them next to the front door, before she said anything that she might regret. 'And take a key tonight, because you know what, from now on, I'm not waiting up for you. And I'm not running around for you at home either. If you're big enough to look after yourself these days, you can do your own cooking and washing too,' Shannon shot at him, wanting to hurt Kian as much as he hurt her. Only, she faltered when she saw her brother stand up, wincing with pain.

'Look. I don't want to fight with you, Kian. I'm just worried about you. I'm not trying to be your mum. I'm your sister. I care about you.'

'Good, cos I don't need another mother. I don't even need the one I've got. She's bloody useless.' He jerked his head towards the stairs, guessing his mum was still in bed and probably doing her usual of not resurfacing until lunchtime, safe in the knowledge that the flat would be empty then. 'Lounging around in her bed all day, expecting everything to be done for her.'

'Oi, don't you be bad-mouthing your mother, kid!' Gary's voice boomed from behind them, startling them both.

Turning to where the voice had come from, Shannon and Kian saw a dishevelled-looking Gary sitting up on the sofa where he'd passed out the night before. He had clearly been listening in to their conversation and couldn't help sticking in his own five pence worth.

'You wanna learn some manners, kid. There's no need to be slagging your mother off. She's sick,' Gary sneered, leaning across the table and retrieving one of the discarded cans of cider, before taking a swig out of it, and lighting up a cigarette.

'Oh she's sick all right, she must be, if the only bloke she can manage to keep hold of is you,' Kian muttered back sarcastically. Kian couldn't stand Gary and since day one, he'd never disguised the fact. Gary was always sticking his nose in where it wasn't wanted, making out that he knew what was best for their mother, when the truth was, ever since Gary had come along, their mother had become considerably worse.

'Oi, you cheeky little fucker!' Gary retorted. 'Watch your lip.' Not rising to Kian's rare foul mood, Gary purposely flicked his ash into an empty beer can, before sitting back on the sofa and letting out a huge belch.

It was no secret that Shannon and Kian didn't like him, they'd both made that perfectly clear from the start. The pair of them barely gave him the time of day, but that didn't bother Gary one bit. He didn't like them either. Pair of whiny little brats the both of them, always acting so hard done by, when the truth was they both had an easy life compared to some.

'You're such a disgusting pig!' Kian said, unable to let the row go.

'Kian!' Shannon warned, flashing her brother a stern look.

Gary was the type who was capable of all sorts if pushed enough, and Shannon didn't want Kian to be the one to push him. Especially with drink and drugs still in Gary's system. There was no telling what the man might do.

'No, Shannon, I've had enough. Why should you have to work doing shifts at the chippy after you've been at school every day when all she does is get pissed and lay about in bed? And this waster sits on his arse in our flat with all his scummy mates here. How's that fair?'

'Fair?' Gary laughed then. 'Ah, diddums, poor little Kian. Life ain't fair, mate! You'll find that out for yourself once you've grown up. Your sister is fifteen. In my book, that's old enough to start paying her way in the world. You don't get nothing for nothing as they say…'

'Well, you seem to be doing all right!' Kian snapped, glaring at the man and ignoring Shannon as she squeezed his arm in warning for him to stop. 'Apart from pouring drink down our mother's throat, you ain't put your hand in your pocket for jack shit since you've been here. All you do is sit there and preach to us about our mum as if you know her better than we do. As if you actually give a shit. My mum's been nothing but worse since she met you.' Kian got up and charged towards Gary, pointing his finger at the man, his face turning puce with rage.

'And you know it's true, too, Shan. She's always off her head on drink and drugs. You think I don't see? You think I don't know? But I see it all, and it's bullshit. He's poisoning her. He's making her worse.'

'You wanna watch that gob of yours, Kian! Throwing allegations like that around. I look after your mother. I give her exactly what she needs,' Gary said, throwing Kian a crude wink and smirking to mask the fact that the boy's sudden move towards him had rattled him. 'And, you ain't too old to get a slap, kid. It would pay you to remember that!'

'Oh yeah? Just you try it, mate!' Kian said, taking another step towards Gary to let the man know that he wasn't scared of him.

'Kian, don't!' Shannon pleaded, standing at her brother's side, her hand on his arm protectively as if to gently hold him back.

But Gary was on a roll now, in his element, knowing that he was winding the boy up good and proper.

'Yeah, listen to your big sister, Kian. She knows the score. I mean, I'd hate to see your mother's face later when she finds out how unwelcome you two little scrotes have been making me feel. I wonder how she'll react when I tell her that I don't think I should come over anymore...' Gary glared at them both triumphantly. Knowing full well that if Michelle had to choose between him and her kids, she'd choose him. Twice over.

Shannon and Kian knew it too. Their mother had always done that. Become emotionally and physically dependent on whatever bloke she had hanging around her at the time. Gary might not provide her with any kind of financial security, but he supplied her with the one thing that she truly craved in life: oblivion, in abundance.

'Oh, no. We're not saying that you ain't welcome. You've got that wrong, mate,' Kian shouted back. 'We're saying that if you are so intent on sticking around, how about you put your hand in your pocket and contribute towards the bills and the rent? Seeing as you care about our mum and all that...'

Kian raised his eyebrows expectantly, laughing then, as Gary looked momentarily lost for words. He knew that the man would never agree to those terms, because the bloke was a freeloader. He didn't give a shit about their mum. He was just using her. Just like they all did, until the next easy option came along.

'I do my bit!' Gary sneered finally, annoyed that he was being made to answer to a snivelling little kid. Kian was acting cocky now, getting too big for his boots and Gary didn't like it one bit.

'I know the way to that woman's heart. And your mother likes a drink. That and a few other tricks I have up my sleeve.'

Gary stuck his tongue out then, making lewd gestures to purposely rile Kian up further.

'You piece of shit…' Lunging for Gary, Kian had had enough.

Only Gary was up on his feet to retaliate now, too, ready for the boy after purposely goading him. The two were butting foreheads, their fists clenched at their sides, as they both willed the other to make the first move.

But Shannon wasn't prepared to stand back and watch the two men fight.

'Stop it, both of you!' she said, pushing herself in between them. What her brother was saying was true, there was no doubt about that. But he wouldn't win against Gary. 'Just leave it, Kian. He ain't worth it.'

She grabbed her brother roughly by his arm and wrenched him away from Gary. Kian pulled away defiantly, twisting to get out of her hold, and as he did something dropped with a loud clang from his tracksuit pocket and hit the floor. He looked startled.

'What's that?' Shannon asked suspiciously, eyeing up the iPhone, as Kian quickly scooped it up and stuffed it safely back inside his pocket again, hoping that Shannon wouldn't get a good look at it. But she had seen it.

'Isn't that the new iPhone? The one that's just come out? How can you afford one of those?'

'I can't. It's a mate's. He lent it to me.' Kian shrugged, still seething from Gary's words.

'A mate? What mate? Why would they just lend you a brand-new phone like that? Won't they need it?' Shannon said, unconvinced.

'For fuck's sake, Shannon. Can you just stop with the fucking interrogation? My business is exactly that. My business. Don't you get it? I ain't a little kid anymore. I don't have to tell you everything about my life.' Grabbing his jacket, Kian made his way towards the front door.

'Where are you going now?' Shannon called after him.

'Out. Because if I stay here any longer, I'm going to lose my head! Either that or I'm going to end up battering that prick.' He pointed over to Gary.

'Oh I'd pay to see that, mate, I really would,' Gary shouted back, thoroughly enjoying the show and the effect he seemed to have on the boy.

'You know, you want to be careful, Gary, cos one word to the wrong people and I could make you disappear!' Giving Gary one more look of contempt, Kian slammed the front door behind him.

'Woo! Someone's very touchy, ain't they?' Gary smirked. 'Mark my words, I know the signs. Staying out all hours, then the beating the other day, now this new phone. Tut tut! Someone's definitely up to no good.'

'He said he got it from a friend and he wouldn't lie to me,' Shannon said with more certainty than she really felt. Gary's words were only igniting what she was already thinking herself, but she would never let him know that.

'And you know what, my brother was right about something else, too. Our mother has got worse since she met you, and you have overstayed your welcome. The sooner you move on the better for us all.' Kian might be in trouble, but one thing was for certain, no matter what, they'd always stuck together.

Gary just laughed at that.

'You and your brother are in for a long wait, Shannon, love. I ain't going anywhere. And the sooner you accept that the better.'

'Well, I am! I'm going to school!' She slammed the front door behind her, unable to stomach the vile man any longer.

But as she made her way down the flat's stairwell, she couldn't help thinking that maybe Gary had a point. Something was going on with Kian. Something really bad. And as much as Kian tried to pretend it wasn't, Shannon could just sense it.

CHAPTER SEVENTEEN

'The lift was out of order on Monday too, Sarge. In the other block. When myself and DC Holder came to take the witness statement from the assault on the PCSO,' Lucy said, pointing the broken lift sign out to DS Morgan and making her way to the stairwell door.

'Well, I guess it could be worse,' he said, feigning positivity. 'There're twenty-four floors; thankfully, we only want number thirteen. Plus, I think my wife would probably encourage the extra cardio. Especially if she found out that I binned the salad she made me for lunch and had that greasy cheeseburger instead.'

'Yeah, Sarge, I think going by how often the lifts are out, and the number of times we get called out here, we certainly don't have to worry too much about taking out any gym memberships anytime soon.' Lucy smiled as she followed her superior up the stairs.

'So do you think someone got to the witness on Monday, Sarge?' Lucy asked a minute later, knowing how disappointed the entire team had been when she and Holder had come back to the station without their witness report. Margaret Piper had refused to even let them in the flat, telling the two CID officers that she had made a mistake and she couldn't remember the incident. They'd left empty-handed with the strong suspicion that Margaret had been threatened, somehow, to keep her mouth shut.

Not only that, but to add further insult to injury, DC Holder had also come away suffering a bout of concussion and had needed ten stitches from the brick the two boys had launched at his head.

'I'd say it's likely, but we can't prove anything. It happens all the time around here.'

'What if I paid her another visit, Sarge. Seeing as we're here anyway. She might talk?'

DS Morgan shook his head.

'If she has been threatened and we turn up again at her door, and someone sees us, we could end up putting her in real danger. If she contacts us then fine, but sometimes we just have to know when to let things go. She's an elderly lady. She probably just wants a quiet life and, living round here, who can blame her.'

Lucy nodded in agreement. DS Morgan had a completely different energy than Holder. The job hadn't made him bitter. In fact, if anything it had had the opposite effect on him. DS Morgan still actually cared about the safety of the general public. He was proud of the force in which he served and of his DS rank. Lucy also liked the fact that DS Morgan always spoke so earnestly about things. Lucy liked that quality in a person. It made her feel as if she knew where she stood with them.

'Ugh! Watch where you're walking, Murphy,' Morgan said then, as he stopped on the next landing and nodded down at the used condom strewn in the corner. 'Nice to see that romance isn't dead, eh!' He turned to smile at Lucy.

'Are you all right?' he asked, seeing the pained expression on his trainee's face as she gripped the handrail tightly. 'You can't be out of breath already, we've only done a couple of flights. You're supposed to be running rings around me, Murphy. You look as if you're struggling.'

'Sorry, Sarge. The only thing I'm struggling with is this place. It's just disgusting. Gives me the creeps, that's all,' Lucy said with a tight smile, trying to play down her anxiety about being back on the estate yet again. Every time she stepped foot in the place, she was overcome with the same feeling of wanting to get the hell out of there. 'And it stinks too,' she added, screwing her face up as the acrid stench of urine hit them both with full force as they continued making their way up the concrete steps.

'I know. Social housing at its very worst, isn't it? The estate doesn't seem to be getting any better no matter how much time we spend here. In fact, lately the levels of violence and criminality have escalated beyond control. Which is why there was so much hostility towards our PCSO the other day. The residents here don't want a police presence on the estate, because they feel as if they are being discriminated against and controlled. But at the same time, they need our protection. It's a catch-22.'

'It's always had a bad reputation, though, hasn't it?' Lucy said, acting casual as she posed her question. 'I mean, you've been on the job for years, haven't you, Sarge? Have you always worked around these parts?'

DS Morgan laughed.

'God, that makes me feel old, but thinking about it, I've been in the job longer than you've been alive. For my sins, eh! And I've investigated some horrific crimes that have taken place here over the years, let me tell you. Some that we've had fantastic results with in catching the perpetrators, and some where we didn't have any leads at all. There's some cases that still haunt me even now.'

Lucy nodded in agreement. She understood that only too well.

'Anyway, let's not start the day getting all morbid. You sure you didn't run into today's witness when you were in uniform? The delightful Mr Johnson…'

Lucy shook her head.

'Well, that is a surprise! Johnson is a serial complainer.' DS Morgan shook his head, making his way up the final flight of stairs. 'The last call-out he made he'd reported a kidnapping. It was only after he'd given us the descriptions of two apparent assailants that had committed the crime that he mentioned the victim was in fact his pet cat. Bertie. And worse still, the animal only came in through the cat-flap mid-statement and pissed in the middle of the hallway carpet. You couldn't have made it up!'

Lucy couldn't help but laugh at that.

'Another time, he'd reported an attempted burglary. Johnson had witnessed a man casing out the flats and seeing which ones were occupied or empty. Only on further investigation, we learned that the man in question was in fact one of the local residents who was going door-to-door collecting money for a legitimate cancer charity.'

'So do you think today will be a waste of our time, Sarge?' Lucy asked, wondering why they were even bothering.

DS Morgan held open the doors that led to the thirteenth floor, grinning as Lucy stepped outside onto the balcony and dramatically breathed in a huge lungful of clean air.

'We have to take all complaints seriously, and if Johnson says that he witnessed the assault, we'll soon find out if it's legit. And if so, he's our only lead.'

Lucy nodded, distracted for a few seconds by the view across the common. The grey London sky, stretching out above the huge field of green. This concrete monstrosity such a contrast to the natural beauty around them. She shivered despite herself. The wind was picking up, carrying the sound of kids playing further down the balcony, the noise echoing around them. She was waiting for the nostalgia. For the jolt of a memory to suddenly hit her. But there was nothing. Just numbness as she stood there, looking out at the bleak grey view.

Her eyes fixed on a group of toddlers playing down in the small playground with their mothers nearby. Over by the fence, a gang of older teens huddled around in a group, no doubt up to no good.

'I can't even imagine what it would be like to grow up in a place like this,' DS Morgan said thoughtfully, then, looking at Lucy and realising that the woman was lost in her own daydream, he added, 'Earth to Lucy?'

'Sorry. I was miles away and just thinking the same!' she said with a shrug. The trance was broken.

'Come on. Let's go and see what old Victor Meldrew has to say for himself,' Morgan quipped.

'Victor who? I thought his name was Mr Johnson?' Lucy looked confused as DS Morgan groaned dramatically.

'Christ, I really am old if you don't know who Victor Meldrew is. Never mind.' Morgan chuckled to himself as they both made their way down the balcony towards Mr Johnson's flat.

CHAPTER EIGHTEEN

'Philip, love. It's me, Karen.' Calling out, but not getting an answer, Karen let herself in to Philip Penfold's flat. She was pleased that he hadn't bothered using the security chain, otherwise she'd have been locked out. She hadn't thought about that when she'd arranged to have it installed for him.

'You not up yet, Philip?' she said, surprised to see that the curtains were still drawn and the place was in darkness. Something was most definitely up. Normally Philip would be up and dressed ready when she got here bright and early on a Wednesday morning, full of beans and grateful for some company after not seeing her since Monday, bless him. The poor bloke barely stopped for breath some days, busy telling Karen all about the plans he was going to make for the day. Which, of course, he never really got round to doing. But still, his intentions were always good and he was always full of optimism, which never failed to make Karen smile. She found herself enjoying their little chats and their nice morning cuppa together. Even if she did struggle to get a word in edgeways. But this morning there was a very different mood to the place. Narrowing her eyes, she glanced up at the clock on the wall. It was almost eleven a.m. Reaching for the light switch, she scanned the room, shivering as a cold blast of wind hit her.

'Philip, love? You've left the window open.' She pulled it shut. Judging by the freezing temperature in the room that window must have been left open all night.

But Philip didn't answer. Worried that something might have happened to him, Karen made her way to his bedroom, inspecting the flat as she went and checking that there was nothing untoward going on. As far as she could see the place seemed clean and tidy enough.

It stank of air freshener though. The pungent, artificial smell was so strong that Philip must have used an entire can on the place. She could smell something else too. A bitter, nasty, stale cigarette smoke lingering in the air. Was the blast of air freshener Philip's abysmal attempt at trying to mask it? That must be why he'd left the window open all night too. To air the place out. Maybe he didn't want her to know that he had started smoking?

She pursed her mouth then, and shook her head. Philip could be funny like that, bless him. Despite being a man of twenty-three years of age, he still acted like a child in a lot of ways. As if he would get told off, when the truth was, it was none of her business what the man did. As long as he wasn't hurting himself or anyone else in the process, he could do what he liked.

Philip was a grown man, and Karen was his carer not his keeper. And by Christ, if she had to spend as much time as Philip did alone in her flat, she could think of a lot worse things than smoking to kill her boredom. Reaching Philip's bedroom, Karen knocked lightly on the door. 'Philip, love, you okay?' Peering through into the darkened bedroom when she didn't get any answer, Karen eyed the mound on the bed. Presuming it was Philip under there, still sleeping, with the duvet drawn up around him. 'You're not ill, are you?'

'I'm just tired.' Philip's voice was muffled by the duvet that swamped him. Karen wasn't convinced.

'Only it's not like you, Philip, to stay in bed this late…'

'I didn't sleep last night. I'm tired that's all.'

Karen narrowed her eyes suspiciously at Philip's bluntness. Staring back out into the lounge, she noted the Xbox that had been moved onto the coffee table in the middle of the room, away from where it normally sat on the TV stand, underneath the telly. Philip had gone on and on about getting himself that console. He'd pestered her to take him into town one Friday, claiming he needed to buy it right then, for the weekend. And she hadn't been able to refuse him, because he'd acted as if his life had depended on it. Though it was funny, because she'd never actually seen Philip play on the thing. And the fact that it was still out, the cables stretched across the carpet, the controller discarded on the floor next to it, was equally surprising. Because Philip rarely left anything out of place.

Part of his diagnosis was that he suffered from acute OCD. He seemed a lot better these days, though according to his case file, he couldn't even leave the flat a couple of years ago without knocking on the wall eight times before he left. And he had to check the handle four times after he'd locked a door, otherwise he would get very upset. He was still very clean and tidy though. Karen had thought it was a blessing at first. Being allocated as a carer to someone who ensured that their living space was always immaculate. It meant that she didn't ever need to worry about doing lots of housework like some of her colleagues had to do. She'd heard all the stories. How they'd had to scrub all sorts of disgusting substances from bathroom floors or boil wash soiled bedding, or they were constantly hoovering up crumbs and dirt. Philip was always so tidy. But that also came with a price, and Karen had seen how much Philip suffered with his anxiety, never really being able to relax unless everything was just so. He'd turned into a bit of a recluse in doing so, his home becoming his only real sanctuary.

'Have you been up all night playing your computer games?' Karen asked, realising that maybe he really was just tired. What else would the poor boy do in his evenings, to break up the monotony of being on his own all the time?

'Well, listen, love. I have to go to the bank today anyway. So, how about I leave you to your nice lie-in and come back in a couple of hours? I can do us both a bit of lunch if you like? We can have our cuppa then?'

'Whatever,' Philip grunted.

'Okay then, love,' Karen said, standing awkwardly in the doorway for a few seconds more, unable to shake the feeling that there was something more going on here.

She felt hesitant to leave suddenly, a horrible thought crossing her mind that maybe Philip was struggling a bit with his mental health. That he might be depressed? This was a symptom of it, wasn't it? The feeling of not wanting to get out of bed. And now that she thought about it, he'd been showing signs over the past few weeks too. Acting strangely. Stranger than normal, anyway.

Karen had only been caring for him for a couple of months now, yet she had already noticed a rapid decline in Philip's personality since she'd first started. He really seemed to be going into himself, becoming much more withdrawn and edgy than normal, and lately he seemed a bit paranoid too, she thought, thinking about all that business last week with Philip declaring that he didn't feel safe on his own at night and insisting that he wanted a chain on his front door. Karen had tried to reassure him that he was safe here, that no one was going to break into the flat, and if he was ever scared she was only ever a phone call away, but Philip wouldn't let up about it; he had been adamant that he wanted one. So Karen had organised to have one fitted.

But the fact that he hadn't used it while she'd been away showed that he couldn't have been that fussed about his security. She was going to have to keep a closer eye on him, because this sort of thing happened all the time, didn't it? No matter how good your intentions were as a carer, no matter how much you convinced yourself that you'd never take your eye off the ball. This job was full on and, sometimes, carers did miss things that were happening right underneath their noses, through no fault of their own.

If people really didn't want you to know things about them, there were ways of hiding them well. And if Philip was feeling down in the dumps, then Karen was determined to cheer him up.

'Tell you what, I'll get some of those fresh bread rolls that you like from the bakery in town, and some corned beef,' she said, knowing how much Philip loved his food. If anything would put him in a better mood, it would be a decent bit of grub and a nice strong cup of sweet tea. Just how he liked it. Then she'd break the bad news to him that she was going to have to go away for the rest of the week. She felt bad about it now, seeing Philip like this. But what choice did she have? Her mother had called her late last night to say that she'd had a bad fall and Karen had no choice but to go and look after her. She'd have to leave Philip to his own devices.

Though now she wondered if she could inform her manager, and get someone allocated to cover her shifts, so that Philip wouldn't be left alone, especially if he was in this state. But she'd only been doing this job for a few months, and she didn't want to come across as unreliable. Besides, Philip was more than able to cope on his own for a few days. She only normally popped in three mornings a week, and left him all weekend, didn't she? It wasn't as if he really needed to be supervised round the clock or anything. And it would only be a few extra days.

Karen was more a support system for the lad than a proper carer. Someone to help him with his bills and finances and do a bit of shopping for him every few days. But mainly she was company for him. And nothing needed to change over the next few days – Karen could fetch him some shopping today, and get a few extra goodies to keep him happy, and she would phone him every day that she was away to make sure everything was all right. He'd be fine.

'Okay, well I'll see you in bit, Philip, love.' Hearing Philip grunt in acknowledgment to the conversation, Karen let herself back out of the flat.

CHAPTER NINETEEN

DS Morgan rapped loudly with his knuckles on the man's front door, and he and DC Murphy waited patiently for an answer.

'I just saw the curtains twitch, Sarge. Before we'd even knocked. He knows we're here,' Lucy whispered to her boss.

DS Morgan nodded knowingly.

'He likes to cause a fuss.' Irritated now, Morgan knocked on the door for a second time. 'Though he's stupid if he thinks leaving us standing out here on his doorstep won't draw attention to him. Especially if he's willing to give us a witness statement—' He stopped mid-sentence as the door suddenly swung open.

'Ah, Mr Johnson. My name is Detective Sergeant Morgan and this is Trainee Detective Constable Lucy Murphy.'

'About bloody time!' the small elderly man interrupted, glaring at the officers, before stepping out onto the doormat and staring down the balcony, as if to make sure that no one had clocked the Old Bill at his house, then seeming almost disappointed when he realised that there wasn't anyone else around.

'Well, don't just stand there looking gormless, come in then.' Leading the two officers into his lounge, Mr Johnson took a seat in his chair by the TV, motioning to the two detectives to take a seat opposite him.

'I called your lot over two hours ago,' he said, still clearly disgruntled. He turned the volume down on the telly so that his voice filled the room. 'That's the problem these days, isn't it? No one cares anymore. No one takes anything seriously, and you lot are so bloody laid back you're almost horizontal.' Mr Johnson nodded in agreement to his words as the two officers kept their expressions neutral, staying professional despite the old man clearly trying to rile them.

'Thank Christ I didn't call about something serious like an attack or something. I could be dead by the time you lot pulled your finger out.'

DS Morgan took a deep breath.

'Mr Johnson, please let me assure you if you are ever so unfortunate to be attacked, that if you call the emergency number, which I'm sure you are aware is nine nine nine, we will deal with the matter with great urgency. As we do every call out. We gauge each job by its level of urgency, and this was marked down as a routine call so that we could take a witness statement from you. I'm sure you can appreciate that we are extremely busy, Mr Johnson,' DS Morgan said, doing his utmost to stay professional.

'I told your officers on the phone that I didn't see much. But it might be something, so I thought I'd call it in. You never know, do you?' Mr Johnson said then, indignantly. 'There was a group of lads hanging about the estate on Monday morning. Local lads. And they were giving out a lot of grief to residents walking by. Myself included. Swearing and calling names. That kind of thing.'

DS Morgan placed his notebook down on his lap before glancing over at DC Murphy. They exchanged a knowing look. This was all just one big waste of time.

'And did you see the actual assault take place?' DS Morgan asked.

Mr Johnson shook his head.

'Well, no. But as I said, this lot were hanging around the place, purposely looking for trouble. I saw them vandalising the lift downstairs so that none of us residents could use it. And then they stood at the end of the stairwell and gave out to anyone trying to get past them. All I'm saying is, I reckon someone told the Special Constable about them. And that's probably why he got a beating by them. Makes sense, doesn't it?'

Mr Johnson was eyeing the two detectives smugly now, as if he'd just single-handedly solved their case for them.

'And you're certain that this was Monday morning?' DS Morgan asked.

'As sure as I am that my balls are in my pants,' Mr Johnson said crassly, nodding his head. 'That's the day I collect my pension from the post office. It was definitely Monday.'

'Right, well. The attack actually happened on Sunday, Mr Johnson. So, thank you for your "help", but on this occasion, we'd need a much more solid witness account of the incident in order to take your statement.'

DS Morgan got up and indicated to Lucy that it was time to leave.

'Wait. There's something else, too,' Mr Johnson said, going over to the dresser now and picking up his own notepad. 'I've been keeping a log of some very strange behaviour going on in the flat below me.' The old man lowered his voice, as if somehow the tenants below him might be able to hear him. 'It all sounds very sinister if you ask me.'

'Can you tell us what you mean by sinister?' Lucy said then, sensing the tension between her boss and the elderly man and hoping that her gentler, more concerned approach might appeal to the man's softer side.

Mr Johnson eyed Lucy, as if seeing her now for the first time. He twisted his face in scrutiny.

'You're a bit young, ain't you? To be a detective constable? But I suppose it's all this equal opportunity stuff these days, isn't it? The police force has got to look as if they're doing their bit I suppose.' And with that Mr Johnson dismissed Lucy completely and turned his attention back to DS Morgan.

'I can hear someone crying and screaming at all times of the night and day. I was kept awake most of the night, last night. I thought it was just kids at first, having a party. I wouldn't mind if it was a one off, but it's all the time lately.'

DS Morgan bit his tongue, realising that they'd been called out here under false pretence. Mr Johnson hadn't witnessed an assault at all. Yet he'd managed to get two CID officers out to his home to deal with a noise complaint.

'Well, I can't hear any noise now,' he said, listening for a few minutes and only being met with silence.

'I know what you're thinking,' Mr Johnson said, eyeing the officer shrewdly. 'That I'm wasting your time. But I'm not. I lay down on the floor, with my ear to the ground, and I could hear it. Last night it sounded like someone was being attacked. Like they were scared. The young lad who lives down there, by himself, I think he's a bit retarded or something. He's got a carer.'

'We don't use words such as retarded, Mr Johnson. It's actually a very offensive term. We say disabled, or SEN – special educational needs – these days,' DS Morgan said tightly.

'Disabled then, whatever. It might be her though, mightn't it? The carer, she might be abusing the poor lad! You hear about it, don't you, on the news. People victimising the elderly, harmless people like me that wouldn't hurt a fly. Because they think that we're vulnerable. Well, I'm standing up and being counted. I'm making sure my voice is heard…'

DS Morgan glanced at Lucy, pursing his mouth tightly closed so that he didn't voice something he might later regret. 'Well, Mr Johnson, while we are here, we will pop down to the flat and check that the young man is okay and that there's nothing untoward going on.' DS Morgan got up and made his way to the front door with Lucy following him behind. 'But in future, if you do hear any noises coming from the flat, like parties or loud music, then we'd encourage you to report it to your local authority.'

Mr Johnson opened his mouth to argue further but DS Morgan wasn't prepared to listen to Mr Johnson's far-fetched accusations any longer.

'Thanks for your time, Mr Johnson.'

'Well that was a waste of time,' DS Morgan said, through gritted teeth, his anger getting the better of him as they took the stairs.

'We are going to check it out though?' Lucy asked, her instincts telling her that as much as a pain in the arse Mr Johnson might be, they couldn't just leave today without at least checking that this lad downstairs was okay. 'I mean, if he's right about this lad having problems, shouldn't we at least check? It might be that he just needs some extra support?'

'Oh without a doubt,' DS Morgan said, still clearly disgruntled. 'It would be more than our jobs are worth not to follow up the complaint, but I'm willing to bet my money on this being just another of Mr Johnson's fabricated stories.'

CHAPTER TWENTY

Listening to the sound of Karen shutting the front door behind her, Philip threw the covers off of him and stared up at the ceiling, sweating profusely now from the heat of hiding away under the thick covers. He licked his dry lips, his throat felt as if he'd swallowed sawdust and his head was still pounding. But at least the room had stopped spinning now. He rubbed his red, puffy eyes from where he'd been crying alone in his bed the last few hours. He was glad that Karen had gone. He didn't want her to see him like this, because he knew that she'd only be worried about him, and Philip didn't want to have to lie to her. Because Karen was nice to him. He liked her.

He couldn't really remember his own mum; he'd been so young when he'd been placed in care. But he sometimes imagined that Karen was like a mum to him in some ways. Not his real mum, who had chosen drugs over him and treated him badly because she was ashamed of him being disabled, but like the mum he dreamt about sometimes, like the ones in the movies. The type of mum that, if Philip was brave enough, he could confide in. Only he wasn't brave enough, not one bit. He couldn't tell Karen about Jax and his boys turning up all the time and taking over his flat. About how they humiliated and hurt him. About what they did to Bobcat. Because Jax would know. Jax knew everything. And what if he hurt Karen too? Philip couldn't let that happen.

Lifting the covers, he stared further down the bed to where Bobcat lay tucked into Philip's legs. He was hiding away, and Philip didn't blame him. Bobcat was exhausted from being tormented all weekend. Which was exactly how Philip felt, too.

Hearing a loud knock at the front door, Philip froze, his heart pounding loudly again in his chest, terrified that Jax might have come back. Only he knew that Philip had his carer coming over, he rationalised. That's why Jax and the boys had finally left last night. But what if Jax had just seen Karen leave? Hearing another knock, Philip held his breath. Maybe it was Karen? She might have left her purse and keys behind by mistake. Whoever it was didn't seem like they were going to go away.

Dragging himself reluctantly from the warmth of his bed, Philip trudged across the living room floor as quietly as he could and tiptoed when he neared the door, so that he could stare out through the spy hole without being spotted. Staring down the lens, Philip started to panic at the sight of the two people standing the other side of the door. They were dressed smartly in suits and he wondered if they were from the council or social services. What were they doing here?

Then he heard the word 'Police,' and shrank away from the doorway. Did they know that Jax had forced him to take drugs last night? Was that why they were here, so that they could arrest him?

Was he in trouble? Philip didn't want to go to prison. He didn't want them to take him away.

Leaning up against the wall, he prayed that they'd think he wasn't home and that they'd both go away.

CHAPTER TWENTY-ONE

'Have you heard anything, Jax?' Kian said, approaching Jax as he hovered on the stairwell by the main doors that led out to the twelfth floor.

'Not here!' Jax said, silencing Kian with a shake of his hand. He signalled to the kid that he was busy and continued to peer out along the balcony, all the while making sure that he remained out of sight, hiding just inside the stairwell so that nobody could see him. Kian bit his lip and waited patiently, not wanting to rile the older boy. He'd been dreading seeing Jax this morning, because he knew that they were both in deep shit and Jax would probably blame last night's fiasco on him. Because Kian hadn't stuck to the plan and done as he was told. Instead he had frozen, and because of that, Jax had acted on impulse and hit the man too hard, and now the man was dead.

Kian hadn't slept a wink all night thinking about it. Every time he closed his eyes, he'd seen the man sprawled out on the pavement, his skull cracked open and blood everywhere.

They'd done that. They'd murdered someone.

'The bloke's dead, isn't he?' Kian whispered, almost crying now as the words tumbled unconsciously from his mouth. Jax turned and glared at Kian.

'I said, not fucking here! Can't you see I'm busy?' Jax nodded towards the woman he was watching. She was standing on Philip's doorstep and rooting around inside her handbag as if she were looking for something.

'Who's that? Philip's mum?' Kian asked. He hoped that the poor guy had someone looking out for him, and maybe whoever she was would put paid to Jax and his boys going round there all the time and taking the piss out of the poor bloke. But Jax shook his head.

'Nah, it's his carer. Though she should be long gone by now… Philip ain't got a mum. She didn't want him apparently. Gave him up when he was little. Said he was too special in the head for her to cope with, didn't she?' Jax shrugged. He looked annoyed now. Philip's carer should be long gone by now. That was why he'd told Kian to meet him here.

'Oh, shit!' Jax said, ducking out of the way as the woman began walking towards them then. 'You better get out of here. I'll send one of the boys around to yours when the coast is clear. Then we'll talk. Until then, keep your head down and if anyone starts asking any questions, you say nothing. You got me?'

Kian nodded.

'Go on then, fuck off!' He watched as Kian did as he was told and scarpered back to where he'd come from, then made his way down the stairwell ready to head back to his own flat on the other side of the estate. Just then the woman stepped out into the stairwell where Jax had been standing.

'Jax? What are you doing here?' Karen asked with a smile, not expecting to see her son before she left.

'I was just coming to see if you had gone yet, Mum,' Jax lied. His mum was supposed to have left for Margate first thing this morning, to visit his miserable old bag of a nan. The old witch had taken a bad fall and hurt her hip apparently. Jax had spent the whole morning listening to his mother harping on about it over breakfast. As if he actually cared. But when she started fretting about how she was going to have to leave Philip to fend for himself for the rest of the week, he'd started taking an interest in the conversation, insisting to his mother that his nan would need her, that she should go. Only now he wondered if she'd changed her mind again.

'I wanted to check on how Nan was doing,' Jax lied. His nan had never really taken to him. Even when he was little the old battle-axe had declared that Jax was spoilt and Karen let the boy get away with murder. And she might have had a point, but even so, Jax had never given her the time of day after that.

'Oh, you are a sweet boy!' Karen Priestly beamed at her thoughtful son. 'I'm leaving soon; I said I'd pick up a bit of shopping for Philip before I go.'

'I can do that for you,' Jax said with a shrug.

'Oh, no, son, I couldn't ask you to do that. Besides, I haven't really seen Philip yet, he's still in bed, and he seemed a bit under the weather…'

'It's no trouble, Mum, honestly. You can concentrate on Nan; she'll be waiting for you to get there. You know what she's like. Especially if she's hurt herself as badly as you said. She'll end up doing herself even more damage. I'm sure Philip's fine.'

'Well, I guess it would be helpful if you could just pick up a few bits. Some bread and milk, oh and I said I'd get him some corned beef. And maybe pick up a few bars of chocolate too?' Reaching into her bag and taking out her purse, she handed her son a twenty pound note along with Philip's door key. 'Maybe a friendly face like yours would cheer him up. He's got an Xbox in there. Maybe he'll let you play it with him.' Karen wondered if having some male company close to his own age might be just the thing to cheer Philip up. 'He does get a bit funny with people he doesn't know, though. He suffers terribly from anxiety.'

'Mum, it's fine. I'll just drop his stuff off and go,' Jax said, trying to convince the woman to hurry up and leave.

His mother had no idea of the torment she'd caused Philip. It was her fault that Jax had found out about Philip in the first place, running her mouth off and telling Jax all about her new client, with no regard whatsoever for patient confidentiality. Jax's ears had pricked up the minute his mother had first mentioned that she was caring for a man who lived on the estate. *A poor vulnerable man with mental health and physical disabilities, not much older than you, Jax,* she had said, when she'd come home from her first shift. *He's a bit simple, but he's as soft as anything! Poor thing, lives all alone in his flat. He hasn't got a soul in the world to visit him. Must be ever so lonely. What a desperate life, eh? At least he has me visiting during the week to break things up a bit. I can't even imagine how he must feel to be stuck in that flat on his own twenty-four seven all over the weekend.*

Believing that Jax had a genuine interest in her job, and that he was showing real compassion for the man that she was caring for, Karen started sharing stories about all her shifts working for Philip, wanting to encourage the rare caring side to her son that she was seeing whenever she discussed him. She had been giving Jax regular updates on her visits ever since. Jax knew that his mother's shifts were Monday, Wednesday and Friday mornings. And that Philip was left alone every weekend.

Jax had even managed to get his hands on his mother's keys one afternoon when she was having a nap, taking them to get his own set cut. He'd returned them to her purse without her ever knowing they had gone.

And as it turned out, Philip's flat was the perfect base for him and his boys. Somewhere for them all to doss during the week and all weekend and get stoned off their faces. They could do what they liked for most of the week, and who the fuck was going to stop them? Certainly not Philip. The bloke was shit scared of him and rightly so.

'Honestly Mum, he'll be in safe hands,' Jax said with a grin, enjoying the fact that his mother was so clueless to the little set-up he had going on here. Which also meant that Philip had been true to his word; he hadn't mentioned a thing to anyone.

'Well I guess I could ring him later and explain that I've been called away in an emergency. And if you're getting some food in for him, he'll have enough to keep him going for a few days… Do you think he'll be all right? I mean, he doesn't really need much help, but what if something happens while I'm away?' Karen mumbled, nervous now, unsure if she was doing the right thing.

'Mum! Stop it,' Jax laughed. 'It's all cool! Everything's under control. If anything happens, call me, and I'll help out okay? Now go, Nan needs you! Send her my love, yeah?'

Karen smiled then, kissing her son on the cheek and walking away before she changed her mind completely.

Waiting until his mother had reached the bottom of the stair-well and stepped outside, Jax grinned to himself before pocketing the cash she'd given him for Philip's groceries and making his way back out on the balcony towards the bloke's place, looking forward to giving Philip the unexpected surprise of his company.

Whistling to himself smugly, Jax was stopped in his tracks a few moments later as he spotted the two figures that were now standing on Philip's doorstep. Dressed in plain clothes or not, Jax could sniff out a copper from a mile off. They must have used the entrance at the other end of the tower block.

Waiting a few minutes, Jax watched as the two police officers walked off, before retreating back down the stairwell himself. Not wanting to take any chances, Jax decided that he would come back tomorrow once the coast was clear. The fact that the Old Bill were knocking on Philip's door didn't bode well at all. If that fucker had grassed on them, it would be the very last thing he'd ever do.

CHAPTER TWENTY-TWO

Giving the door one more knock, only to be met with complete silence, DS Morgan shook his head. 'No one's home. And it wouldn't surprise me if this was another of Mr Johnson's vendettas against yet another neighbour. He's fallen out with so many of them upstairs he's probably run out of targets, so now he's making his way through this floor, too.' Morgan sighed, ready to leave. They'd already wasted enough time today and he was willing to bet his next month's wages on the fact that this wouldn't be the last time Mr Johnson summoned them out to the flats this week for something equally ridiculous.

'Hold up, Sarge,' Lucy said, about to follow her colleague, before hesitating as a sound came from behind the door. She pressed her ear up against the wood and listened. 'I thought I just heard someone moving around in there.'

Morgan stopped and waited as Lucy knocked again, this time louder.

'You're persistent, Murphy. I'll give you that,' he said unconvinced.

'I swear I just saw a shadow sweep across the gap in the bottom of the doorway,' Lucy said, staring down at the floor, convinced that someone was hiding on the other side of the door.

'Hello? We know you're in there! You're not in any trouble. We just wanted to have a chat with you. Make sure that you're okay...'

Silence. Staring back at the spy hole, Lucy wondered if the lad who lived here was standing the other side of the panel, watching her. She was sure she could feel that he was.

That he was there, just feet away from her; though for some reason he was pretending he wasn't home.

'Here, Sarge! Can you hear that? It sounds like a baby crying.' Lucy turned to her boss to see if he could hear it too. Morgan stepped forward and pushed his ear up against the door then. He nodded as they both heard the strange high-pitched wailing noise from inside.

Louder this time.

'Yeah, I can hear it,' DS Morgan said, rolling his eyes. 'It's a cat!'

Lucy blushed then, realising that the crying sound was indeed the noise of a cat meowing to get out from behind the door.

'I wonder if that's the noise that Mr Johnson's been hearing, too?' DS Morgan questioned.

'Do you think something might have happened to the lad in there and the cat's on his own?' Lucy said. She was already feeling stupid about thinking she could hear a baby; she didn't want to add her fears about the tenant of the flat being incapacitated, or dead. Bending down she peered in through the letterbox at the small hallway leading to what looked like a lounge.

'I can see the cat's bowls over by the wall. They're full of kibble and water. Ahh, hello little kitty,' Lucy said, spotting the scruffy-looking tabby cat sitting by the doormat looking up at her. 'Sorry, mate, I can't let you out. Hopefully your dad will be home soon.'

'No dead bodies?' Morgan joked, as Lucy stood back up, guessing what the younger officer had been thinking.

'Not that I could see, thank God. And the cat's obviously being well looked after, Sarge. But there's no sign of anyone else home.'

Morgan shook his head.

'The poor cat's probably only crying because he can sense us out here, and he wants to be let out,' he reasoned. 'Come on. Let's get back to the station. We can always come back and try again the next time we're called out here. And there will be a next time. There always is.'

*

Hearing the officers walk away, Philip breathed a sigh of relief before sliding down the wall behind him. For a second, he'd actually considered opening the door. Especially when the female officer had peered in through the letterbox, and Philip had been forced to press himself up against the wall in the small alcove next to the front door. His hand had hovered near the latch after the letterbox had slammed closed. He'd twitched his fingers dubiously, willing himself to do it. To open the door. Part of him wanted to run out there and ask the officers to help him. To tell them the truth about how Jax was hurting and threatening him. To show the police what Jax and his mates had done to his poor Bobcat.

Reaching out to Bobcat then, he gave him a loving stroke, his hand moving over the uneven clumps of fur that remained after Jax and his mates had hacked at it with a razor while they were stoned. Philip bit his lip to stop it from trembling, to stop the tears from coming again. He felt sick just thinking about what those bastards had done. It made him even angrier than what they'd done to him, making him smoke that awful spice stuff. Though it hadn't tasted spicy to Philip. It had tasted like poison.

And at first that was exactly what Philip had thought was happening to him after they'd forced him to smoke it. He had been sure he'd been poisoned and that he was going to die. His heart had been thumping so hard inside his chest as the room started spinning out of control that he'd had no choice but to lie as still as he could on the floor so that he wouldn't throw up.

Like a zombie. Jax had said. *A fat fucking zombie.* And then they'd all laughed at him as he'd lain there, unable to move, unable to speak, even when he'd seen them shaving Bobcat while they goaded him to get up and stop them.

Part of him wished that he could have opened the door and told the police everything.

But he was too scared. Jax had warned him what would happen if he grassed to the Old Bill. He'd said that the police wouldn't believe a retard like him anyway. And the chances were news of Philip telling the police would get back to Jax, and Jax would really hurt him then. And that was why Philip had cowered silently next to the door until he was all alone again. Glancing up at the security chain, Philip reached up and pulled it across, in a fruitless attempt to keep everyone else out.

He started to cry then, sobbing loudly as he realised that he wasn't locking anyone out at all, he was only locking himself in. A prisoner in his own home. And no one could help him.

Not the police, not Karen, no one. Philip was completely and utterly at Jax Priestly's mercy.

CHAPTER TWENTY-THREE

'Lucy, can I have a word?' DS Morgan asked, standing in the doorway of his office that sat off to the side of the CID room. Glad to take a break from the numerous reports that she had been writing up from the many cases that they'd been working on over the past few days, Lucy was only too happy to oblige.

'Please, close the door,' he said, as Lucy stepped inside his office.

'Is everything okay, Sarge?' she asked, suddenly apprehensive of her boss's sombre mood.

'Take a seat, Lucy,' DS Morgan offered, waiting for the young DC to sit down before he proceeded. Her eyes went to the phone that sat on his desk, off the hook, as if someone might still be on the other end of the line.

'There's a call for you. It's just come through from control room,' Morgan said, confirming Lucy's suspicions. No one called her work unless it was an absolute emergency.

'It's a Vivian Alton. She said it's urgent.'

'Oh God!' Lucy said, immediately thinking the worst. *Something has happened to Nan. Why else would Vivian call her at work?*

'Please, go ahead. I'm going to go and put the kettle on,' DS Morgan said, passing the receiver, and excusing himself from the office so that she could take the call without feeling as if he was watching over her.

'Vivian. Is it Nan? Is she okay?' Lucy said, not able to disguise the evident panic in her voice as her heart pounded inside her chest. Her breathing suddenly restricted at what she might be told. Morgan heard her breathe a sigh of relief at the caller's answer before sounding distressed again at their next words.

'What do you mean she's missing? How long ago?' Her voice went up a few notches as she started to panic all over again. 'I finish my shift in an hour…' Lucy walked to the office door, and catching Morgan's eye, before placing her hand over the receiver, she explained what was going on.

'I'm sorry, Sarge. It's my nan. She's gone missing. Vivian is her carer,' Lucy said, her face pale now, visibly distressed. 'My nan has Alzheimer's. She's only really got me. We live together. Do you think it would be okay if I could leave early?'

'You're only filing reports. Of course, go!'

Mouthing the words thank you, Lucy got back on the phone and told Vivian that she was on her way.

'Oh, and Vivian, I think I know where she might be… I'll meet you there.' After reciting to her the location where she thought her nan would be found, Lucy hung up.

'Thanks so much, Sarge. I'll make up the extra hour before my shift tomorrow morning and get those reports all finished.' Lucy got up to leave the office with urgency now.

Morgan nodded.

'Do you want me to ask patrol to take a look too? See if anyone's free in the area?' he offered, feeling bad for the girl that she had so much weight to bear, looking after a sick relative on top of working in CID. The job was a nightmare at the best of times for fairly stable families. It was common knowledge that the unsociable shifts and stress the job caused put huge strain on relationships and dependents.

'No; thanks though, Sarge,' Lucy said gratefully, making her way to the door. 'Fingers crossed, I think I know exactly where I can find her. Thanks again, Sarge. I really appreciate it.'

Morgan waited until Lucy had left the office entirely, before opening his desk drawer, pulling out a file and taking a seat back down at his desk.

When DC Lucy Murphy had first come to his attention it had been because of her impressive arrest record in uniform. But Morgan had done some digging around about the girl since. Because ever since he'd laid eyes on Lucy Murphy, he'd had a strange feeling that he knew her from somewhere. And now he knew where.

Walking back over towards his desk, he pulled open the drawer and picked up the cold case file that he'd been reading earlier. The file that had haunted him for the past twenty years of his career. DS Morgan had met Lucy Murphy long before her career in the force. Like her, the day would be for ever ingrained in his memory.

CHAPTER TWENTY-FOUR

2000

'Hi, I'm DS Cowley and this is DC Morgan.' The DS introduces himself to the scene of crime officer as they make their way inside the cordoned off flat on the Griffin Estate, and newly appointed DC Jason Morgan scans the bedroom, instantly recoiling at the amount of blood at the scene. Though he tries desperately to keep his cool in front of his superior and not react, he's never seen anything quite so horrific.

The bed is completely covered in blood and the splatter flickers right up the walls, peppering the edges of the ceiling.

'It doesn't matter how many crime scenes you'll attend in your career, Morgan' his sergeant had said to him before they arrived, 'it still never fails to horrify you how much blood can seep out of one person.'

'Hi, I'm Jaqueline Burton. Jacqui,' the CSI officer says, not bothering to look up from her notebook as she writes down her findings.

'Whoever did this, really went to town on her,' she says, raising her eyes at the officer and nodding down to the female victim who is still sprawled out on the bed.

'What have we got so far?'

'The victim is twenty-eight-year-old Jennifer Murphy. There are signs of forced entry – the door was kicked in – but so far there's no sign of the murder weapon here at the scene. I'd guess that the attack was premeditated, that the murderer used their own weapon and they've taken it with them to dispose of. The next-door neighbour called it in. Said that she heard shouting and screaming. When officers attended the scene, they didn't hear any noise, but they saw the forced entry and entered the flat. There were no signs of the perpetrator according to the officers. The killer had already fled by then.' Jacqui watches both detectives scan the room again, just as she had done at least a thousand times since she arrived on scene, taking in the vast amount of blood everywhere, the broken furniture, the lifeless body still sprawled across the bed.

'The victim struggled?' DS Cowley asks, wondering how long her horrific ordeal must have lasted.

'She fought for her life with everything she had, I'd say, going by the mess.' Jacqui had noted the dressing table contents that were scattered all over the floor. The bedside table was upturned, the small chair broken. The chair leg was splintered on the floor beneath it.

There had certainly been a struggle.

'I'm fairly certain that we will find some skin cells under her nails when they do the full autopsy. Or perhaps some DNA from inside her mouth if she bit him. It's hard to say just by looking at her, but she definitely put up a fight. The bruising around her neck is extensive, so I'd say that she was more than likely overpowered in the end. Pinned down, possibly held by her throat, before being stabbed repeatedly.'

'Do we have any suspects to focus on? Is there a husband or a boyfriend?'

'We've spoke to the victim's mother, who was extremely distressed, as you can imagine. She said that there was no boyfriend that she knew of, but that doesn't rule anything out. It could have been a relationship that this woman was keeping quiet for whatever reason, or perhaps it was a recent thing. The mother did say that her daughter was a very private person. But there was no one who has been mentioned by name or was known about. The officers have taken away all the electrical devices, to see if we can find out who she was talking to recently. Maybe that might give us some kind of clue.'

'I'll get my officers to do a door-to-door, to see if anyone saw or heard anyone hanging around the place. Or if they knew of her having any regular visitors here at the flat,' DS Cowley interrupts.

Jacqui nods before continuing. 'I can't say with certainty at this stage, but I don't think it was a random frenzied attack. The crime scene is pretty clean in general. I'm not holding out any hope of finding traces of the killer's fingerprints in the room. But I'd say he left some DNA, unwittingly, on the victim's body.'

'And the witness?' DS Cowley enquires.

'She's barely a witness, Detective Sergeant. She's a five-year-old child,' Jacqui says tightly, before adding. 'The officers found her cowering inside the wardrobe. We had to get a female officer to practically physically prise the poor kid out from where she was hiding. She's completely traumatised. As you'd expect.'

Jacqui is unable to keep the raw emotion from her tone. It reminds her that she is still human, no matter how hardened she sometimes pretends to be, thanks to her line of work. Some days she kids herself that she's become immune to this kind of stuff by now. No matter how inhumane people could be to each other, no matter how much depravity they could inflict on each other, she'd somehow learned over the years how to close off herself to it all. She has had to, in order to do her job properly, and in order to do it well. She's trained herself to keep her emotions out of it and think with her head. It's one of the reasons why she loves being a crime scene investigator. It means she can just switch off and focus on the science behind the investigation, not the killer's motive. She concentrates on processing the crime scene, because that's where they'll find their answers more often than not. But this little girl has got to her.

Walking over to the wardrobe, DC Morgan peers inside, careful not to touch anything in case of contaminating the crime scene. He can't fathom how a small child must have felt watching such a violent attack on her own mother.

'So, she might have seen the attacker? She could possibly describe him?' he asks, wondering how much the child could have possibly seen from inside a wardrobe.

'Seen him? Heard him? Your guess is as good as mine. We don't have the answers yet. She isn't speaking. I can't even imagine…' Jacqui lets her words trail off.

How would a small child ever come back from seeing her own mother brutally murdered in front of her?

'Well, let's hope we get something out of her,' DS Cowley says finally. This was a high-profile murder case. The perpetrator had fled the crime without leaving any clue as to who he was or the motive for the attack. 'That child is our only witness. She holds the key to catching whoever did this.'

CHAPTER TWENTY-FIVE

'I'm so sorry about this, Vivian! Is she okay?' Lucy asked, getting out of the car. Vivian Alton was standing at the edge of the park waiting patiently for her.

'How did you know she'd be here?' Vivian said, as she looked over to where Winnie sat just a few feet away, perched on the swing. 'I've been afraid to take my eyes off her, in case she goes off wandering again.' Vivian attempted to smile. 'I stayed back though, for this one. I thought perhaps she'd do better if she saw you instead of me.'

'Thanks, Vivian. And I'm so sorry for all the worry she's caused. She did this last week too. Wandered off, only to end up here. I'm so sorry, I should have told you! I've had so much going on lately…'

'Lucy, my darling, you need to stop apologising. This is not your fault. It's no one's fault.'

Lucy nodded, trying her hardest not to break down with relief that they'd found Winnie. Vivian had been driving around the streets for almost half an hour before she'd frantically called the station and told Lucy that her nan was missing. Lucy had known instantly where they'd find her. The same place she'd found her last time she'd given Lucy the slip and gone off wandering on her own. The small children's park on the outskirts of Wandsworth Common was the place her nan used to take Lucy when she was little.

'She hasn't moved from the swing; she's barely even acknowledged I'm here, if I'm honest,' Vivian said, as Lucy followed her gaze to where her nan sat on the swing.

'Christ, look at her,' Lucy said, a lump forming in her throat at how suddenly small and vulnerable her nan looked sitting there all alone, her hands holding the chains as her legs dangled, childlike. She was staring vacantly out into space.

'She refused to move; she just kept saying that she's got to wait here for you…' Vivian paused, speaking softly now. 'And your mum.'

Taking a deep breath, Lucy nodded at Vivian, understanding the weight of the words.

She'd known that this was coming. She'd been gearing herself up for yet another heart-to-heart with her nan the entire journey here. Because she knew that the woman would be working herself up into a state, confused and angry, because nothing made any sense to her anymore.

It had been just little things at first, like forgetting that she had food cooking in the oven, or not being able to find something that she'd only put down just minutes before. Lucy had made light of it all then, thinking that it was endearing when her nan couldn't find her reading glasses that were on her own head. She'd thought that her nan was just getting forgetful in her old age.

Only it wasn't long before her nan couldn't remember other things, simple things, like her conversations seconds after the words had left her mouth. Or the time when she had gone to the shops and forgotten what she'd gone there for, then forgotten where she lived and been unable to get back home again. The doctors had said that Alzheimer's was a disease that killed off brain cells gradually, causing its sufferers to forget more and more important things, until eventually they forgot how to feed themselves, and even how to breathe. They'd estimated that her nan's deterioration could take between four and eight years. They'd been wrong. It had only been two.

Lucy felt cheated. Her nan's episodes of memory loss were happening more and more, almost on a daily basis now. And there were other symptoms too that Lucy never expected, like the dramatic change in her nan's personality. At times it was as if she was a completely different woman. Gone was her gentle, loving Nan and in her place was an angry, frustrated stranger. Suffering from abrupt mood swings, she'd become stern and brutal with her cutting remarks and unkind words. She acted sometimes as if she no longer cared whose feelings she hurt. Other times, there were glimmers that her nan was still there. Lucy could see her, really see her, behind her eyes. But that was rare, and more often than not, her nan was lost in her own little world. A world that Lucy couldn't reach, but often found herself wondering about.

Life wasn't fair. But then, Lucy had learned that the hard way long ago too.

'You can get off if you like. I'll take over from here.' She gave Vivian's arm a grateful squeeze.

'Are you sure, darling? I don't mind sticking around for a bit to give you some help.'

Lucy shook her head, knowing that more people around only made her nan worse. She had more chance of getting her nan to open up to her if she was alone. It was less distressing for her. Less of an ordeal.

'No, honestly. It's fine. She'll listen to me.'

'Well, if you need anything, you just give me a call, okay?'

Lucy nodded gratefully before making her way over towards the swing.

'Nan!' Lucy said. She approached the woman slowly and kept her voice low, not wanting to startle her. Winnie turned, full of expectation, but her expression dropped when she saw Lucy's face.

'I'm sorry?' Winnie said, screwing her face up, confused, before shaking her head at her as if she didn't know who she was.

'Nan? It's me, Lucy.'

'Don't be ridiculous.' Winnie shook her head. Then taking another look at Lucy she narrowed her eyes. 'You do look a bit like my daughter, Jennifer, though. Do you know her?'

Lucy bit her lip, unable to speak for a few moments, as a pool of emotion formed in the pit of her stomach.

'She's got her own baby now. My little Lucy-Lu. Oh! Same name as you,' Winnie said proudly, staring off into the distance, patiently waiting for her daughter and granddaughter to join her.

'We're going on a picnic.' Looking down at the floor, she screwed her face up. 'Oh, darn it, I forgot to bring my picnic bag.'

Lucy sat for a few seconds, subtly watching her nan's face, searching for traces of her to finally reappear. The real her. Not this imposter. But her face didn't change. Her stern, stubborn expression remained the same. Finally, Lucy spoke.

'Nan, it's me. I'm Lucy.' She smiled lightly as her nan eyed her with scrutiny, trying to make it easier for Winnie to admit that she had simply got muddled up. 'I'm not little anymore. Look, I'm all grown up. You remember, don't you?'

She braced herself for the pain that this conversation always caused her nan, because she knew exactly where this was going. The disorientation, the confusion. Then the pain and the tears.

'You're just a little confused, Nan.'

Winnie looked at Lucy again. Properly this time, taking her in.

'You have the same eyes as her,' she said, staring at Lucy now with such intensity that it was as if she could see right through her. 'But you're not my granddaughter. You can't be. Don't be so silly. Lucy's only five. Oh, she's going to be trouble that one. She's got a fire in her belly just like her nana!' Winnie laughed then, throwing her head back affectionately, before turning to Lucy with a shrug, her eyes sparkling. So sure of herself. 'Maybe it's you who's confused, dear?'

Lucy couldn't help but smile at her nan's sharp tongue.

'Do you remember that time we came here when I was little, Nan? And you pushed me round and round on the mini-roundabout, forgetting about the giant chocolate ice cream you'd given me on the way here? And I threw up everywhere. All over myself and all the other kids on the roundabout. You were morti-fied.' Lucy chuckled, imagining the scene she must have caused in front of all the other children and their mothers.

Winnie turned her head, eyeing Lucy suspiciously, a flicker of a memory resonating within. Lucy smiled, not wanting to alarm her nan. Keeping things normal.

'How about we go home, hey, Nan? It's cold out here and it's getting dark. Let's go and put the TV on. I'll make you some of that chicken noodle soup that you like? Vivian's gone home now, but she said she'll see you tomorrow.'

Lucy spoke slowly, keeping her voice soft, just like the doctors had advised her, throwing as many familiar things into the con-versation as she could that might gently jog her nan's memory. She needed to act normal. To pretend that this, the pair of them sitting in the park, waiting for the five-year-old version of herself to turn up, was normal.

'Oh, and I picked up that magazine you asked for this morning, when I was in the newsagents. You know, the one with the knitting pattern you saw on the TV. That will keep you out of mischief, eh Nan? For a few minutes anyway!' Lucy grinned, reaching into her handbag and pulling out the copy of the magazine her nan had mentioned the night before, relieved when she saw the small, fleeting flicker of recognition flash in her nan's eyes.

Winnie's expression completely changed then, as she suddenly seemed to come back to the present. Taking all her surroundings in around her, she looked down at the swing that she was currently perched on, as if seeing it for the very first time, and realised where she was. Turning her head, she cast her gaze out across the field to where all the noise was coming from. The excited chatter and laughter from a group of older kids all huddled together. Her eyes squinted at the bright orange sunset, as the sun peeped out from behind the looming tower block in the distance. And Lucy looked then, too. Both of them staring over towards the Griffin Estate, aware of how the two huge buildings loomed so menacingly over the beautiful stretch of emerald green common. Aware of the power the estate still held over them both.

'That place is a bad, bad place,' Winnie said then, shaking her head sadly. 'Bad things happened there.'

'I know, Nan. I know,' Lucy said, nodding in agreement, wondering how much she would remember this time. Maybe, this time, Lucy wouldn't have to explain. 'Shall we go home, Nan? It's getting chilly out here...'

She hoped that tonight would be easier than most. That Winnie would comply. That Lucy could get her home and give her some dinner before making sure she was safely tucked up in bed. But Winnie wasn't completely coherent yet. She still didn't remember it all, and today she wanted answers.

'We can't just leave, Lucy! What about your mother? She'll be wondering where we are if we don't wait for her.' Pursing her mouth, she shook her head, lost all over again.

'She's not coming, Nan!' Lucy said, taking a deep breath, and gearing herself up for the rest of the conversation that she knew would follow.

'Where is she then?' Winnie said, narrowing her eyes. 'Too busy for her old mother, is she? You'd think she'd come and see me once in a while and check that I'm okay.'

Lucy bit her lip, ready with the excuses and the lies that she normally used to placate the woman. The beautiful art of distraction. She'd play along normally and tell her nan exactly what she wanted to hear: that her mum was running late, and that she'd meet them both at the house. By the time they'd got home, Winnie had normally forgotten all about it and moved on to something else. But Lucy couldn't keep lying to her nan, no matter how good her intentions were, because she wasn't sure if she was just adding to the poor woman's confusion; filling her head with lies and memories that weren't really there.

'She's gone, Nan. You know that, don't you. You remember?'

Lucy waited, watching her nan's eyes, waiting for the switch, for the realisation to hit her. But Winnie only looked even more bewildered. Her eyes were wide now, as if on red alert.

'Gone? What do you mean gone?'

There was no other way to say it. No way of making this any easier. So Lucy just said it.

'She's dead, Nan.'

'Dead? No. Jennifer can't be dead. Not my Jennifer!' Winnie's voice came out as a jagged screech. She sounded panic-stricken, as if hearing the news for the very first time. But she'd been told hundreds of times. The trouble was, she always seemed to be able to block it out, needing to be told over and over again; and every time it was just as painful.

'What an awful thing to say, Lucy! Why would you do that to me? Why would you tell such disgusting lies?'

Lucy took her nan's hand in hers.

'Nan, I'm not lying. You remember, don't you? You remember that she's dead? It was so long ago now. I was only five.'

And now Winnie did remember. She shrieked, falling to the floor, and Lucy wasn't quick enough or strong enough to catch her. Slipping from the swing onto her knees, the woman screamed loudly, like a wounded animal, silencing all the children nearby, who turned to look at her.

A woman approached them to see if Lucy needed help, but Lucy waved her away.

The last thing her nan needed was spectators. That only made her more distressed. More faces around her that she didn't recognise. More words of reassurance from voices that she'd never heard before. Just magnifying her confusion.

'Nan, you remember, don't you?' Crouching down, she cradled her nan in her arms as Winnie gave in and nodded. 'I know it's awful and I know it's hard. But I'm here for you, Nan.'

She did remember. Lucy could see it in her eyes. The grief that lingered there was so strong, so consuming, that every part of her shook violently as she sobbed in her granddaughter's arms.

'It's okay, Nan. We're going to be okay. Me and you. We've got each other. I'm not going anywhere.'

'Oh, Lucy. How could I forget something like that? That she's gone. How could I not remember? What's the matter with me?' Winnie wailed, the raw panic that she hadn't remembered, that she'd had to be told, evident in her voice.

And Lucy was crying then, too, her heart breaking for her poor, old Nan.

'You're not well, Nan. It's not your fault. Sometimes you just forget things. You're going to be okay. I promise you, Nan. I'm going to look after you,' Lucy said, trying to keep her calm and reassure her; though Lucy knew that she was playing her concerns down. This was bigger than she could cope with. She felt so overwhelmed. You forgot what you walked into a room to get. You forgot something off your shopping list. You forgot a date booked in your diary. You didn't forget that your only daughter had died. That she had been brutally murdered.

'Oh God!' Winnie said, then, as if remembering that one last detail that destroyed her over time. 'She lost the baby too, didn't she? He killed the baby too.'

'Yes, Nan. She lost the baby too.' Lucy nodded, then stood up and hooked her arm through her nan's. She lifted her up off the ground and walked her slowly over to her car; her arm around her tightly now to keep her upright. To stop her from collapsing again from the grief of it all.

Lucy focused all of her attention on to her grandmother now, so that she didn't have to think about that day when she'd cowered inside that wardrobe, terrified for her life. For her mother's life. Lucy hadn't known until years later that her mother had been pregnant. She'd been too little to understand at the time that she would have been a big sister.

'Come on, Nan, let's get you home.' Placing her nan in the passenger seat of the car and closing the door behind her, Lucy took one last deep breath and leant up against the car. She wondered if her nan would forget about all of this by the time she reached home, like she normally did. Until the next time she remembered and Lucy was forced to tell her the dreadful news all over again, both of them reliving every emotion, every ounce of pain.

Getting into the driver's seat, Lucy plastered a smile to her face so that her nan wouldn't see that she was struggling. Because the truth was that Lucy wasn't sure she was able for much more of this. Her nan needed more help now than Lucy could give her.

CHAPTER TWENTY-SIX

Checking that the coast was clear, Jax made his way back to Philip's flat, turning the key in the door and shaking his head when he realised the chain was on.

'Oi, Philip. It's me Jax. Open the door will you!'

Philip did as he was told, fear spreading across his face at Jax's surprise visit, running his sweaty hands awkwardly up and down his pyjama bottoms. He'd hoped that he'd be safe today. That he could sprawl out on the sofa and watch some of his programmes in peace.

'Now, are you going to tell me why the Old Bill were sniffing about yesterday? You better not have been telling tales, Philip. You know what will happen if you do!'

'The Old Bill have been here?' Having received a text from Jax instructing him to get his arse back over to Philip's pronto, Kian arrived at the flat just in time to catch the tail end of the conversation, immediately thinking the worst. 'What were they here for? Were they here for us? Is the man we jumped dead?' Running his hands through his hair and cursing to himself at the mention of the police, Kian started to panic.

'That's what we need to find out from this mong! What did they want?'

'I don't know. I swear, Jax, I didn't say anything. I didn't even open the door. I swear on Bobcat's life.'

'You better be telling me the truth, cos if I find out otherwise, you'll be in deep shit!'

Philip nodded frantically, grateful that Jax believed him. Jax pursed his mouth. He'd watched the coppers walk off, so he knew that Philip was telling the truth and hadn't let them in.

'They were probably just doing a door-to-door after that numpty community police officer got a kicking at the weekend,' Jax said, directing his comment to Kian. 'And the chances that they've linked anything to do with the assault the other night to this flat are less than zero. I mean they'd have to have superpowers!'

Jax made a mental note to tell all the boys when they got here later that they'd have to keep the noise down. If the police were snooping around the estate, the last thing they needed right now was to draw any more attention to themselves, and it would be just their luck that they ended up being raided, all because of some nosy neighbour reporting noise.

'Your carer not been about then?' Jax said then, testing Philip to see what he'd say.

'She popped in yesterday. And she's probably going to come back again today. She said that she would get some food for me. She'll probably be here any minute…' Philip said, trying his luck and hoping that the mention of the imminent visit from his carer would scare Jax off.

Though he couldn't help but feel worried because Karen hadn't come back yesterday like she'd promised she would. Philip had waited for her all day.

And Jax was unwavering.

'Funny, cos I heard your carer has been called away on a family emergency. My sources have informed me that she's going to be away for at least a week.'

'She didn't tell me that she was going anywhere…' Philip said quietly, dropping his head and staring at the floor like a scolded schoolboy, wishing he'd got up now when Karen had come around yesterday morning, instead of hiding away underneath the bed covers. Philip hoped that Jax was lying, that he was just trying to wind him up, but something about the confidence in his voice told him that he was telling the truth.

'Don't look so surprised, Philip,' Jax said, tapping himself on the temple. 'I keep telling you that I see and hear everything, don't I?'

'I don't feel very well. My head hurts,' Philip said, wishing that he was back in bed again. That he could go to sleep and make Jax and his friends all disappear.

'Well, it's a good job I'm about to keep an eye on you then, isn't it? You've got a whole week of company. Won't that be nice?' Jax smirked, seeing the look of horror spread across Philips face just at the thought of it. 'I mean, we can't have you here all on your tod, what if something happened to you? Or you got bored, eh?'

'Nothing will happen to me, Jax. I'll be fine,' Philip stuttered. 'And I've got Bobcat to keep me company…' Philip was almost pleading with Jax now, hoping he would change his mind and leave. He couldn't cope with the thought of having to spend a whole week with Jax and his boys here tormenting him.

But Jax wasn't listening. He was already making himself right at home, slumping down on the sofa in the same spot that Philip had just got up from and placing his feet up on the table as he started skinning up a joint.

'You gunna put the kettle on and make me and Kian a decent cuppa or what? Bit rude not to look after your guests, mate,' Jax sneered, using his thumb to tell the man to move his arse, as Philip stood there staring down at him gormlessly, feeling suddenly like a trapped animal.

'TEA! Now! Chop chop. Me and Kian have got some business to discuss and the lads will all be around later too, so there won't be any lounging around and watching TV happening for you I'm afraid.' He laughed as the cat took one look at him before doing a runner from the room. 'Ooh, the mangy furball's a bit temperamental today, ain't he! Go on then, fucking do one, Philip, and bring us in some biscuits, too, while you're at it.'

Kian sat down, too, then and shot Philip a small look of sympathy when Jax wasn't looking. He watched as the bloke skulked off into the kitchen to do as Jax had told him.

Picking up the kettle and filling it with water to make Jax his tea, Philip's hands shook violently and it was all he could do not to burst into tears.

'Why do you think the police were here? Are you sure it ain't about us? Do you think they are going to come back?' Kian said, close to tears now that Philip had left the room and they could finally talk. 'There was a lot of blood! And he wasn't moving, Jax. Do you reckon he's dead?'

'Kian, chill the fuck out, man!' Jax said sternly. He sparked up his joint and, taking a long slow draw, purposely played with Kian before he finally spoke. 'The bloke ain't dead. But he's in a bad way. It's been on the news. He's in a coma.'

'Thank God,' Kian said, letting out a huge sigh of relief. 'I haven't slept the past two nights, I've been worried sick at the thought that we'd murdered someone. Every time I've closed my eyes, I've seen him lying there, splayed out on the pavement in a huge pool of blood. I can't get that woman's screams out of my head.'

'It probably would have been better for us if he'd have snuffed it though,' Jax said with a shrug. 'Let's hope he don't remember what we look like, eh? Cos we'll be in deep shit if he does.' He was purposely putting the shits up Kian; he enjoyed seeing the fear on the younger boy's face. That would teach him for fucking everything up the other night. 'You need to lay low, Kian. They might have clocked a better look at you.'

Kian paled at the realisation that they weren't out of the woods yet.

'So, what did we get?' Jax said, waiting patiently for Kian to hand over the phone and the money that he'd seen Kian grab from the man's jacket pocket before they'd run.

'Fuck all,' Kian said, shutting his eyes, unsure how to break the news to Jax. 'There wasn't any money, Jax. His wallet was empty apart from fifty pence and an old library card.'

'Fuck sake!' Jax said, staring at Kian as if waiting for the punchline. But Kian was being serious.

'I got his phone, though, it's a new one…' Routing around inside his pockets, Kian pulled out the phone and passed it to Jax, then searched in his other pocket for the wallet and started to panic when he realised that it wasn't there.

'Shit!' he said, taking his jacket off and patting himself down. 'I can't find the wallet. I must have dropped it on my way over here!'

'You better fucking be kidding, Kian!' Jax said, blowing out a huge puff of smoke, and glaring at the younger boy. 'Because if it's got his library card in it, that means that someone will see his name. They'll work out that it belongs to him, and it will have your fucking fingerprints all over it!'

Kian wanted to cry again then. He started replaying the argument he'd had with Gary yesterday morning in his head. When Shannon had dragged him away from the man and he'd dropped the phone, had he dropped the wallet too? If so, chances were that Shannon would have found it, and it wouldn't take long for his sister to start asking questions and working out where it had come from. It was either with her, or at home still. On the floor.

'I think I know where it is,' Kian said, almost certain that the wallet would have fallen out and he'd find it under the sofa or down by the TV cabinet. 'Don't worry, I'll sort it.' He got up and started making his way towards the front door, just as Philip came back into the room with two mugs of tea.

'Oh, I ain't worried, mate,' Jax said. 'If you've fucked this up, you're going to be the one taking the fall, not me. They are your fingerprints, not mine. Let's wait for the boys to get here and I'll send some of them with you to find it.'

Kian nodded his head, recognising the veiled threat behind Jax's words.

He didn't trust Kian to do anything anymore and Kian couldn't really blame him.

This was the second time he'd done a job for Jax and the second time he'd fucked everything up. He wasn't cut out for this life and, what was more, he no longer wanted any part of it. But he was in too deep to get out now. Until he paid the debt back to Jax Priestly, the man had him well and truly by his balls.

CHAPTER TWENTY-SEVEN

'Kian, lad!' Benny Lynch beamed at the boy over the fish and chip shop counter. 'How's things, my man? You here for some grub?'

'Nah, I've already eaten, thanks,' Kian said, guessing by the friendly reception he'd got so far that Shannon couldn't have said anything bad to Benny about him. Kian was certain if Shannon had got the wallet, it wouldn't take her long to piece together why Kian had it in his possession, and she wouldn't have been able to help herself but confide in Benny. Kian took that as a good sign for now.

He needed to get the wallet back, but the last place Kian wanted to get hold of it was through Shannon.

'Your sister's out the back, taking the bins out for me. You can go through if you want?' Benny said, guessing that if it wasn't food Kian wanted then it would be his sister.

'Cheers, Benny!'

'No worries, Kian. Nice to see you! Tell Shannon she's due her ten-minute break, while it's quiet. Here, grab a couple of cans of Coke from the fridge if you want.' He stepped back and opened the fridge so that Kian could help himself.

'Cheers, Benny! You're a star!' Kian grinned, seeing why his sister always sang Benny's praises. The man seemed like a genuinely nice guy. He paid Shannon well, and always sent her home with food at the end of her shifts. Doing as he was told, Kian grabbed the cold cans of drink, before making his way out the back to see his sister.

'Kian?' Shannon said, surprised to see her brother here as she stepped back inside the back door and locked it behind her, before dragging the empty bin back over to its place. 'Is everything okay?'

Noticing the friendly smile on her brother's face, and the can of drink in his hand that he held out to her, she guessed his bad mood from yesterday had clearly softened.

'Benny said you can have a ten-minute break. Call it a peace offering, Shan,' Kian said, opening the drink and passing it to his sister.

'A peace offering, well that's a first.' Shannon smiled.

'I owe you an apology.' Kian shrugged, looking coyly down at his trainers.

'Ahh, Kian! You know I can't stay mad at you,' Shannon admitted with a grin.

'I've just had a lot going on lately, and I know I've been taking it out on you, when I shouldn't have. I'm sorry! It's that Gary. Man, he properly pushes my buttons, Shan! I can't stand him.'

'Don't let him get to you! That's why he does it! He winds you up, because he knows he'll get a reaction from you.' Shannon knew that Kian was being straight with her. He'd never behave like this unless something or someone was really getting to him. And that someone was Gary. The man was pushing Kian to his limits.

'Yeah you're right! I'll try harder. I just wish he'd do one, Shan. He's making everything a million times worse. He's making Mum worse.'

'I know,' Shannon said sadly. 'But what can we do? Nothing. And he knows it, too. Which is why he's always lording it up in the flat and acting like he owns the place. He's right, isn't he? If it came to it, Mum would choose him over us.'

Kian shrugged, knowing that his answer wouldn't be one that Shannon wanted to hear.

Of course their mother would pick Gary over them. It's what she did. It's what she'd always done.

'We're just going to have to wait it out. You know that her relationships never last. He'll get bored of her eventually, and then she'll move on to the next one,' Shannon said, referring to the long string of failed relationships her mother had had over the years. Though it pained her to even think it, Gary seemed to be sticking around much longer than most. This relationship had been the record for her mother. Which didn't bode well for their chances of getting rid of him anytime soon.

'I've just been trying to stay out of his way, Shan. I can't be at the flat when him and his mates are all there, and when Mum gets herself into those states. It's horrible to watch. It makes me feel so useless. Like there's nothing I can do. That's why I'm out all the time.'

'I get it.' Shannon nodded. 'God, as knackered as I am some days, I'd much rather come and work a shift here than go home after school, trust me. It's shit, isn't it? But it won't be for ever, I promise. We'll sort this. You've just got to trust me…'

Kian nodded. He did trust Shannon; from day dot she'd always had his back and looked out for him, but he doubted that there was anything Shannon could do about Gary hanging around. Though he didn't voice that thought. Not when he had other pressing matters that he still needed to sort out.

'Listen, Shan, while I'm here…' he said carefully, 'you didn't happen to clock my wallet yesterday morning, did you?'

'What? As well as that expensive phone?' Shannon said, narrowing her eyes, immediately suspicious of her brother's motives for coming to see her. She'd forgotten about the phone for a few hours, but now that Kian had brought it up, Shannon wanted to know where he'd got it.

'What mate would just give you that?'

'Just someone I know. I told you. It's not mine, I was just keeping hold of it for a bit,' Kian said, looking shifty once more. The last thing he needed was them both getting into another row after they'd just cleared the air.

'You didn't come here tonight to apologise to me at all, did you?' Shannon said then, seeing straight through her brother suddenly. 'You're just after this missing wallet. Admit it. Apologising to me was just your way of seeing if I'd found it. Why so sneaky, Kian? What are you hiding?'

'It ain't like that, Shannon…' Kian protested, knowing that it was exactly like that and that Shannon knew it, too. 'I did come here to apologise; I swear it…'

'I'm not stupid!' Shannon said, shaking her head as her brother lied to her face, unable to hide her disappointment. 'Do you know what, Kian, I'm busy working, so you're going to have to go.' Her voice was deadpan as she led Kian back out to the shop front and lifted the countertop for him to leave.

'You off already, Kian?' Benny said, before picking up on the tension between the two siblings and the look of fury plastered across Shannon's face. Benny followed her gaze to the group of boys all hanging around the parade outside, as one of them nodded to Kian. Kian nodded back.

'They're waiting for you?' Shannon said, shaking her head. 'They're the mates you've knocking about with now? The Griffin Boys. Jesus, Kian. I thought you were smarter than that. They sell drugs, Kian, did you know that? They hang around the estate and dish them out to kids!'

'It ain't what you think, Shan. I ain't hanging out with them. Not really,' Kian said, feeling his cheeks redden. 'But I need that wallet, Shan; it belongs to them.' Kian suddenly felt way out of his depth. He knew that Jax would be watching him, waiting for him to come out with the wallet, but his sister's scrutiny was even harder to bear. Part of him wanted to confide in her and tell Shannon that he was in trouble. That he'd got in too deep with these boys and he didn't know how to get out. Because Shannon always knew what to do. She'd help him.

But another part of him knew that if she found out what he and Jax and done, she'd never forgive him. Not only that, but Kian knew he couldn't ever let his sister get involved in this.

'I told you, I don't have *your* wallet. And I don't have time for this, Kian. I've got work to do,' Shannon said with finality before turning and making her way out the back again.

'See you, Benny,' Kian said quietly, leaving the shop and returning to his group of mates, trying to put on a front.

When he reached the group, he shook his head.

'She ain't got it.'

'Well where the fuck is it, then?' Jax glared impatiently.

Kian pursed his mouth.

'It must be back at the flat. I'll go and check and meet you back at Philip's in a bit, yeah? I'll be ten minutes max, I swear!'

Making his way back to the estate, he just prayed that his worst fears weren't about to come true. Because other than the Old Bill, there was only one person worse than his sister finding it. And that was Gary.

CHAPTER TWENTY-EIGHT

Dragging all the cushions off the chair and tucking his hand down the edge of the sofa, Kian ran his fingers across the coarse material, trailing through the crumbs and loose change that had managed to fall down between the cushion gaps, before he sank down despondently to the floor. He'd searched everywhere without any luck. The wallet must be around here somewhere.

This was where he'd dropped the phone yesterday morning. The wallet must have fallen out then, too. He had to keep looking. Rolling onto his stomach, he lay down flat against the carpet, peering underneath the sofa as he reached his arm out as far enough as he could stretch, frantically patting the floor with his hand, just in case he'd somehow missed it. But it was no use; it wasn't here. It wasn't anywhere.

He was glad that his mum and Gary were out, because it had given him time to rip the whole flat apart looking for it. Only the place looked as if a bomb had hit it now. Kian guessed he had a while until they came home so that he could clear it all up. He wasn't worried so much about them; the pair of them were probably both down at the pub, propping the bar up for the evening before they made their way back here for the usual afterparty. Off their faces no doubt. Kian intended to be long gone by then. The only reason he'd need to move his arse and get this place back together again was because of Shannon. His sister would be finishing her shift at the chippy soon and the last thing he needed was another run-in with her tonight.

'Shit!' he shouted, banging his fist against the floor, realising he was going to have to face Jax empty-handed once again. Jax was going to murder him for this.

Standing up, Kian stared around the lounge in dismay, scanning through the mess and chaos to check the floor one last time, to make certain that he hadn't missed it. Maybe he hadn't lost it in here at all. Maybe it was outside, when he'd made his way over to see Jax earlier. Though he'd already walked the communal garden that stretched out between the two tower blocks, as well as both stairwell and balconies between here and there, at least four times. Unless someone had found it? Which meant Kian would be royally screwed. Jax had said as much, hadn't he? How the police would be able to link the wallet back to him by taking his fingerprints.

And Kian would have to accept the blame; there was no way that he could grass Jax up, and tell the police that it was Jax who had punched the man. And even if he did speak up, Kian had still been there, hadn't he? He was still an accomplice. He'd committed the actual mugging, too. He'd been the one to take the wallet and phone straight out of the injured man's pocket, before doing a runner from the scene of the crime and leaving the man for dead on the pavement. They'd send him away. He'd have to spend time in one of those young offender's institutes, with older lads all just like Jax. Worse than Jax. Kian wanted to cry.

'Oi, dopey bollocks!' Gary called out from where he stood at the kitchen counter. His voice dripped with sarcasm. 'Fucking hell, you want to borrow my hanky?'

Kian wiped his face, embarrassed at being caught out sitting here crying.

'I didn't hear you come in.'

'Yeah I got that!' Gary smirked. 'What the fuck's going on here? We been burgled or what?'

'I was looking for something.'

'Yeah, what's that then? Your brain? Take it you couldn't find it!'

Kian reminded himself of his sister's advice not to give the man any reaction.

'You better clean this shit tip up; your mum's just picking up some smokes from the petrol station, she'll be back any minute.'

Kian shrugged. Picking up the cushions one by one, he threw them back onto the sofa.

'Leave it as you found it, mate. It's not a doss house and your mother will only get upset coming home to find it in this state. We're gunna have a game of poker in a bit; I've got some of the lads coming round. I'm feeling lucky today,' Gary said, his eyes twinkling as he stood and watched Kian do as he was told for once, putting all the furniture back to where he'd found it all without so much as an argument.

'Good for you. I'm going back out,' Kian said, not rising to Gary's comments.

'Go on then, what you lost?' Gary said, eyeing Kian curiously now. 'I mean, it must be important if it's got you doing housework and sitting there crying on your tod like a little girl?'

Kian bit his lip, ignoring Gary as he carried on tidying up the mess he'd made.

'Oi, you listening to me? I'm talking to you. And you should be nice to me, Kian. Cos I could make your life very difficult, mate. I could really fuck things up for you. Big time!'

'You already have, mate, just by breathing,' Kian said sarcastically, ignoring Gary's empty threat as he grabbed his coat from the armchair and made a bolt for the front door. 'Tell Shannon I'll be late again, yeah!'

'Here, what about all this mess? I take it you won't be wanting this then either?' Gary said. The sing-song tone to his voice stopped Kian dead in his tracks just as he'd reached for the front door. Turning slowly, his heart sank as he saw what Gary was clutching in his hand.

'My wallet...' Kian lied, trying his hardest to play it cool and not stutter; he didn't want his nerves to give him away. 'Cheers, I've been looking for that everywhere...' He stepped forward to take it from Gary, but Gary held the wallet up higher, hovering it in the air just out of the boy's reach.

'I didn't know that we had a bookworm in our midst. Is that where you've been skulking off to, Kian? To read books in the local library?'

Gary laughed then, confirming Kian's suspicions that the greedy ponce had already gone through the wallet to see if there was any money up for grabs. He would have quickly seen that he was shit out of luck, and Kian just hoped that the bloke was his usual thick as shit self and hadn't come to any other conclusions about where the wallet had come from.

Though the smug look on the man's face told Kian that maybe Gary was more on the ball than he gave the bloke credit for.

'Give it here,' Kian said, jumping to make a grab for it; only Gary was too quick.

'Fuck me, you really want it back, don't you? Must be real important. This scruffy old wallet with fuck all inside it...' Gary said, laughing now as he taunted Kian by holding the wallet higher. 'Only a funny thing happened, and you're not going to believe it when I tell you.' Gary put the wallet in the back pocket of his jeans and walked over to the fridge, helping himself to a can of cider and taking a long swig, immensely enjoying taking his time tormenting Kian with what he knew. 'See, after you stormed out of here yesterday, after you had your little strop, I saw this thing on the breakfast news. They were saying that there was an assault on Wandsworth High Street the other night. Right near us. Turns out that some little wannabe gangsters only mugged and almost killed a man over an iPhone and a wallet. Sad, ain't it? That that's all a life is worth to some people. I mean, these news people, they didn't have a very good description of these lads that did it. They said something about both boys wearing dark tracksuits with hoods,' Gary said, his eyes scanning Kian's outfit that matched the description exactly. 'Though that's pretty much standard uniform around these parts of the estate, ain't it? It could be anyone. Only, I was sitting there and I began thinking to myself. I was thinking, what were the chances, huh? Of you getting in so late the other night and then being all cagey with your sister the next morning? Proper angsty to her for no particular reason. Then dropping that expensive-looking phone you had on you? I mean, who lets you borrow their phone? No one, that's who, and I'll tell you how I know that, Kian. Because, you can't bullshit a bullshitter. I can sniff one of my own out from a mile away.'

Gary grinned then, taking another huge swig of cider before continuing.

'So when I stumbled on this little beaut after you left…' He tapped the wallet gleefully, 'everything just slotted into place. I knew you were hiding something and now I know what.'

Gary tapped his temple then, as if he was some kind of genius. 'I should have been in the police, me. Only I couldn't work with that shady lot.'

'You've got it wrong,' Kian said, his heart pounding inside his chest. 'I found it,' he said, desperately trying to talk his way out of it. 'Out on the road. Honest. So, if it does belong to some bloke or whatever, then whoever attacked him must have dumped it.'

'Ohh, right! Well that makes sense, I guess. Phew, and there was me thinking that you'd been a naughty boy,' Gary said, nodding his head understandingly. 'And what, you just found it, did you? The phone and the wallet both together? That was lucky, wasn't it?'

'I guess...'

'Well, there's only one thing for it, Kian. We need to phone the Old Bill and hand it in. You might help solve a crime. There might even be a reward...' Picking up his own phone from the side, Gary started pressing the buttons.

'No!' Kian shouted, spittle spraying from his lips, his face bright red. 'Don't do that. Shit!'

Placing the phone back down, Gary laughed out loud, showing Kian that he was only messing with him all along.

'You got something to hide, have you?' Gary said then, seeing the guilt written all over Kian's face, making him look every bit his thirteen young years. He'd been well and truly caught out and now Gary had him backed up in a corner.

'I ain't a bad bloke, Kian, despite what you think of me. And I'll happily give you the wallet back,' Gary said, leaning up against the kitchen worktop and crossing his arms over his chest, a smile on his face at the fact he was doing such a good deed. 'Only my generosity and silence is going to cost you.'

Kian stared at Gary then, just as he heard the front door open and his mum come in.

'What in God's name is going on? Why's the place in such a tip?' Michelle said, slurring her words, as she stared around at the state of the flat.

'It's all right, love. Kian was just looking for something. He's found it now,' Gary said, eyeing the boy, knowing full well he had the upper hand now.

'Well, you can bloody well clear this place up, Kian. Look at the state of it,' Michelle said, making her way into the kitchen to pour herself another drink before Gary's mates all turned up for their game night.

'I'll give the kid a hand,' Gary said, letting Michelle know that everything was in hand. He picked up the last of the cushions with Kian traipsing around behind him at a much slower pace, feeling physically sick that Gary now had one well and truly over on him.

'You're too bloody good, Gary! Kian should be clearing up his own mess; he's big enough and ugly enough. Kian, you should be bloody grateful to Gary…'

'Oh, I'm sure he's grateful really, Shell!' Gary grinned, before lowering his voice and whispering in Kian's ear.

'I want five hundred notes. Or else I'll be handing that wallet in to the police myself, kid. You got it?'

CHAPTER TWENTY-NINE

'You all right back here, Shannon?' Benny called out, making his way around the back of the shop to check on her. Having locked the front door of the chippy and put the closed sign up ages ago, he'd been busy cashing up the till, waiting for Shannon to come back out the front and collect her wages. But the girl had made herself scarce, and Benny had a feeling that her brother had upset her when he'd popped in earlier, because she hadn't been her usual self since.

'Yeah, I'm fine, Benny. Just tired that's all. I'll be glad to get home to my bed tonight.'

Benny nodded, not wanting to push the girl. He knew Shannon well enough by now to know that she kept her private business exactly that, private. She'd open up to him only if she wanted to.

'I've got your wages here. There's a couple of extra quid in there tonight we made in tips, too,' Benny said, passing Shannon the envelope of money and watching as she opened her tatty old make-up bag, which was full of notes, before stuffing her wages inside.

'Whoa, you've got more money in there than they've got at the cashpoint down on the high street!' Benny said, making light of the fact he'd just spotted Shannon's little stash of money. Money that he didn't think she had, seeing as she was always so desperate for extra work.

'I thought you were strapped for cash?' Benny said, wondering why Shannon had kept pestering him for so many extra shifts when she was clearly doing all right by the looks of it.

'I am. This isn't for me. I'm saving up for something,' Shannon said, looking embarrassed then, as if she'd been caught out.

'You ain't in trouble are you, Shannon?' Benny asked carefully, not wanting to imply anything that would offend the girl. 'I saw your brother earlier and those boys that were hanging around outside…'

'Well, he doesn't have a girlfriend,' Shannon said sadly, shrugging her shoulders. 'He's knocking about with a bad lot. Those boys earlier. You heard of the Griffin Boys?'

Benny closed his eyes. He knew full well who the Griffin Boys were. Trouble with a capital T. He'd had his eye on a few of them earlier, when they'd been hanging around outside the shop. He'd been nervous that they were there to make trouble. It wouldn't be the first time that they'd tried to intimidate local shop owners for free food or money out of the till. Or worse, smashing the place up if the owners didn't comply. Lucky for Benny, the boys had stayed outside, but he'd seen Kian walk off with them all, and already guessed that this was why the boy had been getting into trouble lately and stressing Shannon out.

'I know. It's just that he's not like that. He's not like them. He's soft, Benny. Too soft. And he might not realise it yet, but those kids are just out to use him. And he'll be the one that gets himself in trouble. I can just see it now.'

'Listen, Shannon. I know that you might not want to hear this, but you are not responsible for your brother's actions. If he's chosen to knock about with a bad lot, then that's on him. All you can do is give him advice and hope that he sees the light. You know. You don't need to get involved in any of it…'

'Involved?' Shannon said, the penny dropping at where Benny thought the money had come from. 'You think they gave me this?

That they sent Kian in with it, what? So I'd look after it for them?' Shannon couldn't help but laugh then. 'Benny, this is the money you've been paying me. I've been putting a bit of cash away after every shift. Well, half of it anyway. I give the other half to my mum to try and help her out with the bills and the shopping…'

'You must have been saving up since you first started here, going by that lot! Stashing it away every week,' Benny joked; then, seeing the embarrassed look on Shannon's face, he realised that's exactly what she had been doing.

Shannon had been helping Benny for almost a year now. She'd been fourteen when she had first walked in here, bold as brass, and begged Benny for a Saturday job.

'I'll do anything you want. Cleaning, sweeping up. I can even help you peel all the spuds…' she'd said innocently, eyeing the mountain of chips in the warming counter and not realising that most of the food that Benny sold was bought in, prepped and ready to chuck in the fryers. Still, Benny had liked her confidence and her willingness to earn a wage, so he'd decided to give the girl a chance and, to be fair to Shannon, she'd been true to her word ever since. She was a good little worker. 'What's the money for then? You going to buy a house or something?'

Shannon shrugged, stuffing the make-up bag down into her school bag, wishing that she'd kept it hidden out of sight now that Benny was asking questions.

'I tell you what, my Anita should take a leaf out of your book, Shannon. That woman spends the bloody stuff as if it's going to burn a hole in my pocket if she don't.' Benny laughed affectionately. It was no secret to anyone that knew Benny and Anita that Benny absolutely adored his wife. Anita and their two young daughters were all he ever spoke about, and Shannon knew that Anita felt exactly the same about Benny. They were like one of those perfect families that you saw on TV shows, the type of family that Shannon would never have believed really existed until she'd met Benny. Benny would give Anita the world if he could make it possible. So she knew that he was only making the joke to lighten the mood a bit.

'Though seriously, Shannon, if you're strapped for cash and want to help your mum out with the bills and stuff, why are you hiding it away? It isn't a crime to want a bit of money for yourself, you know, sweetheart. You worked hard for it, why shouldn't you treat yourself now and again?'

'It ain't for me,' Shannon said quietly, before adding, 'Promise you won't laugh if I tell you what it's for?'

Benny eyed her suspiciously, hoping that Shannon wasn't going to tell him something bad.

'Course I won't,' he said, praying that he could keep his word.

'My mum ain't sick, Benny. Well, not in the way I made out to you, anyway.'

Benny nodded to show that he was listening, but didn't let on that he knew exactly what Shannon was going to tell him. Michelle Winters was an alcoholic. A slave to drink, and it was common knowledge around these parts that it was taking a toll not only on her, but on her kids too. It was another reason why Benny had given Shannon a job. Not that he'd ever let Shannon know that; the last thing the girl would ever want was a sympathy vote. She was way too proud for that.

'She's got a drink problem,' Shannon said. Relieved in a way to finally say the truth out loud.

'I'm so sorry, Shan. That must be really hard to have to deal with,' Benny said softly, knowing how much courage it would have taken her to finally confide in him.

He was surprised that Shannon hadn't opened up to him about it all sooner; they spoke about most things and they'd formed a nice little friendship over the past year. But in that time Shannon had never once spoken of, or bad-mouthed, that woman. She was far too loyal for that, and Benny could only imagine the pressure that had put the kid under.

'She's not a bad person, but she's got worse. A lot worse, and I just wanted to earn some money, so that maybe I could look into getting her some help.' Shannon was stuttering now, the words pouring out of her mouth quicker than she could keep up with them, not wanting Benny to think badly of her mother. 'Some proper help, like get her booked in at a rehab centre or something. And I've almost got enough.'

'You know what, Shannon, that's a really lovely thing to do,' Benny said, sincerely. 'Your mum's lucky to have you, darling! You know that, don't you?'

Shannon nodded, though she doubted Benny's words completely.

'I've got to get home, Benny. See you tomorrow, yeah?'

Benny nodded and watched as Shannon made her way across the parade of shops towards the estate, with her bag tucked tightly under one arm and the weight of the whole world on her shoulders.

Benny shook his head sadly, and pulled the shop's shutters down.

CHAPTER THIRTY

Squinting as he made his way into Philip Penfold's lounge, Kian winced as the thick cloud of smoke made his eyes water and blurred his vision. The smell of weed was so strong and pungent that he'd been able to smell it out on the stairwell at the end of the balcony.

He'd already guessed that Jax and his boys were having another of their parties and he didn't want to stick around. He'd be stoned himself just by breathing in the dense, drug-filled air. Holding his breath, he made his way down the dark hallway, peering into the darkened lounge and seeing if he could spot Jax. The curtains were pulled and the only light in the room came from the bright blue hue of the television. All Kian could see were the silhouettes of people dotted all over the lounge, sitting in huddles on the couch and at the dining table. He didn't spot Jax, but Philip saw Kian and was on him in seconds.

'Have you seen Mr Bobcat?' Philip said, gripping Kian's arms tightly.

'Mr Who?' Kian said, shaking his head.

'My cat. Mr Bobcat. He's gone,' Philip said, not bothering to wipe the tears that started to fall, though he did have the decency to wipe the long trail of snot that dangled from his nose with the sleeve of his jumper.

'Jesus, mate. Calm down. I'm sure he'll be back.' Kian grimaced, noting how red and puffy Philip's eyes were. By the looks of it, he'd been crying for hours.

'No, he won't. He'll get lost. He won't know his way back here. Someone will let him out the main doors. How will he get back in? He won't come back here because Jax scared him.' Philip was sobbing openly now, not caring how pathetic he sounded. Because that's what Jax and the boys had told him; that he was pathetic for crying over a poxy cat. But Mr Bobcat wasn't just a cat. He was Philip's family. His only real friend. And now he'd gone.

'I think he ran out when one of the boys left the door open. He's a house cat, Kian. He doesn't know how to act outside. And he'll be scared out there all by himself. He'll be looking for me, but I can't go out and find him because Jax won't let me go outside. Will you have a look for me, Kian? Please?' Grabbing a photo of the cat, Philip shoved it into Kian's hand before the boy could protest.

'All right, Kian lad!' Interrupting the conversation, Jax eyed the photograph that Philip had just thrust at Kian and put his arm around Kian protectively.

'Philip, mate! You're not still harping on about that bloody mangy cat again, are you? You need to get a grip, lad. I told you, he'll be back when he's hungry.'

'But he won't be able to get back in. And what if he ends up near the busy main roads? Please let me look for him, Jax. I'll come straight back,' Philip said, knowing how close he was to making Jax angry; but he didn't care. It would be worth Jax giving him yet another slap around the head or telling the boys to hurt him and make fun of him if it just meant that Jax would listen to him. All he wanted was his Mr Bobcat back.

'I told you, you ain't going out there!' Jax said, gritting his teeth. Philip's constant whining was starting to wind him up. The bloke was an embarrassment. 'I know you. You'll start chatting shit to people with that fat gob of yours. And before we know it, we'll have Old Bill back here again, asking what we're doing in your flat. To be fair, mate, it's probably for the best anyway. I mean, with the amount of gear getting smoked tonight, Mr Mangy Bobcat would be off his bloody nut.' Jax grinned. 'And the noise ain't good for him either, is it? Too many people about, too. He'd probably end up getting stamped on.'

Philip stared at Jax, aware of the veiled threat. He looked as if he were about to say something else, but thought better of it and, instead, he walked off.

'Fucking nutter!' Jax muttered, shaking his head. 'Anyway, fuck him. Where's the wallet?'

'Look Jax, I know this is going to piss you off. But there's a problem...' Kian started, trying to remember the speech he'd rehearsed on the way down to the flat, but he couldn't think of the words now with Jax standing over him, staring so intently at him. 'I haven't got it. But I know where it is.'

'You what?' Jax said, narrowing his eyes. His face twisted with disbelief. 'Well, if you know where it is, why ain't you got it?'

'Someone else has got to it and they know...' Kian blurted out the truth, knowing that Jax would be annoyed no matter what. 'Gary. My mum's waster of a fella.' Kian was stuttering now as he tried to explain. 'He found it when it fell out of my pocket. He's a proper arsehole, Jax. And he hates me. He said he won't let me have it back unless I pay him five hundred pounds to keep his mouth shut...'

'Are you having a laugh or what?' Jax said, shaking his head and laughing out loud. 'You better not be trying to have me over, Kian. This better not be your way of trying to get five hundred notes out of me. You already owe me two grand!'

'It's not, Jax, I swear. He knows. He said he'll give it back and keep his mouth shut, but he wants paying. Otherwise, he said he'll grass me up to the police. And he will. I know he will. He's the type who'd grass.' Kian was close to tears now.

'And how the fuck does he know where the wallet came from?' Jax said, biting down on his lip.

'It's been on the news apparently. The bloke's wife put out an appeal.' Kian shrugged. 'I mean, Gary is a prat. But I guess he ain't as stupid as he looks, because he saw me with the phone, and we had an argument and I must have dropped the wallet. And then he saw the news piece, and the name of the bloke was written on the library card inside and he just put two and two together.'

'The bloke sounds like a fucking genius, mate!' Jax said, rolling his eyes sarcastically. 'Fucking hell, Kian, you may as well have drawn him a fucking diagram!' Jax shook his head in complete disbelief. 'Or made a fucking public announcement telling the bastard that we bloody did it.'

'I'm sorry, Jax,' Kian said, staring at the floor then, unsure what else he could say to appease him. He knew what Jax was thinking. That he was a moron and that he'd fucked up, yet again.

Jax stood there silent for a few minutes, taking several long drags of his cigarette, his face blank, as if deep in thought. He moved out the way as a couple of the lads walked past, leading some of the girls from the estate into one of the bedrooms. The music was pulsing, the air still thick with smoke. Kian felt sick. He needed air. He needed to get out of here. But he knew that he had to wait until Jax gave him permission to do so. His fate right now was in Jax's hands.

'Well then, we're going to need to get our thinking caps on, ain't we? Because we need it back,' he said finally, stubbing his cigarette out in the ashtray on the coffee table nearest to them.

'What? We're going to pay him?' Kian asked, unsure that that would be the end of it even if they did. Gary was the type to hold this kind of information over his head for ever, rinsing him for whatever he could get.

'Don't be stupid, Kian. Course we ain't paying the bloke.' Jax laughed. 'He doesn't know who he's fucking with, throwing his demands about, but trust me, he's about to find out.'

Kian nodded, still uncertain what Jax intended to do to Gary in order to get the wallet back, but relieved that Jax didn't seem too angry with him.

'He ain't good for my mum. She's been worse since she's been with him…' Kian said, unable to keep the hate from his tone.

Jax nodded again. Sucking at his teeth, he didn't say a word. He didn't have to, remembering his own dad. That bloke had been a waster, too. Always cheating on his mother and slapping her around the place. When he'd finally walked out on them both, when Jax had been not even five years old, social services had deemed them a broken home. Which Jax's mum had always laughed about afterwards, insisting that that man finally upping and buggering off meant that their home was finally fixed.

He summoned Philip over to where Kian stood. 'Here, Kian, make yourself useful and take this whiny bastard out from under my feet, will you? Go and look for that poxy cat. Maybe he'll give it a rest then, with all his harping on.'

'Thanks, Jax. Thank you!' Philip beamed, rushing to get his shoes and coat on as Kian stood there, nodding to the instructions Jax was dishing out, grateful that Jax wasn't blaming him for the fuck up.

'One hour, and then you get your arses straight back here, with or without the cat, do you understand? One hour, and make sure that this div doesn't start chatting shit to anyone, you get me?'

Kian nodded, desperate to make it up to Jax.

'And when you get back, we'll work out what we're going to do about this Gary bloke; he sounds like an absolute prick. It's going to be my absolute pleasure to sort him out once and for all.'

CHAPTER THIRTY-ONE

'Mind your head, Mr Gibson!' Lucy Murphy said, guiding the elderly man's head into the police car so that he didn't hit it off the metal door frame, as he continued his barrage of abuse and swearing.

'Mind my head? I've got more things to worry about than my bleeding head. I don't know why you are arresting me. It was that treacherous bastard who started it all. Let me out of here, I'm going to bloody kill him!'

'You need to calm down, Mr Gibson. You're only going to make things worse for yourself talking like that,' Lucy warned politely, before shutting the door on the older man and leaning up against it, taking in the small crowd of people congregated outside the Dog and Bone pub on Wandsworth High Street. Luckily, they were starting to disperse now that the show was over and they'd had their five minutes' worth of free entertainment. And it had been a show.

Even Lucy had been dumbfounded when she and DS Morgan had seen the fight break out, just as they'd been making their way back to the station after investigating the scene of an attempted burglary at the local betting shop further down the high street. The intruders had assaulted the young female cashier who'd tried and eventually succeeded in fighting them off, but not before she'd got herself a beating for her efforts.

The last thing Lucy had expected as they made their way back to the station was the sight of two men in their early eighties rolling around the pavement outside the pub and taking swipes at each other.

Lucy had barely been able to believe what she was seeing, and the situation had become even more laughable when she found out that the argument was actually about the landlady, who both men had seemingly taken a liking to; she was at least forty years their junior.

'And they say chivalry is dead!' she'd murmured to herself with a smirk, as she swooped in and grabbed Mr Gibson from where he'd been, down on the ground straddling his very drunk companion.

'Has he calmed down yet?' Morgan asked, bending down and peering into the back of the car as they waited for the van to turn up so that they could take him in.

'Not a chance, he's still going at it. Adamant that the landlady has a crush on him.' Lucy shrugged, rolling her eyes at the man's persistence as he continued to bellow and throw himself around in the back seat of the car, despite his hands being bound together with handcuffs.

'How's your guy, Sarge?' Lucy asked, nodding over to the other patrol car that had turned up, where they'd placed the night's other offender.

'Not a peep out of him. Think he's already sleeping it off!' DS Morgan said with a weary sigh. 'And the landlady doesn't want to press any charges. She said that they are regulars and apparently they're always at it. Said there's no harm done. In fact, if anything, the bar's packed now and they've all got something to talk about. Let's just take them in and hold them both in the cells until they sober up. We'll keep them both apart for a bit. Let things calm down.' He yawned. 'This is why I couldn't go back to being in uniform. Dealing with pointless, drunken spats like this, when there's far more important crimes we could be focusing on.'

Lucy nodded understandingly. She knew that DS Morgan was still seething after the state the betting shop assistant had been left in. The poor woman had been carted off to St George's in an ambulance, and Lucy and DS Morgan had heard the paramedics say that she had a suspected eye socket fracture as well as a broken jaw. The job got to them some days much more than it did others.

'Looks like we're in for a busy old nightshift, eh Sarge?'

'Is there any other kind?' Morgan said, picking up his radio from the front of the car and rolling his eyes as the dispatcher informed him of a disturbance nearby.

'Two male youths making a noise disturbance and damaging someone's back gate. Just around the corner, on West Street, just before you turn in to the Griffin Estate. Uniform are all busy. Can anyone there attend?'

'I'll go, Sarge,' Lucy offered. 'You wait here for the van to turn up, and then you can come and find me.'

DS Morgan pursed his mouth, about to say that he'd go, but then he realised that Murphy wanted to prove to him that she was more than capable of dealing with this on her own.

'Go on then,' Morgan said, glancing back at the man in the back of his unmarked car, who was still kicking the back of the seat and swearing. 'I'll probably have my work more than cut out for me by staying here. I'll come and pick you up as soon as the van gets here.'

Lucy nodded. 'See you in a bit, Sarge.'

She made her way quickly to the location the dispatcher had mentioned on the radio. She hadn't been exaggerating when she'd said to DS Morgan that tonight had been busy. They'd been rushed off their feet and she didn't even want to think about the amount of paperwork they'd accumulated in the process.

Instead, she thought about her nan, at home tucked up safely in her bed, with Vivian looking after her. The woman had a heart of gold for doing all that she did as it was, always being so patient and kind to her nan. Vivian often stayed over to cover Lucy's night shifts when she'd been in uniform, but working in CID would hold much more responsibility and the extra hours needed only mirrored that. And as much as Vivian hadn't complained about the sudden extra hours that Lucy's move to CID would naturally incur, it wasn't fair of her to expect Vivian to be happy with this arrangement for very much longer, especially as the woman had a young family of her own that needed her.

Not only that, but her nan was getting so much worse. The other night in the park had genuinely scared Lucy. Vivian was right about that, too. Caring for her nan was too much for the two of them to take on. Even so, just the thought of putting her nan into a home made her feel physically sick. Her nan had been there all her life for Lucy, and Lucy wanted to give her nan that back in return. It was a dilemma that she had no idea how to solve. Walking faster now, out of breath, Lucy pushed all thoughts of her nan to the back of her mind. She needed to find these kids and deal with them first. Then at least she'd be another job closer to finally finishing her shift and being able to go home.

CHAPTER THIRTY-TWO

'Mr Bobcat?' Kian called out, stepping inside the communal bin shed and wrinkling his nose in disgust as the putrid smell instantly hit him. 'Mr Bobcat?' he called again, scouring the floor for any sign of the missing cat, whilst shaking his head with embarrassment at how stupid he must sound right now. 'Surely you could have picked a better name for the poor bastard than Mr Bobcat, Philip?' Kian joked, crouching down on the floor and staring underneath the large communal bin. 'We must sound like right prats, walking through the estate shouting that out.'

'No. Mr Bobcat suits him,' Philip said defensively, not getting Kian's humour one bit.

The bloke hadn't smiled or spoken once since they'd left the flat. The only thing he was focused on was getting his cat back, but so far they'd had no luck. They'd searched high and low across the entire estate, checking every stairwell, every balcony, knocking on every door that they'd passed. Kian had even lain down in the middle of the road and looked underneath the wheels of all the parked cars, just in case the cat was hiding under them.

'Seriously, Philip, if he ain't here, then God knows where he's gone. We've looked everywhere,' Kian said, grimacing as he lifted up one of the large bin lids, before immediately slamming it back down as the pungent stink of dirty nappies and rotten food hit him with full force, almost making him gag. 'Come on, mate.

We've been looking for almost an hour. You heard what Jax said, we better get back now or Jax will send his boys out looking for us.'

As they made their way back up West Street towards the estate, Philip ran after Kian and grabbed at his jumper, pulling him back.

'But we can't go back without him, Kian. We need to find him. He'll be cold out here and scared,' Philip said, his voice going into the same high-pitched panic that Kian had heard earlier when Philip had first begged him to help look for his beloved cat.

'What if he isn't out here though, Philip? He might be inside someone's flat right now. All warm and cosy and drinking a nice big saucer of milk. And we're the mugs out here, freezing our nuts off,' Kian said, trying to sound hopeful. But Philip shook his head.

'I've got a bad feeling, Kian. I know Mr Bobcat. He's run away because he doesn't like Jax.' Philip started crying then. Sobbing loudly, working himself back up into a state. 'I don't like Jax either. He's a bully. And he's mean. And he's always horrible to me and Mr Bobcat. I want to run away, too. I don't ever want to see Jax and his stupid mates ever again.' Philip raised his voice, his fists clenched at his sides.

'Here mate, calm down, yeah. It's all right. It's all going to be all right,' Kian said, trying to pacify Philip, as he noted the curtains in the window of the nearby ground floor flat twitching.

But Philip was already hysterical. The stress of the last few days at Jax's mercy, and now losing his beloved cat, was all too much for him. He couldn't cope anymore.

'My head hurts, Kian. I haven't slept for days. And I miss Karen, my carer. I want her to come back and help me.' Philip was bawling loudly now, not caring that he was drawing attention to them both. That people were looking out their windows or leaning over the balcony to watch some nutjob having a meltdown; that all he was was a bit of entertainment for them until the next drama happened.

'I'm not going back there, Kian. I don't want to and you can't make me. I hate Jax. I hate his friends. I hate the disgusting drugs they give me that make me feel sick. They shaved Mr Bobcat's fur off and they made him run away. And they are eating all my food and drinking all my drink, and they are all making too much mess, and they are too loud! The music is too loud! I can't sleep. I want him gone.'

Philip lashed out, kicking and punching the gate that was nearest to him, in pure frustration.

'Philip, come on, mate! People are looking...' Kian warned as a light flickered on in the flat nearby, just as another resident further up opened a window and shouted down at them.

'Oi, I've got a baby in here I'm trying to get to sleep. Bugger off you bloody morons or I'm calling the police.'

But Philip didn't stop. He kicked and punched harder, pummelling the wooden panel with his boots and fists until it splintered, crying louder, shouting hysterically. He wanted someone to call the police. He wanted someone to help him.

'Mate, come on. Calm down. We're going to get in trouble otherwise,' Kian said, pulling Philip away from the gate, but Philip shrugged him off. So Kian tried another tactic.

'Philip, if they call the police on us, they'll take you away. And trust me, mate, as much as you want to get away from Jax, that ain't the way. Because they will take you away and lock you up. And what's Mr Bobcat going to do then, eh? When he comes back home and you're not there? What if Jax takes him?' Kian said, glad to get Philip's attention finally, as the man stopped his kicking and listened to what Kian was saying.

Sitting down on the kerb, Philip took some deep breaths to calm himself down. The outburst and the stress of the past couple of days were finally taking their toll on him. He was exhausted. Both mentally and physically drained.

Kian could see it too.

He waited patiently for a few minutes as Philip composed himself, then finally continued.

'Mr Bobcat might be there right now, at the main doors of the block, trying to get back in. We should go and look, Philip. I saw a documentary on cats the other night, about how they always find their way home,' Kian lied. 'It's like a primal instinct that they have. They just know. Come on, mate, let's go and have a look, shall we?'

Relieved when Philip finally nodded in agreement, Kian grabbed him by the arm and led him away before he could change his mind. Away from the shouting neighbours and the broken gate that was hanging on loosely now by its hinges.

'Do you really think Bobcat will be there?' Philip said, suddenly sounding a lot more positive as he quickened his pace in order to keep up with Kian. As they rounded the corner, they bumped straight into a woman who had been heading their way.

'Evening, boys, I'm DC Murphy. We had a call about a noise complaint. Is everything all right?' Lucy said, eyeing them and noting that they matched the description given of the two boys. Lucy stared at the older lad, noting the streaks of tears running down his cheeks and the way that he looked down at the floor instead of giving her any eye contact.

'We've lost his cat,' Kian said quickly, speaking first in fear of what Philip might say. 'Mr Bobcat. And my mate, Philip, he's a bit upset.' Grabbing the photograph that Philip had pressed into his hand earlier, from his pocket, Kian showed it to the officer as if to prove he was telling the truth.

'We've been out looking for ages, and so far we haven't had any luck, so we're just going to go back home, aren't we, Philip, because we think that's where Mr Bobcat might be.' Kian was desperate for the officer to believe them and let them go on their

way before any of the neighbours came out and told the copper
about the damage that Philip had just done to someone's front
gate. 'Cats usually know how to find their way home, don't they?'
Kian paused, hoping that the officer would back him up, and
her words would be enough to appease Philip about the whole
situation.

'Yeah, they do. I'm sure you'll find him,' Lucy said to Philip,
wanting to give the poor man some hope that he'd find his beloved
pet, before turning her attention back to Kian. She had recognised
him as the kid they'd seen on the stairwell at the Griffin Estate
on Monday morning.

'I've seen you before, haven't I? You're the kid who was going
to the chemist to get some painkillers, because you'd had a fall.'
Lucy eyed the boy suspiciously now. 'Kian, isn't it?'

'Yeah, that was me.' Kian shrugged, praying that the officer
wouldn't follow them both back to the estate to make sure that
they got back okay.

'And what's your name?'

'Philip Penfold,' Kian said quickly, his heart pounding in his
chest as he prayed that Philip would keep his mouth shut and
not say anything about Jax and the others.

Lucy nodded. The name sounded familiar but she couldn't
think why.

'Do you want me to walk you back to your flat, Philip? Help
you look for your cat?' Lucy asked as Philip looked down at the
floor, not willing to give her eye contact. She was unable to shake
off the niggle inside her telling her something was up. She couldn't
put her finger on it, but she was certain that the older lad was
upset about something more than just his cat.

Kian waited, holding his breath, his eyes boring into Philip's
as he silently prayed to himself that Philip would keep schtum.
Because if this officer came back to the flat now, Jax and his boys

would end up in a whole world worth of shit, and that meant Kian's neck would be on the line too. It would all come out. The drugs, the money, the man they'd put in a coma and almost killed. They'd all be done for.

'Philip?' Lucy said softly, before she was interrupted by the controller on her police radio asking for an update. She told them that she was with the two suspects and was giving them both a stern warning to keep the noise down. Ending the call, Lucy looked to the two boys again.

'Philip? Shall I walk you back?'

'No. I'm fine. We're fine. Like Kian said, we're going to go back and wait for Mr Bobcat at home. Make sure he's safe,' Philip said, knowing that as much as he wanted to ask for some help, it would be more than his life was worth. Kian was right. He needed to get home for his cat; otherwise, Mr Bobcat would be left at Jax's mercy and Philip couldn't bear the thought of that.

'Okay lads,' Lucy said, reluctantly. But as far as she could see there was nothing untoward going on here. Their story about trying to find the missing cat seemed genuine. 'I hope you find him!'

As she let the boys continue their way back towards the Griffin Estate, Lucy saw the headlights of DS Morgan's car approaching to pick her up. Opening the door, she rolled her eyes jokingly.

'Just kids, Sarge. They're looking for a missing cat.'

'Just when you thought our special training and expertise couldn't have been put to better use tonight…' he said as they drove off, making their way back to the station and the mountain of paperwork they had waiting for them until they had their next call out. Roll on five am when her shift would finally be over. She could finally get home and relieve Vivian, so that the poor woman could get home to her own children. But part of her was dreading what she might be walking in to when she got there.

CHAPTER THIRTY-THREE

Turning the key in the lock as gently as he could, Kian snuck inside the flat. The warm glow of the TV lit up the lounge. His eyes going straight to the sofa, he was relieved to see Gary passed out on it, exactly where Kian had guessed he would be, surrounded by a deck of playing cards and a coffee table full of empty cider cans. His mates were long gone. Kian had been counting on that.

He tiptoed along the hallway, as quietly as he could, knowing full well that Shannon would be waiting up for him to come home, despite their argument. His sister couldn't help herself, he thought, as he reached her bedroom and saw her bedside light glowing from underneath the gap in the door. Opening it gently, in case she was asleep, Kian peered in.

'You're back early!' Shannon said, glancing at the clock and seeing that it was not even eleven thirty yet. It was the first time he'd been home before midnight in days. Perhaps her little lecture had worked. 'Is everything all right?' she said, sitting up, surprised that her brother had come to her room and guessing that, like her, he felt bad about their argument earlier. She hated rowing with Kian.

'Yeah, I just got back. I'm knackered so I thought I'd head straight to bed. Thought I'd say good night…' He looked awkward, as if there was something else he wanted to say, but couldn't.

'You know, you've driven me mad lately, Kian, but you know I'd forgive you anything, don't you? Well, almost anything,' Shannon said, hoping that her brother had at least listened to her warning about the boys he'd started hanging around with. But she knew that alienating her brother now would be playing into those boys' hands, and Shannon didn't want her brother involved with them anymore than he already was.

'I know, Shan.' About to close the bedroom door, he faltered, his hand on the handle. 'And Shan? I did mean what I said earlier. I know I've been a miserable sod lately, I'm sorry. But there's nothing for you to worry about. I'll sort things.'

'I get it, Kian. You're growing up. Just don't push me out, okay? I'll always be here for you. You know that, don't you?'

Kian nodded. Unable to find any words, he blew his sister a kiss and then closed the door behind him. Shannon was right. She'd always been there for him. No matter what. And he felt bad for lying to her tonight and pretending that he was coming home to go to bed. But he knew she wouldn't be happy with his and Jax's plan, and he also knew that just popping in to Shannon's room bought him a much-needed alibi. Because Kian knew his sister wouldn't lie to anyone, and he was counting on that fact. Because if there was any comeback from what they were about to do, he would be depending on his sister screaming his innocence to anyone who'd listen.

Making his way over to his mother's room, he pushed the already ajar door open slightly more and stared in through the darkness, screwing his mouth up as he saw his mother sprawled out on top of the duvet, still fully clothed. He held his breath. The room smelled musty and sour, a mixture of cheap booze and body odour.

Kian swallowed down his anger. From as far back as he remembered Shannon had fed him the line that their mother was sick, and for a while Kian had believed it. When he'd seen her unable to stand on her own two feet, crawling across the floor. Or the times she'd been crying hysterically as if she was in pain for no reason, or no reason that Kian had been able to see. Or the times when she couldn't even get her words out. When she mumbled and slurred her speech so badly it was as if she was talking in a different language. But as he'd grown older, Shannon hadn't been able to shield him from the truth of their mother's addiction. No amount of excuses would mask the truth. Their mother was an alcoholic.

There had been times, he remembered, when she'd seemed okay for a while. Times when he'd been small and she'd played games with him or helped him build his Lego. Or the times they'd snuggled up under a blanket and watched Christmas movies together. But he could count those good times on one hand. Most of his memories were bad. And it was Shannon who had always been there for him, not his mother. Which is probably why he didn't have the patience for the woman anymore. In fact, some days he actually hated her. Because it stayed with you, seeing someone you love in that state, when you were so small and vulnerable. That panic and fear never left you. And there had been so many times over the years when Kian had worried himself sick that one day his mother would go too far; she'd drink too much, and he or Shannon would find her dead.

And since she'd met Gary, that thought had only been magnified. Because Gary took the piss out of their mother. He knew her weaknesses and he used them all against her, getting her drunk and out of the way so that he could lord it up in their flat, in their home, with his degenerate mates. Well, Kian wasn't having it anymore. And he wasn't going to allow the bastard to dangle something over his head and blackmail him with it either.

Making his way back into the lounge, Kian lingered in the doorway for a few seconds, taking a slow, deep breath as he looked over at Gary, gearing himself up for what he was about to do next.

He hated the man with a vengeance. And he'd decided that, for once, he was going to deal with this alone. Instead of going along with Jax's plan, Kian was going to take this moment to prove to Jax, at last, that he could do something right, without having to let Jax into his home, where Shannon and his mum were both sleeping. Without all the drama and the aggro.

Taking a few steps towards Gary, Kian stared at him. He was out cold, breathing heavily, his mouth wide open as his snores filled the room. One hand was resting inside the crotch of his trousers; the other was behind his head. Kian eyed Gary's jeans, guessing that if he had the wallet on him, it would be in his back pocket. Which meant he was lying on it. Moving slowly, Kian leant over Gary's body. He held his breath as he slid his arm down the back of the sofa, pressing his hand against the chair's material as he tucked his fingers under Gary's waist.

Reaching into the back pocket, his fingers gripped the square of hard leather. Bingo. Kian pulled it out slowly.

'Oi! Are you trying to touch me up, you fucking pervert!' Gary said, lurching forward suddenly, bolt upright now on the sofa as he made a grab for Kian's wrist.

'Shit!' Kian tried to wrench himself free from the man's tight hold, the wallet still firmly in his hand, but Gary quickly figured out what was going on. Lifting his eyebrows, he laughed, tightening his grip on the lad.

'Oh, I know what you're up to; you're trying to steal that wallet back. Well tough shit, mate. I told you, you ain't having it until you pay up,' Gary sneered, just as a glass beer bottle smashed against the side of his head.

Kian stared in horror as Gary slumped back down on the sofa, a trickle of blood running down his face. Turning, he stared at Jax, who was standing behind him, the bottle still in his hand.

'Fuck me, if you want a job doing properly, you've got to do it yourself, eh? Seems to be a theme with you, Kian!' Jax said, grabbing the wallet from Kian's grasp and tucking it inside his own back pocket. Then, turning to the lads behind him, who'd all been waiting outside with Jax for the signal from Kian that never came, Jax ordered them to move their arses.

'Get him back to the flat, pronto! When this fucker wakes up, he's not going to know what's hit him. Literally!' Jax laughed at his own wit, placing the beer bottle back down on the coffee table amongst the rest of the bottles and cans.

CHAPTER THIRTY-FOUR

Placing her handbag down on the dining table, Lucy rubbed her pounding head.

'Bad day?' Vivian asked, coming out from the kitchen and handing Lucy a tray of hot food and a cup of tea. 'Your nan's still in bed, darling. But I've made her some breakfast for when she wakes up, and I thought you might appreciate some after your night shift too.'

'Ah, you didn't have to do that!' Lucy said, feeling foolish then for letting tears form in her eyes at the kind gesture. Vivian had no idea how hard Lucy was fighting to keep herself together at the moment. 'You honestly don't know how appreciated this is.' Lucy paused. Vivian had her jacket on, which had become her usual attire each time Lucy had seen her lately. Coat done up, handbag over her shoulder, ready to race out of the door and back to her own growing brood the second Lucy got home.

'I don't know how you do it, Vivian,' Lucy said. 'Caring for my nan each day and then going home to your own family too. You have no idea how appreciated you are. I'm so sorry for keeping you waiting for me yet again.'

'I know, my darling,' Vivian said softly. 'And trust me when I say this: it's been an absolute pleasure caring for your lovely nan, and I hate to spring this on you…' Vivian reached into her handbag, retrieving the envelope from inside, before handing it to Lucy. 'That woman is a tonic, really she is. But I just can't do it anymore, Lucy. I've got to think of my own family, darling. If your job had more set hours then it wouldn't have been an issue. And now you're working in CID, even you don't know if you're coming or going half the time,' she said truthfully. 'I'm not blaming you, darling. I knew what I was getting into when I took this job on, but I seem to be getting home later and later and it's not fair on my lot.'

Lucy nodded. She'd known that this was coming for a while now. Of course, it was too much to ask someone to hang around each night until Lucy finally walked through the front door. It wasn't fair on Vivian, and Lucy had known it would only be a matter of time until the woman decided enough was enough.

'We'll be gutted to lose you, Vivian, but I understand. Of course I do,' Lucy said, trying her hardest to keep the false smile plastered to her face.

Her mind was whirling. Changing her nan's carer would be a nightmare because her nan really didn't take well to change. As much as Winnie sometimes made Vivian's life difficult, taking all her frustrations out on the woman, she loved the bones of her really. They had a real friendship of sorts, and more importantly her nan trusted Vivian implicitly.

'Look, Lucy. I know that you don't want to think about it, but maybe it's time to look at Winnie's options. Being here at home, with a carer, it's full on; and if you do find someone who can do it, and that you trust to do it properly, then great. But I really think she'd be better off looking at residential care…'

'You know I can't, Vivian,' Lucy said, shaking her head, immediately dismissing the idea, doing what she always did and cutting the conversation dead, just as Vivian knew she would.

'But why not? It doesn't mean that you've given up, Lucy, or that you've failed her in any way,' Vivian said, trying to reason with the younger woman. 'It just means that your nan will have more help around her. All the time, around the clock. She's a feisty woman, Lucy, you know that. Stubborn as a bull that one. It's not good for her to be stuck between these four walls all day every day – at least in a residential home she'd have other people around her, too. She'd make friends maybe. She'd have a better quality of life, Lucy. You could visit her all the time. Every day.'

'I don't want to visit her, Vivian,' Lucy said, unable to keep the emotion from her voice. 'She wouldn't want that. She wants to be here, at home with me, with all her memories and things around her.'

It was Vivian who shook her head then.

'Darling, her memories are diminishing daily and her things are exactly that, just things. What your lovely nan needs is proper care and support. She needs as much help as possible to have the best quality life for the time she has left.' Vivian spoke gently, aware that Lucy didn't want to hear any of this, but she loved Lucy and Winnie as if they were part of her own family and it needed to be said, no matter how hard it was for Lucy to hear it. 'I mean this with the best will in the world, Lucy, darling. Your nan is struggling. Really struggling. With everything. You must see it?'

'Sometimes she's okay…' Lucy said weakly, trying to justify her decision, even though she knew that was becoming less and less true lately. That her nan was often away with the fairies in her own make-believe world.

'Sometimes!' Vivian shrugged. 'Yeah, she's present. Back in the room with us. Full of all her funny stories and sayings. But the next minute she doesn't even remember her own name, Lucy. She can't go out on her own in case she forgets where she lives. She can't cook for herself, in case she forgets that she's left the oven on. She needs round the clock care and I truly believe that's too much for a sole carer. And it's too much for you, too. How are you supposed to do your job?'

Lucy was quiet then. She couldn't argue with Vivian because, as much as she didn't want to hear it, she knew it was true.

'Look, darling, I'm not saying that you have to decide right away, but just think about it yeah?' Vivian said, placing her hand on Lucy's arm and giving her a warm smile. 'Maybe this is the right time to do it, instead of introducing her to someone new? I'll work a month's notice so that you have time to make whatever arrangements you decide. And if it's all right with you I'd love to keep in touch with Winnie afterwards, if you'll let me?'

Lucy hugged Vivian tightly then. The woman had been with them for almost two years and had become like a member of the family. She was going to be lost without her. They both would be.

'She'd like that,' she said softly, then added, 'We'd both like that.'

Then, seeing the woman to the door, Lucy closed it behind her and made her way back into the lounge. She stared at the tray of food on the table, her appetite suddenly gone now. Instead, she poured herself a large vodka. Drinking it down in one, she grimaced at the sharp taste. She wasn't a big drinker but she knew that she needed something to take the edge off her mood and to help her sleep for the few hours before her nan woke up. Otherwise she'd lie awake in bed fretting.

Slumping down in the armchair then, alone in the silent room, Lucy stared over to the photograph on the mantlepiece. Her grandmother's favourite photo of the three of them the last time they had all been together, back when Lucy had been just five years old. She shook her head in wonderment that her nan seemed to always gravitate back to that time, imagining that Lucy was still young and that they were all still together. It was funny how the human brain worked.

Because Lucy couldn't remember much about that time at all now. And Christ knows she tried, willing herself to remember the sound of her mum's voice, or her smell, or her laugh. Willing herself to remember what he looked like. Her mother's killer.

Lucy wondered what that must feel like now, for her nan, not being able to remember that fateful day. To not feel that great weight of sadness, that sinking feeling inside her chest every time she thought about her mother. In some ways, Lucy envied her that.

What she would give to not still feel that wave of terror that swept over her every time she closed her eyes and found herself back there inside that wardrobe, huddled beneath the pile of clothes, staring out of the small gap in the wood, willing her mother to run, to hide, just like she was hiding. Her mother hadn't stood a chance.

But then there were other things that she physically willed herself to remember. Other things that she'd scolded herself for not being able to reach. Like the man's face. Squeezing her eyes shut tightly now, Lucy fought to keep back her tears, angry with herself once more. It had been twenty years; surely she should have remembered by now? The therapist had told her that it was shock that caused her memory lapse. That some things were too painful for the mind to comprehend, so sometimes, subconsciously, our minds just completely blocked entire memories out.

And it pained her deeply because she was the only living person to have seen the man's face who had murdered her mother. She was the only person to witness the heinous, horrific crime. But every time she closed her eyes and tried to recall that day, all she could really properly focus on was all that blood. Red on white. Her mother's dressing gown soaked in it as she lay bleeding out across the bed. And the man's face, when he turned, had somehow morphed into a mask of black, with no features. To her he was just a monster. The irony was that it felt like a tiny taste of what it must be like for her nan, not to be able to remember things without really having to try.

And Vivian was right. Her nan's memory was depleting much more rapidly. The doctors had warned Lucy that Alzheimer patients could suddenly plummet before stabilising again, but that those periods of stability would get shorter and shorter.

It pained her to even think it, but maybe it was time to think about more permanent care for her nan. She just wasn't sure she could bring herself to do it, though.

Her nan had brought her up: she'd raised her from the age of five, doing her best by Lucy always, even though the entire time she'd been fighting herself to hold her own life together, fighting to stay sane after her own daughter had been taken from her in such a brutal and tragic way. Lucy's mother's death had affected her nan severely; of course it had. Any mother would have been the same. But her nan had always had to be brave for her. She'd always put Lucy first. Wasn't it only fair now that Lucy at least try to do the same?

CHAPTER THIRTY-FIVE

Every part of him ached. That was Gary's first thought as he regained consciousness, his eyes flickering open as he stared out across the dimly lit room. *Where the fuck was he?* He couldn't see any familiarity in the room, or any of the furniture in it. *Shit!* His head was pounding too. Wincing, he decided that he must be getting too old to handle these nightly benders of his, drinking himself into oblivion, until he blacked out and had no memory of what he'd said or done. He'd ended up in some dodgy places in his time. Only tonight he must have drunk way more than normal, because he had no idea where he was now. No clue at all.

And the pain in his head was excruciating. He tried to move his hand up to the sharp thud at the top of his skull, to try and soothe the ache radiating inside his head, but he couldn't move his arms. He was tied to the chair that he was sitting on. His hands and feet were bound to the chair legs with rope, and he'd been gagged.

'What the fuck…?'

His words were muffled by the ball of material that had been wedged inside his mouth. Disorientated, he'd thought that his mouth and tongue had just been dry, that he was severely dehydrated. It was quickly dawning on him that his current predicament was much worse than that. He was being held hostage. Panicking, he started to shake his whole body in a futile attempt to break free from the restraints that bound him to the chair. A tiny part of him was still trying to convince himself that this was some kind of sick joke, that someone was just messing with him. Only he knew deep down that wasn't the case. Someone meant business. This was deliberate.

But it must be a case of mistaken identity, because as far as Gary could remember, he hadn't done anything lately that would warrant pissing anyone off this much, had he? He'd been keeping himself to himself, holed up at Michelle's place, minding his own business for once. It was probably the first time in his life that he'd actually managed to keep himself out of trouble for so long. He hadn't been doing anything he shouldn't have; no running around and shagging other fella's birds, or hiding from his dealer for not settling up his ever-growing tab. This was all a big mistake. Of course it was. So it stood to reason that whoever was holding him must have majorly fucked up. All Gary needed was a chance to explain that they'd got the wrong man.

Scanning the room then, he let his eyes dart around the space in search of some sort of clue as to where he was or why he was here. But the room was clear of any personal items and there were no photos on display. It looked like a dump, just like Michelle's place after Gary had had one of his parties. The place reeked of stale cigarettes, booze and sour body odour. It was a doss house of sorts: just a dull-looking room with a tatty grey sofa, and an old boxy-looking television set in the corner. An Xbox was splayed out in the middle of the floor with two controllers nearby, as if the place belonged to a teenager or something.

He closed his eyes and Kian's face flashed up in his memory. A vivid image of the boy standing over him whilst he slept. Was it a memory? Or had he dreamt it? He was almost certain that it had been real and that he'd caught the boy out last night as he lay sprawled out on Michelle's sofa. The little shit had been trying to pull a fast one, rummaging through Gary's pockets whilst he'd slept, searching for that poxy wallet that he'd nicked no doubt. Gary had made a grab for him, he remembered that much, locking the boy's arm inside his fist and dragging Kian down to his level. He recalled the look of fear etched on Kian's face. And then something else had flashed there. An almighty thud, and then nothing. And now Gary had woken up here. It didn't make any sense.

Gary tried to remember, but he couldn't think straight. He had no memory of anything that happened after he'd set eyes on Kian. But this couldn't be down to the kid, could it? Being here, tied up like this. Kian wasn't capable of shit like this; the boy didn't have it in him, and he'd know that Gary would obliterate him for pulling a stunt like this, and take great pleasure in doing so. Gary shuffled in his seat at a sudden noise behind him, hoping that finally, if nothing else, he'd have some answers to his questions.

'Finally, Sleeping Beauty has woken up!' Jax Priestly smirked, stepping out from behind Gary so that the man could see him.

Gary narrowed his eyes, looking from Jax to the two lads standing just behind him, but he was still none the wiser; he didn't recognise any of them. He tried to speak. To say something, to explain. He wanted to tell whoever this lad was that he'd got it wrong, that he had the wrong man. But again, the words were muted by the cloth in his mouth, and Jax laughed.

'I'll take it off, but if you shout for help, if you even make so much as a squeak, I'll cut your tongue out of your head. And there'll be no more fucking gestures of kindness from me. I don't give out second chances,' Jax warned the man, as Gary nodded obediently, agreeing to his conditions.

Jax, true to his word, grabbed the gag from Gary's mouth and held out the bottle of water he was holding.

'Here, drink this. I'm not a complete heartless bastard… besides, can't have you passing out again, can we? We've got shit to discuss.'

Gasping for water, Gary tipped his head back gratefully, gulping it down eagerly and realising too late as the bitter, salty liquid filled his mouth and made him gag, that it wasn't water at all. It was piss. The group of lads all laughed then as Gary turned his head away, but Jax continued to pour the rest of the piss all down him, soaking him. His only saving grace was the fact that the cloth had been removed from his mouth. He could finally breathe properly again.

He could try to explain.

'There's been some kind of mistake. I don't know who you think I am, but you've got it all wrong. You've got the wrong man…' Gary started, unable to keep the high-pitched panic from his voice.

'Oh no, mate, I never get it wrong. You are Gary Miller, ain't you?'

Gary nodded, a ball of fear instantly forming inside his stomach as the one tiny bit of hope he'd been clinging to – that this was all just one big mix-up – was suddenly wrenched away from him.

'I don't know what I'm supposed to have done…' Gary said, his eyes pleading with Jax now. He was unsure who the kid was, or what he was really capable of doing to him, but he recognised the malice that flashed back at him. All he did know was that suddenly he felt scared. No one knew where he was. And they'd tied him to a chair. He couldn't escape.

'Maybe this will clear things up a bit for you, mate!' Jax sneered, as Kian walked into the room.

'Kian?' Gary said, shaking his head in bewilderment. His first hunch had been right. Kian was behind all of this. Now it was Gary's turn to realise that it was him who had fucked up. He shouldn't have been so hard on the boy, not if these were the sort of evil little fuckers he'd been knocking about with.

'Seriously, whatever I said to you the other day, I was messing, all right? It's my warped sense of humour. I was just winding you up. You know I don't mean that shit…' He was shamelessly begging the boy to rethink what he was doing, trying to convince him that keeping Gary here, tied up against his will, wasn't the way to deal with their argument. But Kian's expression didn't waver, which told Gary that the boy didn't give a shit about his actions. He might think about his consequences, though. Maybe Gary just needed to remind him.

'Think of your mum, mate. She's going to lose her shit when she finds out you've done this to me…'

'Nah, she won't.' Kian shook his head, Gary's whiny tone and fake words instantly riling him. 'I mean, she might for a little bit, but she'll get over it. She'll realise that you don't give a shit about her. You're messing her up, Gary. Plying her with so much booze and gear that she doesn't know what day of the week it is. You're no good for her.'

Kian spoke calmly now, his voice steady, masking the fact that inside he was violently shaking. He'd been waiting for this moment, building himself up to face the man who had brought him and his family so much grief the past few months. This was his opportunity to finally get rid of him.

'That ain't true, Kian. I care about her, honest I do. Your mother's sick. You can't blame me for that. I do my best to help her, that's all. The way I see it, is that I'm the lesser of two evils, lad. If she didn't get her gear from me, she'd only go out and score it from someone else, and who knows what it would have been cut with if she got it off some low-life on the streets…'

'What? So you're doing her a favour, are you?' Kian snarled, then bit his lip as Gary nodded. He was aware of Jax and his boys standing close by, so he fought with everything he had inside him to keep his emotions at bay; but Gary was testing every last bit of patience that Kian had. It was all Kian could do right now not to launch himself at the man and batter the bloke.

'Bullshit!' he said, shutting Gary down, incensed by Gary's blatant attempts to blag himself out of the situation. The man was either severely dumb or severely ballsy to think he could argue back, even after having a bottle smashed over the top of his head and being held hostage.

'I want you gone! I want you out of her life and out of our flat. Today!'

About to make some smart-arsed reply, Gary noted the snarly look on the other boy's face, the first one who had spoken, and quickly thought better of it, though inside he was raging. The audacity of Kian to disrespect him in this manner. Acting like a bad man, like he had a bit of clout about him, just because he had these boys backing him up, whoever the fuck they were. Stupid, stupid boy. Because these lads wouldn't be there to watch over Kian every five minutes after today. So, for now, in order to save face and hopefully escape a beating, Gary decided it was the safest option simply to play along.

'Shit, I didn't think it was upsetting you that much, me being there,' he said with a shrug, trying to sound convincing, telling the boys what they wanted to hear so that he could get the fuck out of here. 'To be honest, things with me and your mum ain't really been working out,' he lied as he vowed silently to himself that Kian would pay for this dearly.

'What about the wallet?' Jax said then, waving it in the air in front of Gary to show him what this was really about. 'I hear you've been making demands. Threatening to make trouble about things you know fuck all about…'

'No,' Gary said, too quickly, realising too late that there was much more to this than Kian just being riled at him.

The news report on the mugging had stated two attackers. He'd bet his life that the one who assaulted that poor bastard was this lad right here. He'd put the man on a life support machine.

That meant he'd have no qualms in hurting Gary. What the hell had Kian got himself involved in?

'I didn't realise. I didn't know where it had come from,' he said weakly and then, seeing the look that the older lad and Kian both exchanged, and knowing full well that neither of them were buying into his pathetic excuses, he changed tack. 'I was just trying my luck, seeing if I could make a bit of cash, you know. What can I say, I'm an opportunist?'

Jax sucked his teeth at that. Finally, the man was done with his bullshit and they were getting somewhere.

'Well this wallet ain't got fuck all to do with Kian. It's mine, okay? So next time you feel like making your demands, you come and see me, yeah? See how far that gets you!' Jax said, his steely eyes boring into Gary's. 'I don't take too kindly to being threatened or held to ransom. So here's what's going to happen. You're going to do exactly as Kian said. You're going to leave his mum alone; you're going to leave him alone. Get your arse as far away from the flat and this estate as possible. And I'll tell you why you're going to do all that, shall I?' Jax said, glaring at the man with an evil glint in his eye. 'Because the second that I hear you've been spotted around these parts again, the second I hear you've tried making any trouble for me or any of my boys, then I'm going to come for you. Do you get me?'

Gary nodded, trying to keep eye contact, to show the lad that he could hear what he was being told and that he'd comply. What other choice did he have?

'Oh, I know that you're going to do as you're told, Gazza! You ain't got no other choice.' Jax smirked again, flashing the knife he had in his hand as a warning to Gary about what would happen if he didn't comply. 'And my lads here are going to give you a little taster of what's to come if you bullshit me. Ain't you, lads?'

'Please, I'll do whatever you ask. You don't need to do anything to me. I heard you. Loud and clear. I fucked up...'

Gary wanted to cry. Realising that he was completely at these lads' mercy, and that the ring leader, the older one, was a complete and utter nut job, he knew that he was done for. He should never have wound Kian up and he shouldn't have taken that bloody wallet.

And as the boys started raining down punches on him, he just prayed that it would be over quickly.

CHAPTER THIRTY-SIX

'That bastard's only gone and left me!' Michelle cried dramatically as she wildly thrashed around the apartment. Intoxicated once again, lashing out with her fists, she punched at the cushions on the sofa before launching them across the room in anger, almost knocking the lampshade onto the floor.

'Mum, stop, you're going to break something in a minute! What do you mean he's left you? Who? Gary?' Shannon cried, having just walked in through the door from doing her evening shift over at Benny's.

Shannon had geared herself up for another night of dealing with her comatose mother, and Gary and his cronies taking over the flat and making a general nuisance of themselves. She hadn't been expecting this and she was praying that it was true, because if Gary really had gone then that was music to Shannon's ears. They were well rid of the man, even if her mother didn't see it that way yet.

'I mean, Shannon, he's bloody left me. He's taken all his stuff. Must have sneaked in here and packed his things up when I was out at lunchtime. I came back and everything was gone. His clothes, his shoes, the lot.'

'I'm sure he'll be back before you know it, Mum,' Shannon said, trying to appease her mother, because as much as she was happy that Gary had gone, she hated it when her mother worked herself up into these kinds of states.

It was the drink that did it; it magnified every one of her mother's erratic emotions. Shannon had no idea how much she'd drunk already today, but she knew from experience that there would be no reasoning with her at the moment.

'No, not this time. This time it's different, I can feel it,' Michelle said, getting up from the chair and marching towards the kitchen. She pulled open the fridge door. 'And I've got no bloody booze left. Gary always sorts me out. What will I do without him, Shan?'

Michelle stared at Shannon now, her eyes pleading with her child and Shannon knew exactly what her mother wanted her to do.

'I'm not going back out again. No way. I've only just got home, Mum, I'm knackered,' Shannon said firmly, shaking her head, the penny finally dropping as to the real reason her mother was so distraught. Her mother didn't give a shit about Gary's whereabouts really; what she was really distraught about was that she'd suddenly lost her booze and gear supply.

'Oh come on, Shan. You've got money, you must have got paid tonight by that fatso Benny.'

'Don't call him that, Mum! I've told you before, Benny's nice. And I can't get you anything, Mum, you know that. They know how old I am at the off-licence. They won't serve me.'

'Hang around outside, then. Ask someone. A pretty girl like you, I'm sure someone would only be too happy to oblige.'

Shannon bit her lip then and glared at her mother in disgust, suddenly afraid of what might come out of her mouth if she dared speak. Part of her was shocked that her mother would so flippantly put her in danger for the sake of her next drink, but only part of her. It was an all-time new low for the woman. Finally, Shannon spoke. Calm and in control, her words coming out as if they belonged to someone else.

'It's more than their licence is worth. They only got raided by the police a few weeks ago – you think that they'd risk all that again, just so you can get even more wasted than you already are? No. I'm not going.'

'Oh for God's sake, Shannon, you're so dramatic. You don't give a shit about me, do you? Just like he doesn't. Take, take, take. That's all anyone ever does. Use you until they get a better offer…' Michelle mumbled as she stormed past her daughter, before slamming the door behind her, childlike in her tantrum. 'Well you can ALL leave for all I care. I don't need any of you!' she shouted through the door.

It was so pathetic that it was almost laughable, but Shannon was too exhausted to even do that. Her mother's behaviour was starting to make her feel bitter. She'd had to deal with this all of her life, living with a neglectful, volatile alcoholic as a parent. She'd finally had enough.

*

'Give it a rest, Mum!' Kian punched at the wall before turning up the television so that he could drown out the sound of his mother in the next room. She had been crying loudly for almost half an hour now, occasionally breaking up her sobs with incoherent rants about how unfair her life was and how shit everything was, and Kian was sick of listening to it.

Hearing a knock at his bedroom door, he braced himself for another one of her hysterical outbursts and slumped back on his bed with relief when Shannon popped her head around the door.

'I didn't hear you come in!' Kian said, and then he rolled his eyes as his mother's voice radiated through the walls as if on cue, shouting about how shit her life was. He sighed.

'She's got a point, hasn't she? Though the daft cow is too thick to realise that it's all her own doing,' Kian said bitterly, making no disguise of that fact that he had zero sympathy for the woman.

'You heard that Gary's gone? She reckons he's gone for good this time. He's taken all his stuff. His clothes, his shoes, everything!'

'Good riddance. Let's just hope he don't come back then, eh?' Kian said, concentrating on the game that he was playing, his eyes not moving from the screen. He was glad of the distraction so that he didn't have to look his sister in the eyes, because Shannon would know instantly from the look on his face that Kian had had something to do with Gary's sudden departure.

'Don't you think it's weird, though? That he's just upped and left like that? I mean, he seemed so adamant the other morning about how he wasn't going anywhere and how we had to show him respect,' Shannon said carefully, not wanting to sound as if she was accusing Kian of having anything to do with Gary's sudden disappearance, but she was unable to shake the suspicion from her mind. 'Just, you said that you could make him disappear, and well, now he… he's disappeared.'

'What? You think I had something to do with it? Bloody hell, Shan, I ain't a fucking magician! I didn't wave my magical wand and make the bloke go anywhere, as much as that would have given me great pleasure.' Kian laughed off his trail at his sister, making light of her accusations. He saw the flicker of uncertainty in her eyes.

'Maybe he just had enough, Shan, I dunno. It wasn't exactly the romance of the century, was it? They were both just using each other. I bet he's just had enough. Of Mum, of us. Of all of it.'

'Yeah, you're probably right. I mean, putting up with you first thing in the morning is enough to make anyone do a runner,' Shannon joked finally, rustling her brother's hair playfully in her fingers as he laughed.

'Kian, can I ask you something?' Shannon said then, knowing that her next question could rile her brother up, said in the wrong context.

'Those boys you're hanging out with. You're not doing anything you shouldn't be doing, are you?'

Kian shook his head, turning his attention back to his game so that he didn't have to look his sister in the eye again while he lied. 'No, Shannon. I ain't stupid.'

'Good, because from what I've heard they are into some really bad stuff. Like, really bad stuff.'

'Shan, drop it. I just know them, okay. I'm not doing anything that I shouldn't be doing,' Kian said tightly, concentrating intently on his game then so that they could bring the conversation to an end.

'Good!' Shannon said, still not really convinced, but she knew her brother would just clam up if she kept pushing him. 'I was thinking, Kian. Now that he's gone, what if there was a chance we could help make Mum better?'

'She doesn't want to get better though, Shan. That's the problem.'

'But she's not had a proper chance to do it before now, because she has never had any real help! But what if we can help her?' Shannon said then, coyly, finally voicing the idea to her brother that she'd had spinning inside her head for almost a year now.

'How? By involving Social Services like last time? Yeah right! Do me a favour.' Kian bit his lip. 'The last time they got involved, all they wanted to do was take us out of Mum's care and place us with foster families. Fat lot of good that lot was.'

Shannon was quiet then, unable to argue with that, because she knew that it was true. Social Services had only made everything worse. The threat of taking Shannon and Kian away had only made their mother drink more. Shannon and Kian had learned quickly to keep their home life private from then on, not letting on to the school or anyone official what their situation might be.

It was another reason Shannon needed to work at the chippy, so that she could help out with the bills and food shop. To stop the household amenities being cut off. Shannon did everything she could to keep them off the authorities' radar.

'I've managed to save up a bit of cash,' she shrugged, keeping her voice low, 'and it might be enough…'

Chucking his Xbox controller down, Kian looked at Shannon, curious now. His sister was being deadly serious about this.

'Enough for what?'

'Enough to check Mum into a rehab clinic or something.'

'Rehab?' Kian wrinkled his brow, unsure if his sister had any idea how much that might actually cost. 'How much money have you got?'

'Almost two grand.'

Kian whistled loudly; Shannon had his full attention now.

'I've been putting half of my wages away each time. Saving up so we can get Mum some help. Some proper help this time,' Shannon confessed, searching Kian's eyes, willing him to agree with her.

'Where is it? The money?' he asked, before adding quickly, 'I mean, shit, Shannon. You're lucky Gary or one of his poncing mates didn't find it. They'd have nicked it.'

'I'm not stupid, Kian. I don't leave it lying around. I keep it with me at all times. It's in my make-up bag.' Shannon shrugged, pulling her make-up bag from her school bag and showing Kian the thick wad of notes inside as if to prove she was telling him the truth.

'You saved this all up for her?' Kian said, shaking his head in wonderment. This was typical Shannon all over. Always putting everyone first. Putting him first. This was why she spent her nights working in that stinking chip shop and never really had anything to show for herself.

Because she was thinking of their ungrateful, selfish mother.

'But what if she don't want to get better, Shan? What then? What if she wastes your money?'

'I know it's a risk, Kian, but we've at least got to try, haven't we? How can we not?' Shannon shrugged, standing up, glad that her mother's outburst in the next room was finally silenced. She was exhausted and she needed her bed.

'Sounds like she's finally gone to sleep. I know what you think of her, Kian. But she'd do it for us. I know she would. If she wasn't sick,' Shannon said sincerely, bending down and kissing her brother on the top of his head. 'See you in the morning, yeah?'

Kian nodded, waiting until his sister left the room before lying back on his bed and staring up at the ceiling. The money would be wasted on their mother. Deep down, in her heart of hearts, Shannon must know that too. She just didn't want to admit it to herself. Some people didn't want to be helped. They enjoyed wallowing in their own self-pity too much and playing the victim, and Christ knows their mother had always been good at that.

Shannon was a one off. She only ever seemed to see the good in people. It was a trait that even Kian didn't have. Because all he'd learned so far in his short thirteen years on this Earth was that people let you down. All the time. They only wanted what they could get from you and eventually threw even that back in your face. And his mother was no different, no matter what his sister naively thought.

CHAPTER THIRTY-SEVEN

'Oh, hi, Anita, Benny's just out the back sweeping up,' Shannon said, stepping aside and letting Anita into the shop before she turned the closed sign around. 'How are the girls doing?' Shannon said, disappointed to see that Anita didn't have them with her. Shannon loved it when Anita popped in with Poppy and Jasmine. She always made a point to make a big fuss of them when she saw them, tickling them and making them giggle. The two little girls adored her.

'They're both on a playdate this afternoon. I barely know what to do with myself when I'm home alone.' Anita smiled. 'So, I thought I'd come and pick up my darling husband. You guys had a busy day?'

'Oh, you know. The usual Saturday lunchtime rush,' Shannon said with a shrug, then let out a sigh as she took her white coat off. 'Though I don't mind being busy, to be honest. We've been so rushed off our feet that I hadn't even realised the shift was over until Benny told me to start shutting the fryers down. I probably would have stayed here all day otherwise.' Shannon smiled, not adding that, right now, she wished that she could.

Whenever she worked here, it was as if she just completely switched off the outside world. Helping Benny serve and wrap the fish and chips to customers, chatting and smiling away as if she didn't have a care in the world whilst she took their money – for her it was a few hours away from reality. Time that she didn't have to spend worrying about her brother's or mum's predicaments.

'Are you sure you don't want me to come back in tonight, Benny?' Shannon asked, as Benny came through to the front of the shop and greeted Anita with his usual dramatic kiss and a hug, tipping Anita backwards like a ballroom dancer and holding her there until she squealed playfully. Shannon wrinkled her nose and shook her head.

'You two!' she said, jokingly.

But the reality was that just the sight of Benny and Anita being so affectionate always made Shannon feel so warm inside. They were the only two people that she knew in real life who seemed genuinely contented together. It gave Shannon a little bit of hope, that happy families did actually exist. And it was exactly what she wanted for herself one day.

'What?' Benny said, as Anita tapped him lightly on the arm. 'Oh… right! Er, Shannon…' he said, taking the hint and realising that this was his cue, 'you know what we spoke about the other day, about the money that you've been saving up so that you can help your mum…' Benny said, carefully broaching the subject as Anita had instructed him. 'Well, I hope you don't mind but I spoke to Anita about it. I wasn't gossiping about you,' he added quickly, holding his hands up to stop any protest from Shannon. 'I was worried about you, and well, I thought Anita might be able to help too.'

'Oh, right…' Shannon said, her cheeks burning red, not sure how Anita would be able to help her. It dawned on her then that Anita hadn't just spontaneously turned up today. This had been planned.

'We'd like to help you, Shannon. Benny told me how much you've managed to save up, and, well, we'd like to match the amount of money that you've saved,' Anita said, giving Shannon a sympathetic look.

'Why would you want to do that?'

'There's nothing to feel embarrassed about, love. We just want to help you out. Sometimes people just need a break,' Anita said, sensing the girl's embarrassment as her cheeks flushed pink and she stared down at the floor.

'My mum isn't a bad person, you know. She tries her best, it's just she's not had much luck in her life…'

'And no one said she isn't trying her best, love. Alcoholism is a disease, it's no one's fault. A lot of people don't understand that…' Anita continued, before adding, 'it must be so hard for you, darling. God, if it was our Poppy or Jasmine who was struggling, I'd want someone to help them too. Please, let us help you.'

'I've got enough saved up, thanks,' Shannon said, shaking her head and making her way to the back of the shop to get her coat from the hook.

Anita didn't have a clue what she was talking about. The woman would never have to worry about her Poppy and Jasmine struggling the way that Shannon had, because Anita was a good mum. Anita didn't know Shannon's life. She couldn't even imagine it.

'Enough for what though, Shan?' Benny said, insistent, following Shannon through to the back of the shop and not wanting to take no for an answer. 'Only, we looked into it and here…' Benny handed Shannon the leaflet that Anita had printed out from her search on the internet. 'You've done amazing, Shan. Two grand is a great start, but it's only going to get you two weeks in a residential rehab placement, at the very most.' Benny hoped that Shannon would at least hear them both out. 'At least with a full month's placement she'd be able to get herself properly on the road to recovery. She'd have a rehabilitation programme to follow with counselling sessions and just being there, in a completely different environment for that amount of time, away from bad influences or any kind of temptation – she'd have a real chance of getting better.'

'I can't take your money.' Shannon shook her head.

'This isn't a hand-out, Shan. This is us, me and Anita, wanting to see you do well in your life and to succeed. But in order to do that, something's got to change drastically for you at home. Because otherwise you're never going to break out of the cycle, and neither will your mum. Think about it, Shan. Four grand will mean that your mum could stay in her placement for an entire month. It's the only way she'll have a proper chance at getting better,' Benny said, glancing over at Anita to back him up.

Benny had known how difficult it would be to persuade Shannon to accept his offer, because the girl was so fiercely proud. From the first day she'd bounded into the chippy and asked him outright for a job, she'd always said that she'd pay her own way. That she never wanted to be in debt to anyone for anything. Which is why Benny had to be so crafty with thinking up ways to give her a little bit extra in her wages or send her home with some fresh food every now and again, because Shannon wouldn't take it otherwise.

'We don't just want you to have it, we insist on you having it!' Anita said. 'We'll even come with you if you want, when you talk to your mum about it. We'll help you to persuade her that it's the right thing to do, that she should get some help. You never know, it might help, someone else being there. She might listen.'

Anita held out the envelope. Shannon wavered then. Anita and Benny really meant it. They really wanted to help her. And they were right, the money would get her mother some real help: help that would change her entire life completely. All she had to do was stop being so damn proud and take it.

'I honestly don't know what to say to you both.' Knowing that there was no arguing with the two of them, and that she'd be stupid to turn them down, Shannon shook her head and smiled as the tears started running down her cheeks.

'Oh, God. Look at me!' she said then, flustered, unable to find the words to express just what Benny and Anita's gesture truly meant to her. Shannon threw her arms around the couple and hugged them both hard. 'Thank you. Thank you so, so much.'

'Well, bloody hell, thank God for that. I never realised how hard it was to give money away,' Benny quipped, attempting to lighten the mood, as Shannon stepped back and wiped away her tears.

'Oh, that's nothing. If you think I'm stubborn, you just wait until we try and persuade my mum to actually agree to go to this place!'

CHAPTER THIRTY-EIGHT

Sparks were flying from the angle grinder as the boys cut into the metal shutters. Scanning the road to make sure no one was watching, Jax Priestly tugged at the balaclava he was wearing. If there were any passers-by, or if CCTV was working, no one would get a look at his face. He'd made sure that the other boys had worn them too.

'Fucking bingo!' one of the boys said, as the metal panel fell to the floor, revealing the thick pane of glass.

'Move out of my way,' Jax commanded, running at the shop front with the sledgehammer poised over his head. He slammed it into the thick glass over and over again, as the boys all chanted behind him, whooping with joy every time a new web of jagged cracks appeared in the window, before, with one last almighty smash, the glass fell out all over the floor.

'We're in.' He squeezed through the shutters, the boys all following his lead.

'Get the money out of the till,' he ordered one of the lads, who smiled smugly as he prised the money drawer open with a crowbar, only to shake his head as he saw that the till was empty.

'Fuck it! We've got five minutes to wreck the gaff,' Jax said, wasting no time in starting to smash all the glass out of all the containers that ran the length of the countertops, while the other boys got to work destroying all the stock and spray-painting the walls. 'You lot better do your worst.'

CHAPTER THIRTY-NINE

Traipsing over the glass from where the shop window had been smashed repeatedly, as the shards of fragmented glass glistened from where it lay spread out all across the tiled floor, Benny looked down at a thin sliver of metal that had once made up a panel on his security shutters.

'We think that the intruders gained entry after managing to cut a large hole in the shutters using an angle grinder or something similar,' Lucy said. Benny stood in the middle of the shop floor now that forensics had finished collecting evidence and fingerprints from the crime scene.

'The alarm clearly didn't deter them then?' Benny said, staring around him and trying to take in the extent of the damage the vandals had done to his shop.

'The response team arrived eleven minutes after the alarm sounded, Mr Lynch. Judging by the extent of the damage caused, we think it was very much a planned attack, and from what we've already seen on the CCTV footage, early indications are that it was possibly gang related.'

'You mean this was done by kids from around here?' Benny said, shaking his head, dumbfounded, as he stared around the place, unable to think straight. He'd told Anita to stay at home with the girls when he'd got a call from the police saying that his shop had been broken into. And now he'd seen the place with his own eyes, he was glad he'd made her stay away, because he could barely stomach what he was seeing right now.

'I know it's just a chip shop to you lot. But this is my business. It was supposed to be the start of something. I'd put everything I had into it so that I could give my wife and girls a decent life. Why would someone do this to me?' Benny asked, his voice cracking with emotion as he stared down at the till that had been smashed on the floor, the till drawer wide open. 'They didn't even get anything worth taking. I never keep money on the premises.'

Making his way to the back of the shop, Benny closed his eyes, as he saw the damage they'd done to his stock, tipping out bags of battered fish and frozen chips all over the floor of the kitchen and stock room. And, just for good measure, they'd left all the fridges and freezers wide open, to make sure the rest of the stock that they hadn't touched was ruined. Benny eyed the pool of water from where everything had already started defrosting.

'Have you got insurance, Mr Lynch?' Lucy asked, relieved when the man slowly nodded. 'Well, that's something. I know that this must be very distressing for you, and I can only assure you that we will do everything in our power to catch whoever did this.'

'Benny?' A voice shouted out from the front of the shop.

'We're in the back, Shan!' Benny called out. 'That's Shannon, she helps me out from time to time, doing the odd Saturday shift,' Benny said, playing down the fact that actually Shannon was in here most days. She was only fifteen, and Benny knew that even though he only did it as a favour to the girl, it wasn't strictly legal to let Shannon work the shifts that she did. Nor was she supposed to be paid cash-in-hand. 'I called her and told her what happened.'

'Do you know of anyone who has a grudge against you, Mr Lynch? Have you had an argument recently with anyone? No matter how big or small it may have appeared to be at the time…'

Benny shook his head as Shannon joined them and caught the tail end of the question.

'I can't believe it, Benny!' Shannon said, looking as if she was about to cry as she walked over and threw her arms around him, knowing how upset he must be. Then addressing the officer, Shannon added, 'Benny's got a heart of gold. Everyone around here loves him.'

Benny would be heartbroken over this. This place was his life. He had worked so hard to build his good reputation and make sure the chippy was always busy.

'Ah, thanks, Shannon!' Benny said, blushing, not used to the girl's open display of affection. Things must be bad.

'There's nothing that I can think of,' Benny said to Lucy, trying to wrack his brains to recall any problems he'd had with anyone in the past. But there was nothing he could think of. Not even a minor argument. 'I hate conflict. And to be honest, I get on with pretty much everyone.'

Lucy nodded, before asking, 'What about your staff members? Is it just Shannon here who helps out?'

Benny nodded.

'What's your surname, Shannon?' Lucy asked, poising her pen at her notebook as she looked at the girl.

'Winters,' Shannon said. 'But there's nothing I can think of either.' For a second, she wondered about Gary. Could it be a coincidence that he'd taken off the day before the chippy got broken into? But Shannon quickly dismissed the idea. Gary didn't have a grudge with her or Benny; he had a problem with Kian. He wouldn't do this, surely? It wasn't his style.

'Winters did you say?' Lucy said, tapping at her notebook. The name immediately ringing a bell. She'd heard the same name only days ago. 'You don't have a brother, do you? Kian?'

'Yeah, I do,' Shannon said, suddenly getting a bad feeling. 'How did you know that?'

'I've bumped into the lad twice this week already,' Lucy said, pursing her mouth and guessing that this wasn't just a coincidence as she wrote the boy's name down.

'He wouldn't do something like this. He'd have no reason to. He likes Benny and he knows I work here,' Shannon said, immediately defending her brother now that the officer was taking an interest in him. She glanced over at Benny to back her up, but Benny looked down at the floor instead. He hadn't wanted to admit it to Shannon but Kian had instantly come into his mind, and the fact that the officer had just brought his name up of her own accord didn't bode well.

'Benny? You know Kian wouldn't be involved in anything like this.'

'Do we, Shannon?' Benny asked, unsure what he should be thinking right now. 'Your brother came in here only the other night and he had his mates all hanging about outside, didn't he? The Griffin Boys.'

'The Griffin Boys?' Again, Lucy's ears pricked up at the mention of the gang. They were the gang that the police suspected of assaulting the PCSO the previous weekend. 'Is there any reason why they'd target this shop?' Lucy asked.

'No,' Shannon said, realising that the police officer was suddenly taking an interest in her brother now that Benny hadn't backed her up. 'Kian wouldn't have done this. He's only thirteen, he's a good kid. He might have been knocking around with a bad lot lately but he wouldn't do this.' At least Shannon didn't think he would. Would he?

'Ah, my sergeant's here. Give me a minute, Benny, I just want to bring him up to speed with everything,' Lucy said, not wanting to give either of them any indication of her thoughts about Kian and the burglary possibly being linked.

Shannon decided to make her exit while the officers were distracted. She needed to try and get hold of Kian and make sure that he really did have nothing to do with this before the police caught up with him.

'I've got to get back home, Benny,' she said.

'I'll walk you back out,' Benny said, feeling bad that he hadn't stuck up for Kian.

'No, don't worry. I can manage. I'm sure you've got enough to deal with. I'll be back in a bit,' Shannon said, annoyed that Benny hadn't backed her up; though she knew she was being unreasonable, because even she had her doubts.

A few weeks ago, she'd lay her life on it that Kian wouldn't be involved in something like this. But now, she wasn't so sure.

*

'Do we have an MO?' DS Morgan said, staring at the damage.

'Not yet, Sarge,' Lucy said. 'It looks like a typical smash-and-grab. They used what we suspect was an angle grinder to cut through the external aluminium shutters, then smashed the glass to enter the building. It looks like their motive was to make their presence known. A warning of some sort? There was no money on the premises and they haven't taken anything. They've just wrecked the place.'

DS Morgan shook his head. Another completely pointless crime.

'Forensics have been and gone and we've got some CCTV footage, but they were all wearing dark clothing with hoods, and balaclavas, Sarge. Going by their builds and how many of them there were, I'd say we're possibly looking at a local youth gang being involved.'

'What about the owner, Mr Lynch? Any obvious grievances or run-ins with anyone local?'

'No, Sarge,' Lucy said shaking her head. 'He doesn't seem the type.' Then she continued. 'I did manage to get us a couple of leads…'

DS Morgan raised his eyebrows.

'The Saturday girl who works here, her name is Shannon Winters. She has a brother, Kian Winters. He's the same lad that myself and Holder ran into on the estate when we came out to do the witness report for the assault on the PCSO. And he was also the lad that I stopped and questioned the other night, after we made those arrests at the Dog and Bone pub. He was one of the two lads reported as causing a disturbance, but when I spoke to them, they told me they were looking for their cat. And Mr Lynch has said that the boy came in here this week, and, get this, he had a load of mates hanging around outside the front. Mr Lynch said that he recognised some of them from the estate. The Griffin Boys. Though the sister is adamant that her brother wouldn't be involved with anything like this…'

'Sounds about right; in my experience family members are usually the last ones to know about their loved ones being involved in criminal activity, because they don't want to believe it,' DS Morgan said. 'Well, I don't believe in coincidences, Murphy, how about you? I say we pull this kid in and have a little chat with him. See what we can get out of him.'

Lucy nodded in agreement. 'I'm glad you said that, Sarge, because that's exactly what I was going to do next.'

CHAPTER FORTY

'Yes, Karen. I'm fine, honest!' Philip said, holding the phone away from his ear as Jax stood next to him so that he could hear what Karen was saying.

Jax was taking no chances that Philip might try and drop him in it.

'You don't need to worry about me and Mr Bobcat…' Philip said, his bottom lip quivering, as he fought to stop his voice from cracking with emotion at the mention of his beloved cat. Jax glared at him, warning him to watch what he said.

'When are you coming back?' Philip blurted out, trying to make conversation, his words laced with desperation.

Jax rolled his eyes dramatically and smacked himself hard on the forehead. Philip knew he wasn't supposed to ask that question.

'I just wondered that's all. Because you don't need to come back. I'm really just fine,' Philip said, babbling and trying to make things right again, as Jax motioned at him to end the call. 'I've got to go, Karen. I need a poo.'

Philip hung up.

'You bloody moron!' Jax sneered. 'Why did you ask her when she was coming back?'

'I didn't mean to, I'm sorry. But she said she's coming back tomorrow,' Philip said, secretly relieved. Philip had decided that he was going to tell Karen everything once he saw her.

Now that Mr Bobcat was gone, he had nothing to lose.

'Yeah, I bet she is. Two days earlier than she'd originally said! For fuck's sake, Philip, you only had to speak to her for a minute or two max and yet you couldn't even get that bloody right. I warned you not to pester her about coming back, didn't I? I told you to make out that you were fine.'

Philip nodded. 'I just miss her that's all. It slipped out.'

'Yeah, well you're lucky my fist don't slip out an' all and whack you in the face for pulling a stunt like that!' Jax said, knowing full well that his mum would be worrying about how long she'd left Philip on his own as it is, without the man guilt tripping her too.

'Well, if she's coming back tomorrow, you better pull your finger out and crack on with tidying this place up! You can make a start on the kitchen.' He dismissed Philip from the room, unable to bear the sight of the man's sulky face any longer, then slumped down on the sofa and rolled himself a joint, finally able to give Kian his full attention now that the phone call to Karen had been made.

'Now, where were we? Oh yeah, that's it. We were chatting money. More to the point, the money that you owe me.'

'I know, Jax, and I promise, I'm going to get it for you. All of it, soon.'

'Yeah well you better, Kian. Cos things are going to start happening, mate, if you don't. Bad things,' Jax said, instantly relaxing as he breathed down a lungful of smoke.

'Did you hear about that chippy your sister works in? Terrible shame that is, ain't it?'

'What do you mean? What happened at the chippy?' Kian asked, narrowing his eyes as he felt a horrible sinking feeling in the pit of his stomach.

'Someone did the place over last night. Made a right mess too, so I heard. I guess it's a good job that no one was there working, cos they could have got hurt real bad. Silver lining and all that.'

Kian realised that Jax had targeted the place on purpose; another scare tactic to intimidate him, and it was working.

'Your sister's a bit of all right, actually,' Jax said, knowing that his words were putting the shits up Kian, exactly as he intended. 'I might have to pop over to yours and pay her a visit.' He blew a cloud of smoke into Kian's face. 'See how she's doing, you know. Make sure she's all right. Expect she'll have a lot of free time on her hands for a bit, now that she ain't got a job to go to.'

Jax laughed, seeing that Kian was struggling to listen to his threats, but that he was also too weak and pathetic to do anything about them. Jax loved having the upper hand.

'I could give her some work, you know. Your sister would be a good link. I bet she'd be good at it too. Better than that Kayleigh Walters from over the common. Giving the boys a line up, a fiver a go. You know what that is, don't you, Kian?'

Kian shook his head, guessing it wasn't going to be good.

'All the boys drop their kecks and stand in line. And the link has to sort each of them out.' Jax smirked, seeing the look of dread on Kian's face and pretending that the boy didn't understand what he was talking about.

'She gives them blowies, Kian. The girls make out they ain't up for it but they enjoy doing it really. And it means your Shannon will be paying her way. She'll be earning her place in the gang, innit! The boys work hard, out there pulling the big money in; they need some relief.'

Aware that the other boys in the room were all listening in and watching for his reaction, Kian didn't know what to do. He knew that Jax meant it. Once he got an idea in his head, he wouldn't back down. Kian's only hope was to try and reason with him.

'Shannon ain't like that, Jax. She ain't that type of girl.' He prayed desperately that this was just Jax's way of winding him up. That in a minute the older boy would laugh and they'd forget this stupid conversation ever happened. But Jax wasn't laughing.

'Kian, bruv! They are all "like that": slags. She's your sister though, I get it. You don't want to think of her that way. Don't worry though, kid. We won't make her suck your cock!'

The other boys all started laughing then and Kian could feel his cheeks burning red. Just the thought of Jax and his boys going anywhere near Shannon made him feel as if he had molten hot lava burning inside him. He felt nothing but rage, but he didn't know what to do with that feeling. He was outnumbered.

'I said I'd get you your money, Jax. And I will. I promise.'

'Well that's just it, Kian. Your promises don't really mean shit to me. Every job you've touched so far, you've fucked up. So forgive me if your promises don't really fill me with optimism, Kian.'

Kian simply shook his head.

'I can't do that, Jax. I can't let my sister get involved with any of this.' *With you.*

'You don't have many options left, mate,' Jax said glaring at Kian now.

And Kian knew what Jax was capable of.

'I ain't asking you, Kian. I'm telling you. Either get me my money in the next twenty-four hours or I'm going to pay that sweet-arse sister of yours a visit,' Jax said, making it clear that there was no room for negotiations. That these were Kian's only two options.

'I'll sort it,' Kian said, getting up from his seat, grateful that he was being dismissed from the flat, his face burning with humiliation as he walked down the balcony and towards the stairwell.

Kian leant up against the wall and threw up. He was in deep shit now and there was only one way as far as he was concerned to end this and to make sure that Jax would leave Shannon alone. He had no choice but to get Jax Priestly his money. Any way he could.

CHAPTER FORTY-ONE

'Shannon? Mum?' Glad when he didn't get an answer, Kian walked through the flat and made his way to Shannon's bedroom.

'Shan, you home?' he called out again, knocking on his sister's door just to make sure.

Just as he was about to nip inside, a voice from behind him startled him.

'What are you doing?' Michelle said eyeing her son, taking in Shannon's half open bedroom door and Kian clearly about to go inside.

'Err… I was just seeing if Shan was about. I needed to borrow something from her.'

'What?' Michelle said, narrowing her eyes.

'Some stuff for school. For my homework,' Kian said quickly, silently cursing himself for not thinking of something more believable. He rarely bothered with his homework and his mother knew that.

'Homework on a Sunday? You must think I was born yester-day, Kian.' Michelle raised her eyes before shaking her head in disbelief. 'Whatever! Shannon's gone out. Benny called her. He said something had happened at the chippy? Anyway, I'm jumping in the shower and I'm off out later. I won't be home till late. So you'll have to feed yourselves.'

Kian was about to make a jibe that that was nothing new, but sensing his mother's lighter mood, and aware of the reason he was here right now, he didn't push his luck. Waiting until he heard the bathroom door shut, and the sound of the water running in the shower, Kian started searching his sister's room.

So Jax had been telling the truth about the chippy. He and the boys had gone in there last night and turned the place over, and Shannon could be back at any minute. And, being a Sunday, chances were she wouldn't have her school bag with her either, like she usually did. Especially now that Gary had gone. And not if she'd just popped out.

Kian was sure that he'd find it here, hidden away somewhere. Searching the room, Kian pulled all of Shannon's clothes out from the bottom of his sister's wardrobe, scooping them into a pile, and making sure the bag wasn't hidden underneath them. Looking behind the door, Kian pursed his mouth. Nothing there. Then, crouching down on the floor, he stuck his hand under the bed, and swept the carpet with his fingers. He felt something.

Lying down so he could get a better look, Kian grinned as he spotted the bag hidden right at the back against the wall. Grabbing the thick material strap, Kian hoisted it out and unzipped it. He knew that Shannon would kill him for taking her money. But what choice did he have? Jax had meant every word of his threat. If Kian didn't pay him tonight, then he was going to take the payment directly from Shannon. And not in cash.

CHAPTER FORTY-TWO

'Oh, they've sent you out again, have they? They short staffed?' Mr Johnson said, unimpressed at the sight of the young female officer from the other day standing at his front door. Glancing out he looked down the balcony and narrowed his eyes. 'Where's your Sergeant?'

'I'm afraid, it's just me this evening. DS Morgan is busy with another case,' Lucy said feigning a friendly smile. She'd only told Ops that she'd deal with Mr Johnson's call-out because she was on the estate already, about to go around and make enquiries at Kian Winters's address. She figured she'd get Mr Johnson's grumbles out of the way first.

'Well. You'll have to do, I suppose,' Mr Johnson sighed, turning his back on Lucy and making his way back into his flat.

Taking the man's abrupt departure from the door as her invitation in, Lucy followed him inside.

'You told the call dispatcher that you had a crime to report. That there had been a possible assault or… murder?' Lucy said, trying her hardest to mask her disbelief.

'Yes, that's right. It's a murder. Not an assault. He's definitely dead.'

Leaning down to the coffee table, he picked up a glass of what looked like Scotch.

'A murder?' Lucy repeated, watching the man's hands visibly shake as he brought the glass to his lips and knocked it back in one. Whatever he thought he was reporting had clearly shaken him up.

'I ain't normally one to drink this early in the evening. But my nerves are shot to bits…'

'Okay, well let's start at the beginning, then. Do you want to sit down, Mr Johnson?'

Lucy nodded to the chair behind the man, but Mr Johnson didn't sit down. Instead he walked to the drinks cabinet on the other side of the room and topped up his glass once more.

'I saw them. A couple of days ago. That noise I was telling you about, downstairs in the flat. Turned out that there's some lads in there. They did it,' Mr Johnson started, shaking his head, enraged at the memory. 'They were making such an awful racket, so I stuck my head out the window in order to tell them to shut up. I had a half a mind to tip a bucket of iced water down over the lot of them.'

Mr Johnson took another mouthful of his drink.

'Shall we put the Scotch down for a bit, Mr Johnson?' Lucy hoped that he wouldn't drink too much more, as she could hear the slur in the older man's speech. 'These are very serious allegations,' she said, not adding that she needed to make sure that he stayed somewhat coherent so that he at least made some sort of sense. She hoped he wasn't going to waste her time harping on about a noise complaint again.

'They didn't spot me, but I saw them. I watched the boys throw him from the window.' Mr Johnson flinched at the memory. 'The poor bugger hit the ground from twelve floors up. Splat. Just like that. And do you know what they all did? That bunch of bloody depraved animals. They all bloody laughed and got their phones out, didn't they? Taking photos and videos, the lot of them.'

Lucy walked to the window and looked out, scanning the grass below for a sign of an incident.

'Are you certain, Mr Johnson? Only, there's no one out there now. Surely someone else would have seen it…' she said, carefully, aware that something had left the man distressed. The last thing she wanted to do was accuse him of being wrong about what he saw. But Mr Johnson didn't falter.

'He's not there now. No. I know that. Because I went down there, didn't I? Only he'd gone. And I thought to myself, what's the chances that he survived the fall from this height? He wouldn't have just got up and walked away from it, would he?'

Lucy shook her head. Doubtful. A fall from that height would leave an awful mess.

'Well, I finally found him,' Mr Johnson declared. 'Those rotten little bastards only dumped him in the communal bins downstairs. I found him earlier when I put my rubbish out. I sometimes have a little dig around when I'm down there. It's crazy, isn't it, what some people throw away these days?'

'You found him?' Lucy said, wondering about the state of Mr Johnson's mental health right now.

'Yes, he's in my bathroom.'

Lucy stared at the man as if he had two heads growing from his shoulders.

'Well I couldn't leave him down there in the bin, could I? Come on…' Mr Johnson insisted, leading the way to the bathroom.

She did as he told her, watching as he stopped just inside the bathroom doorway and nodded for her to go inside. Apprehensive at what she might find, even before she stepped in the bathroom, she could smell it. That rancid, rotten vegetable smell, that, in her job, usually meant a lot worse.

Taking a deep breath, she poked her head around the doorway, her eyes going to the bin bag splayed out in the bath. She frowned as Mr Johnson continued mumbling, a mixture of the booze and his frazzled nerves.

'I mean, they say that they are supposed to have nine lives, don't they? Christ, Bertie was the same. He was like the bloody Terminator. He'd been run over; he was blind in one eye; he had a limp and the bugger still lived to the grand old age of nineteen. Nineteen! It's bloody unheard of, isn't it? I loved him, dearly, but those last few years the only thing he was fit for was death. All he did was piss everywhere in the flat, and he cost me a fortune in vet bills. Still, who throws a cat to its death from a window, eh? It's inhumane.'

'A cat?' Lucy said then, realising that Mr Johnson wasn't talking about the murder of a person at all. Stepping back out of the room, Lucy shut the bathroom door.

'Yes, a cat. What did you think I was talking about?' Mr Johnson said, losing his patience with the young officer then. 'The bin men would take him, and, well, he's evidence now, isn't he? Now you have something more concrete to go on when you go down there and speak to that lad who lives there. Philip Penfold should be ashamed of himself. Calling himself an animal lover and letting that happen to his cat. I mean, I know he's got special needs and everything, but surely even he must know that this is wrong?'

'Philip Penfold? That's the name of the man who lives there?' She remembered her run-in with the two lads from earlier in the week and how visibly distressed Philip had been. The boy he'd been with was Kian Winters.

Lucy bit her lip. Curiouser and curiouser. That kid's name was beginning to pop up all over the place.

'And where's his carer? I mean, how can there be so much noise and screaming and cats being thrown out of windows if that lad is being properly looked after by the system? It wouldn't be happening, would it? So where's she? Another cog in the machine that doesn't work, I bet.' Mr Johnson continued with his rant, well and truly on a roll now.

'Oh, you have my word, Mr Johnson. This will be dealt with properly,' Lucy said, intending to pay both Philip and Kian a visit tonight before she left the estate. 'You can be assured of that.'

CHAPTER FORTY-THREE

'Benny! Anita! Is everything okay?' Shannon said, stepping back, surprised to see her boss and his wife both standing at her front door. 'Did the police find anything?' Shannon asked, secretly praying that Benny wasn't here to break the bad news that his suspicions had been right and Kian had been somehow involved in the break in at the chip shop.

'No. Nothing as yet,' Benny said, shaking his head. 'But the police are doing a great job, and I'm sure they'll catch whoever did it.' Then, looking to Anita as if for permission, he added, 'It's not a bad time is it? We said Sunday evening. You still want us to be there when you speak to your mum?'

'Oh, I figured you'd both have enough to deal with at the moment…' Shannon said truthfully. The last thing Shannon had expected was for Benny and Anita to still come around and speak to her mother today, as previously planned. 'Won't you need the money yourselves now?'

'We've got insurance, Shannon. It's all covered. Give it a week or so and we'll be up and running again. It's going to take a lot more than a broken shutter and a bit of spray paint to keep me down, let me tell you!' Benny smiled, looking more positive then. 'Our offer to help you out still stands, Shannon.'

'Who's at the door, Shan?' Michelle called out, putting her coat on, and hooking her bag over her shoulder just as she spotted Shannon letting Benny and Anita in.

'I would have tidied up if I'd known Shannon was inviting her friends over. You should have given me a bit of notice, Shannon,' she added tartly, shooting daggers at Shannon for not warning her that she invited guests to the flat. If you could call Fat-Benny and his stuck-up looking wife 'guests'.

'You'll have to excuse the mess. I haven't had time to do anything today,' Michelle went on, more than aware of the disgusting smell in the flat, mainly from the overflowing bin in the kitchen, full of rotten food and rubbish, combined with stale cigarette smoke that lingered in the air. If Shannon had thought to warn her, Michelle could have at least sprayed the place with a bit of air freshener to mask the smell a little. 'I'll leave you to it, shall I? I'm off to see a mate. I'll be back late, Shan.' Michelle nodded curtly at Benny and Anita, as if to dismiss herself as quickly as possible.

'But Mum, they've come to see you,' Shannon said, surprised to see the woman up and dressed, let alone on her way out the front door. She'd been moping around the flat crying ever since Gary had left her. But today she seemed a lot better, though she still wore her uniform of leggings and a baggy jumper, her face devoid of all make-up and her greasy hair pulled into a messy-looking ponytail.

'Where are you going?' Shannon asked suspiciously. Past experience told her that 'off to see a mate' was code for spending the evening in the pub.

'I said. I'm meeting a friend. I don't have to explain myself to you, Shannon,' Michelle said, losing her patience with her daughter's cynical tone.

She'd already clocked the way that Fat-Benny's hoity-toity wife, Anita, had turned her nose up at Michelle's home, casting a subtle glance of disapproval around the flat, along with her aspersions, no doubt. Michelle had seen the woman's eyes lingering on the stagnant water in the sink full of crockery. She didn't have time for this.

'You're not meeting Gary, are you?' Shannon asked, aware how shifty her mum was acting. As if she was doing something she shouldn't, and she'd just been caught out.

'Course I'm bleeding not! Who needs a man, eh?' Michelle said, rolling her eyes.

'Can you just wait five minutes, Mum? I wanted to speak to you about something.'

'For God's sake, Shan! All right. Five minutes, and then I really need to get going,' Michelle said, as Benny and his wife sat down on the sofa.

'I don't think you've met my Anita, have you?' Benny said proudly, introducing his old school friend to his wife.

Michelle nodded curtly in the woman's direction, making no disguise of her complete uninterest in Benny's dolly bird, who was currently perched on the edge of her sofa looking like her shit didn't stink. Her stupid fake smile plastered to her stupid perfectly made-up face.

Pretending she wasn't sitting there and silently judging Michelle when Michelle knew that she was. She was that type. Well, let the stupid cow judge away.

'You're obviously doing well for yourself these days,' Michelle said, giving Benny a once-over and taking in his expensive-looking coat and his shiny polished shoes. 'Chip shop must be raking it in,' she said, raising her eyebrows as if to imply that his wife he had sitting at his side, who was clearly way out of his league was in fact a gold-digger. Anita ignored the comment and gave Benny's hand a supportive squeeze.

'Well, I was. We had a break-in. We think it's some kids from the estate. We might be out of business for a week or two, but it's nothing that can't be fixed,' Benny said, still reeling from the damage that had been caused to his chip shop. But like Anita had said, they were covered by their insurers. They'd redecorate and buy in new stock and the place would be as good as new again in no time. And in the meantime, they both wanted to honour their offer to Shannon to help her mum out before it was too late. Anita had been insistent on that.

'Yeah, well. There are some wrong 'uns around here. Stuff like that happens all the time. Still, I should have guessed you'd have ended up working with food though, eh!' Michelle laughed, but the sneer of sarcasm was aimed as an insult to the man, as she nodded down at Benny's protruding stomach that even his big coat couldn't disguise.

'Mum!' Shannon said, annoyed now and praying that her mum wouldn't refer to Benny as Fat-Benny like she normally did.

'I'm so sorry,' Shannon whispered to Anita, mortified at her mother's behaviour. 'She's not been having a very easy time lately...'

'It's fine, Shannon!' Benny laughed good-humouredly and patted his stomach. 'They called me Fat-Benny at school, didn't they, Michelle? Ha, the good old days, huh! And you're right. Running a chippy is the perfect job for me. Especially when my Anita here is always trying to make me something "healthy". Bloody eggs and avocados or that other kale stuff that I can't stand. I guess my stomach gives away the fact that I still stuff my face whenever she's not looking.' Benny raised his eyebrows playfully at his wife then, and Anita smiled at him, proud of the way that he was trying to put Shannon at ease again and wasn't taking Michelle's spiteful comments to heart.

So far, her first impression of Michelle Winters matched what she'd heard about her. Michelle was a jealous, bitter woman and in just the few minutes that Anita had been in her company, she could already tell that Michelle clearly thought the world owed her something. But that was all part of the illness, she reminded herself. Michelle was sick. Anita and Benny had already discussed that the woman might be a little defensive today, and they weren't going to rise to her bravado.

'Well, shall we cut the fake pleasantries? Is someone going to tell me what's going on here then? Cos you're clearly not here for the tea!' Michelle said, her tone loaded with dislike.

'You're not pregnant, are you, Shan?' Michelle said, eyeing her daughter suspiciously. 'Is that why you're both here, to help soften the blow when she breaks the news to me? Cos let me tell you now, that ain't happening. The place ain't big enough for a baby. All that crying and those dirty nappies, I can't be doing with any of that…'

'No, Mum. I'm not pregnant,' Shannon said, annoyed with her mum now. She knew that this was going to be a tough conversation, but she hadn't realised how tough it was going to be until now. 'They've come here to speak to you, Mum. About you. About your drinking.'

'My drinking?' Michelle said indignantly as if Shannon had just made the most shocking accusation about her. 'What the hell are you talking about?'

Michelle's drinking had always been an unspoken issue. They all knew she had a problem. But they all pretended that it wasn't happening. She was sick. That's how they referred to it. The elephant in the room. But now Shannon had just thrown it out there, and in front of these two stuck-up bastards, too. Michelle shifted uncomfortably in her seat, staring from her daughter to Benny and Anita. The room was full of tension as they all waited for her to speak.

'I don't know what my daughter's been telling you people, but I think you'll find she is very much mistaken. Everyone has a drink every now and then, don't they? I do not have a problem…'

'I want you to have a look at this, Mum,' Shannon said, ignoring her mother's protests and passing her the leaflet on the rehabilitation centre that Shannon had been in contact with.

Though she had a feeling that she had already lost this battle before they'd even started. She'd thought bringing Benny and Anita with her might help, that her mum would actually have to listen to her if she had adult backup, but them both being here was having the opposite effect; her mum was being even more defensive than normal. She didn't want to admit that she had a problem.

'Rehabilitation? Are you joking, Shannon?' Michelle said, shaking her head.

'It's a treatment centre, Mum. They said they've got space available and that they can help you.'

'Help me? What with?' Michelle laughed as if Shannon was being silly, fabricating lies about her. 'I don't need help, Shannon. I told you.' Staring down at the information on the leaflet, Michelle wrinkled her face to show her confusion.

'Michelle, Shannon loves you and she worries about you. We're not judging you, we just want to help.' Sitting forward in his chair, Benny tried to reach out and hold Michelle's hand. To show her that they were just here to help her too.

'Well I don't *need* your *help*. What I *need* is people to stop butting their nose in to my business and telling me what I should be doing with my life. Especially strangers that don't know me from Adam. This is an ambush, you all coming here! You don't know my life. You don't know what I've been through. What if I don't want your help? What if I'm happy as I am? Did you ever think of that?' Michelle sneered, glaring at Benny. 'And what about the cost? Is that why you're here? Mr Moneybags now, are you? Offering to foot the bill?' Her eyes flickering to Anita's she added, 'What am I? Your next little project to make you feel good about yourself? A bleeding charity case?'

'No, Mum!' Shannon said, shaking her head, incensed that her mum could be so rude to these people when all they were trying to do was help her. 'I saved the money. Me! I gave you half my wages and put half my money away after every shift,' she said proudly, hoping her mum would see how serious she was about this.

Shannon had asked Benny not to mention that he'd offered to match what she'd saved so that her mum could do the programme for longer, because she knew that would be a deal breaker. Her mother would be too proud to accept money for treatment from Benny. Which was ironic, really, as she had no qualms about poncing drinks and money from strangers down at the pub. But that was her mother all over. She had twisted priorities.

'The money is for you, Mum, so that you can get some proper help before it's too late.'

'Oh, nice one. So all this time you've had extra cash stashed away, when we've been forced to scrimp by?'

Without Shannon's extra money each week, they would have been in a much worse state than they currently were. They'd have had no food. They would have been even more behind with the bills, and instead of being grateful that not only had Shannon provided for them, but that she'd put money aside to help her get better, Michelle seemed to completely miss the point, throwing her daughter's kind gesture back in her face.

'I wasn't stashing it away from you… the money was for you. To get you better.'

'And I've told you, it's none of your business!' Michelle screeched. 'What a waste of money! Because that's all it will be, a waste. These fancy clinics only want to take your money. IF, and I mean IF, I ever needed help I'd go through the NHS because I can think of a million better things to spend that kind of money on than this crap!'

'Like what, Mum? What would you spend the money on? Booze and fags? So you could drink and smoke yourself to death?' Shannon said rolling her eyes, knowing full well what her mother would do if she had that sort of cash. She'd drink herself to oblivion.

'You wouldn't get this kind of help on the NHS. The waiting lists are too long, and you won't get the kind of treatment that this place is offering. It's one month, Mum. One month of your life. It could change everything.'

'A month?' Michelle said, appalled. 'I haven't got time to sit around in some treatment centre for a month!'

'Why not?' Shannon cried, angry now that her mother wouldn't even consider it. 'What is it you do that's so important, Mum, apart from lying around in bed most of the day feeling sorry for yourself and getting drunk out of your head the rest of the time?'

She had thought that her mother would jump at the chance to get better. That she'd be grateful that Shannon was trying to help, but all the woman was doing was pretending that she didn't have a problem and throwing all the help she was being offered back in their faces.

'So, what are these two doing here, then? Sitting here gawping at me purely for their own entertainment, are they?' Michelle sneered at the couple, deflecting the attention away from herself; she'd had enough of her daughter's interrogation.

'Michelle…' Anita said, sitting forwards in the chair. 'Shannon just wants the best for you. She loves you dearly and she said that you just need a break. Please don't feel like we are judging you, we're not. We just want to help. That's all. We want her to know she's got our support.'

'I'm her mother, she has all the support she needs right here, thank you very much!' Michelle shook her head, unconvinced by

Anita's declaration. 'So what, you're just here out of the kindness of your hearts, are you? You expect me to believe that?'

Benny nodded to Anita, as if giving her permission to share the real reason that they were so adamant they wanted to help. A reason that they hadn't even shared with Shannon until now.

'My mum was an alcoholic, Michelle. Only she didn't get any help she needed and she died last year. From liver failure. She'd been drinking all her life and the damage was irreversible. In the end, even if she'd wanted to try and save herself, there was nothing she could do. There was nothing any of us could do,' Anita said, giving Shannon's hand a gentle squeeze so the girl would know that she knew exactly what she was going through, because she'd been there herself. The constant worry. The stress it put everyone in. This time, Anita could help. And she and Benny were determined to at least try and make Michelle see sense.

'Well I'm sorry to hear about your mother. But I'm not her. I don't have a problem. Apart from being late!' Stubbing her fag out, Michelle stood up and threw the leaflet down on the coffee table. 'I said no, Shannon, and you can't make me. Now, if you don't all mind, I've got stuff to do.' And with that Michelle stomped from the flat, slamming the front door behind her.

'Oh, well we tried,' Shannon said, defeated. 'I should have known that she wouldn't agree to the treatment. Because deep down she really doesn't believe that there is anything wrong with her, does she? She's lived this way for so long now!'

'Shannon, it's a lot to take in. Let her have a think on things. She might change her mind,' Benny said, getting up and giving the girl a hug.

'It's a big step, admitting that there's a problem,' Anita said, holding Shannon's hands and seeing the upset that lingered in the young girl's eyes. 'It's scary and she probably felt as if she was put on the spot. Give her some time.'

She gave Shannon a kiss and they left the flat. Shannon shut the door behind them. Leaning up against it, she really hoped that they were right and that her mother would come around. For her own sake as much as Michelle's.

CHAPTER FORTY-FOUR

Throwing down the phone on her duvet, annoyed that Kian still wasn't picking up, Shannon grabbed her bag from where she'd tucked it underneath the bed.

She'd been home on her own for hours now and had been hoping that her brother would have popped home so that she could have a word with him about Benny's chip shop being vandalised. Only he still wasn't answering his phone, and as much as Shannon was desperate to convince herself that her brother was too busy with his new so-called mates, she couldn't shake the feeling that he was purposely avoiding her because he knew already about the break-in.

Kian was in deep, she wasn't stupid. The Griffin Boys were bad news. Everyone around here knew exactly what Jax Priestly and his boys were into. They were drug dealers. They were thugs too. Threatening people and waving knives around as if they were untouchable, even from the police. And in some ways they must be, because they were still running the streets, weren't they? And if Kian continued hanging around with them, he was going to mess his life up for good.

Pulling her make-up bag out of her rucksack, she held it in her hand and frowned. The small bag felt light. Deflated. As if it was empty. Which she knew it was, even before she'd unzipped it and looked inside. Her suspicions were right. The money was gone. She checked frantically inside her school bag, in case the money had fallen out. In case she'd somehow stupidly misplaced it, though as she tipped all the contents out, she knew that she hadn't. She was always so careful with the money because she knew how much it meant and how hard she'd had to work for it. It couldn't have just disappeared. And there was only one person who knew about it. Kian.

Throwing the empty bag down onto the floor, Shannon felt physically sick that her brother would do that to her. That he'd stoop so low to steal from her after everything she'd ever done for him. All those years of looking after him and looking out for him, making sure that he was okay and that he had everything he needed. Worse still, he'd taken the money, knowing what Shannon wanted to use it for. He'd ruined their one shot at trying to get their mum better. All he thought about was himself, and how to save his own arse.

The more Shannon thought about it, the angrier she felt. Chances were that he was involved in the chip shop break-in too. Because Benny had been right about that; it was too much of a coincidence, wasn't it, that Kian and some of the Griffin Boys had come to the chippy only a few nights before.

Well if Kian wanted to hang around with Jax and his pathetic mates and start stealing money from his own, then Shannon didn't want anything to do with him. Jumping up from the bed, she grabbed her jacket. It was her money. And she was going to get it back.

CHAPTER FORTY-FIVE

'Well? Where's the money then? And don't say that you haven't got it, Kian. Because the clock's ticking. I told you, twenty-four hours and I meant it, I ain't here for games.' Sitting on Philip's sofa, Jax leaned over the coffee table and snorted a long line of white powder before closing his eyes briefly to enjoy the instant buzz.

'I ain't playing games with you, Jax! Honest. I said I'd get it and I will,' Kian said, part of him glad in a way that when he'd opened Shannon's bag the money wasn't there. She must have moved it. Because he would have taken it; he would have had no choice but to take it, and Shannon would never have trusted him or forgiven him ever again. Even though it was partly her he was doing this all for now.

Opening his eyes a few seconds later, Jax stared at Kian with malice, letting the boy know that his threat still stood. Kian knew it too. Jax could practically see the fear radiating from him.

'Tick tock. Tick Tock.'

High now, Jax was enjoying fucking with the kid. Jax actually liked Kian, despite the fact that the kid kept fucking everything up. Kian had persistence. If anyone would get his money, Kian would. Especially now his sister was one of the stakes. Jax smirked then, glad to have found the boy's Achilles heel. He'd file that one away and no doubt use it again in the very near future.

Because what Kian didn't realise was there would always be a next time. He was in now, and that meant that he couldn't just wipe his debt and walk away. That wasn't how things worked. Kian knew too much. He knew how the gang operated, where they hung out. He knew about the jobs they'd done. The deals they made. Still, Jax wouldn't enlighten the boy on any of those facts until he'd been paid his money. Or he'd been delivered Kian's sister. He'd liked the look of the girl, so either one was fine with him. The situation was a win-win. For Jax anyway.

'When?' Jax said, his steely eyes burning into Kian's.

'Soon, Jax,' Kian lied. He knew there was no way that he could get his hands on that kind of money any time soon. 'I'll do whatever it takes. I'll work night and day for you. I'll make drops, I'll run errands. Whatever it takes until you've made your two grand from me, but just leave my sister out of it, please. She's a good girl. I don't want her dragged into this mess.'

Jax nodded, noting the protective note in Kian's voice as he spoke about his sister. The way that he sounded so desperate for Jax to agree to his proposal. It was actually laughable that the kid had no idea the money from the drop never went missing in the first place, that Jax had had it this whole time. Such a foolproof plan to make these boys realise their priorities and to drag them in so deep that they would never get out. A part of them would always, deep down, feel in debt to Jax. Jax loved that feeling. The elders who he worked for had taught him that lesson. Rule by fear, because obedience is the only chance of survival. And these kids were obedient and compliant, Jax made sure of that. They would do whatever they were told to do, no matter what the outcome. Jax nodded.

'And why should I cut you a break, Kian? Huh? Tell me that. What makes you so special?'

'Because I mean what I'm saying, Jax. You have my word. I'll do whatever you want me to do. But leave Shannon out of it.'

Jax smirked. Wanting to have some fun with Kian he nodded. 'Whatever I want you to do? Okay! Anything?'

Kian nodded. 'Right then, let's put you to the test. Call that mong Philip in here and tell him that you killed his precious furball of a cat. Tell him you lobbed him out the window and watched him splat on the grass below.'

Kian shifted on his feet, wondering if that had really been the fate of Philip's cat, or if Jax was just winding him up. Jax picked up his phone and played a video. Kian closed his eyes, unable to watch as he heard the echoing sound of laughter coming from Jax and his boys as the cat met its horrific fate.

'Anything, you said!' Raising his eyebrow at Kian, he challenged him to do as he had promised. 'And show him the video. Tell him you've got something funny you want to show him.'

Kian paused, unsure if he was able to go through with it. Philip loved his cat more than he loved anything and seeing what Jax and his boys had done – what he was supposed to have done – would probably push the man over the edge. Kian didn't know if he was capable of such cruelty.

'No more chances, Kian. Do it,' Jax instructed him.

'Philip.' Kian coughed, clearing his throat before calling out again, this time louder. 'Philip…'

'Yeah? Sorry, I was just cleaning the kitchen before Karen comes back. I didn't hear you,' Philip said, walking into the lounge and wondering what the boys wanted now.

Kian stared at the bright pink marigolds on his hand. The smell of bleach filled the room.

He closed his eyes, summoning up the courage to do as he was told.

'I've got something funny to show you, mate…' Kian said, his voice trembling.

'What is it, Kian?' Jax said, stifling a snigger and riling the boy.

'I, er, something happened to your cat,' Kian started, unable to look Philip in the eye as he spoke, immediately hating himself when he heard the sudden screech of excitement in Philip's voice at the mention of his cat.

'Mr Bobcat? You found him?'

Kian shook his head, holding out the phone with a shaking hand.

'What's going on?' Philip said, immediately picking up on Kian's discomfort. The boy looked scared. Philip recognised it, because he often felt the very same. And Jax had that look on his face that told Philip he was up to no good.

'I'm sorry… I've got some bad news, mate,' Kian said, quickly changing tack, unable to show him the footage without at least giving the man a fair warning of what he was about to see.

Philip's face dropped, paling instantly as he braced himself to hear the worst. But Jax wasn't going to allow Kian to break it to him gently. He wanted him to recite word for word what he'd told him.

'Stop pussyfooting around, Kian. HA! Get it? Pussy? Go on, Kian, show him the video…'

Kian shook his head, snatching the phone away from Philip as Jax jumped to his feet.

'Show him the fucking video!' Jax commanded. The mood in the room was dark now, the tension building.

'W-W-what's on the video, Kian?' Philip asked. Part of him dreading the answer, because part of him knew.

'Did you do something to Mr Bobcat, Kian?' Philip said quietly, clasping his hands together as he twisted his fingers awkwardly in anticipation of the answer that he didn't want to hear. Everyone in the room was looking his way, waiting for his reaction, so he knew it was going to be bad.

'Jax, please. Not this,' Kian begged.

But Jax had had enough of Kian fucking everything up that he asked him to do.

'He... threw your precious cat out the window, Philip,' Jax shouted, laughing loudly as his words hit Philip like a physical wound.

'No. Kian wouldn't do that. He helped me look for him. He's got a photo of him, haven't you, Kian? You said you'd keep looking for him every day. You promised,' Philip said, shaking his head, his words coming out as a whisper. Tears streamed from his eyes. 'You're all just being mean to me. You're just trying to hurt me. Well you can stop now. I almost believed you,' Philip said, waiting for them all to start laughing at his expense. For Jax to tell the punchline and they could all joke about taking the piss out of him again. But no one in the room spoke.

'He's lying, isn't he, Kian?' Philip said.

Running to the window and leaning out, he scanned the grass, checking to be sure that there was no sign of Mr Bobcat down there. It had been days now, and Mr Bobcat still hadn't come home. And he would have by now; Philip was sure of it. He'd be missing Philip. But not nearly as much as Philip was missing him. As Philip turned back to the room, back to Kian, he saw genuine tears running down the boy's face.

'Please, Kian? Say it's not true.' He could feel the panic rising inside of him that Jax might be actually telling the truth this time.

'I'm sorry, mate. Really I am. I told Kian he was a sick fucker for what he did. I told him you'd be devastated. It's all there on the phone if you don't believe me. Take a look.'

Philip stared at Kian. 'Tell me you're lying,' he begged, dropping to his knees. The pain inside his chest was unbearable. He couldn't make the hurt stop. Sobbing loudly, Philip started smacking himself repeatedly around the head with his locked fists.

Jax smirked. The bloke was a complete nutter. This was the ultimate wind up and using Kian as bait was genius.

'Go on, Philip! Watch it, see for yourself!' Jax said, not realising just how far over the edge they'd just pushed Philip.

Because his cat was all he had. He was all he lived for. And knowing that Mr Bobcat had suffered such a horrific death in the hands of this murderer, Philip was completely broken now. He picked up Jax's knife from the table. It was his turn to fight back.

CHAPTER FORTY-SIX

'It weren't me, Philip. Jax is lying. You know I wouldn't do that to you, mate. I couldn't even show you the video. I've only just heard myself. I had no idea.'

Seeing the blind rage in Philip's eyes, Kian stared around the room for someone to step in and help him and saw Jax raising his hands in his boys' direction, as if instructing them all to step back and not interfere. Kian was on his own. Jax wanted him and Philip to fight. But Philip wasn't thinking straight now. Consumed with grief and fury, he was staring at Kian as if he was going to murder him. Stepping towards Kian, Philip raised the knife.

Kian ran, as fast as he could, out through the flat's front door and along the balcony before taking the stairs down two at a time. He could hear Philip's feet slapping on the steps just behind him. Further up, he could hear Jax and his boys as they followed behind, jeering Philip on to attack him, and Philip, like a puppet on a string, followed the orders obediently.

Kian didn't stop to look back. He needed to get away. His heart was hammering so hard inside his chest that it felt as if it might explode out from his ribcage. His breathing was erratic, coming in short sharp bursts, his lungs feeling as if they were on fire.

'You know I wouldn't hurt Mr Bobcat. He's messing with you, Philip; he's getting you to do his dirty work just like he does with all of us. He plays us all off, and uses us against each other,' Kian gasped desperately, praying that Philip would believe him. Because he had no doubt that Philip was capable of murder tonight. And he was still coming for him. Kian could hear his steps slamming loudly against the concrete floor and the boys behind him shouting and jeering as if this was all just some sort of game. As if they were immune to the danger and bloody violence that was about to come. Kian had no choice but to keep going. *Run.*

He thought about Shannon as he skidded across the muddy verge, heading towards the main door of his block, praying that she would be home, because Shannon would help him. She'd know what to do. He was stupid to ever get involved with Jax and his boys. He realised that now. Even though it was too late. Shannon had always warned him to keep his head down and not to hang out with these people. But Kian thought he knew better. He thought that he could do better for himself. That he could make some real money and show Shannon that he was capable of being the man of the house for once, so that she didn't have to carry the burden of having to contribute to the food and the bills all by herself.

But this life with the Griffin Boys was nothing more than a lie. Sure, he'd get a fancy pair of trainers out of it. A new phone maybe. Some cash. But at what cost? Because so far, he was losing everything. All he really had become was a pawn in Jax's sick, twisted little game. If Kian got a pasting from Philip, or worse still, a knife stuck in him, Jax would just put it all down to teaching Kian a lesson whilst providing the boys with some much-needed entertainment. Jax was a psycho.

He had to get inside. The main doorway was just up ahead. Another ten metres or so and he'd be in. He could put the latch on and lock them all out. It would buy him a few minutes at least until they all kicked it in; enough time to make the stairwell to his flat and get safely inside. He could barricade the flat and call the police. Because he wasn't going to get out of this one alive otherwise. Kian reached for the main door handle but he was too slow. He turned and saw one of Jax's boys next to him.

He slammed his foot against the glass panel and purposely sent Kian flying face down in the entrance hallway. Kian could smell the stale, acrid stench of piss on the cold concrete beneath him. Still, he had hope. Still, he thought that he might make it. If he could just haul his body up from the floor, to make a final run for the stairs…

But now Jax and his boys had encircled him and Philip was there, still clutching the knife.

CHAPTER FORTY-SEVEN

Philip was on him in seconds, finally taking out all his anger, all his pent-up frustration. Raining down brutal kicks and blows that he never thought he had in him.

'Don't all just stand there, help me!' he cried, pleading to the boys standing around him. Their faces twisted with hate and malice as they watched with fascination how the blows kept on coming. Nobody was helping him. Because nobody cared. They all secretly wanted this.

Shielding his head, he cowered on the pissy concrete floor, curling into the foetal position, his body unable to take anymore blows. Yet still they kept coming, hard and fast, making every part of him ache, his arms, legs burning.

It was only when he tried to lift his head that he saw all the blood. That he realised that his body hadn't been punched, it had been punctured. He'd been stabbed. Repeatedly. Too many times to even count.

Philip stepped back, staring down at the mess of the boy in front of him. It was like he'd just stepped out of a trance.

'What have I done?' he screamed, as if seeing the blood for the very first time, wiping his red soaked hands down his shirt before tearing at his hair. 'I didn't mean it. Oh, no, please. I didn't mean to do it. Help me? Please help me!' he called as his victim lay on the floor, bleeding out.

He was staring up at Philip, but Philip's features were starting to blur into nothing. Dizzy now, as the lights started to fade, he realised that he was losing consciousness. The voices around him sounded echoey and far off in the distance.

'Fuck, Philip! Someone call an ambulance. He's killed him.'

They were the last words he heard. He was gone.

CHAPTER FORTY-EIGHT

'Red one. Red one. I need urgent assistance.' DC Murphy radioed for the second time since she'd arrived at the crime scene. She needed some backup, and soon.

'Can everyone please just stand back!' DC Murphy shouted, turning to the crowd of teenagers all closing in around her so that they could eye the bloodshed, as a team of paramedics huddled around the young lad's body, desperately trying to save his life. It didn't look promising.

Lucy turned her gaze back to Philip, now huddled up against the wall, rocking backwards and forwards in his blood-soaked clothes, muttering incoherently that he hadn't meant to kill anyone. The knife that had been discarded on the floor beside him when Lucy got here was now bagged as evidence.

'Thank Christ!' Lucy murmured to herself a few seconds later, hearing the welcome sound of sirens, as backup finally arrived, screeching to a stop directly outside the block. At least one of her fellow officers could hold the crowd of teenagers back and stop them all from filming on their phones, Lucy thought to herself angrily, wondering when these people had become so detached and numb to something so horrific as someone being brutally stabbed.

When had someone's life become nothing more than just an opportunist moment to grab some footage in exchange for more likes and comments on social media?

Turning back to the teenager's lifeless body that lay splayed out on the cold concrete floor of the dingy stairwell, Lucy winced as she eyed the amount of blood that pooled out around him now. Her chest restricted as she thought about being back in that wardrobe as a child and peering out at her mother lying on the bed. *Breathe*, she told herself.

'It's not looking good,' one of the paramedics informed the other. 'His pulse is weak. We're going to have to cut his clothes away to make sure we've stemmed the bleeding from all his wounds. He's still losing too much blood.'

Fighting to keep the crime scene under control, Lucy shouted at the crowd of onlookers once more.

'I said stand back!' she yelled again, losing her patience, as she tried to make room for the paramedics who were working desperately to save the boy, flinching as she saw them peeling away the clothing from the boy's blood-soaked body, exposing his many wounds.

She should be immune to seeing scenes like this by now. She might have only been on the force for eighteen months, but stabbings had become almost a daily occurrence these days in London.

It was very much all part of the day's work for Lucy but it never got any easier to deal with, especially for her. Because she didn't just see the victim lying there. She saw her mum.

And it took her back there again, to all those years ago. Gulping down the hot, acrid bile that threatened at that back of her throat, she tried to push the image of her mum's butchered body from her mind. She was angry now.

These kids running the streets with knives had no idea of the consequences of their reactions. They had no idea how their victims' families would suffer greatly for ever more. They were just wannabe gangsters, some of them as young as eleven or twelve years old.

Wearing their crimes like badges of honour. To most of them, this was nothing more than a game. At least, that was probably how it started out. Until they were in too deep and it became all about survival.

'One of his main arteries in his leg has been severed. He's lost too much blood,' one of the paramedics said, confirming to his colleague what they were all already thinking. That they were too late: there was nothing more they could do. Glancing out of the main doors and across the grass in front of the flats, Lucy could see the Air Ambulance circling before going in to land.

This was the best shot the kid had, and Lucy prayed silently that the boy would make it, despite the predicted prognosis and his already greying skin. His eyes were staring off into the distance, already vacant.

'His pulse is weakening.' The evident panic in the paramedic's voice pulled Lucy back from her trance. She could see the crew from the Air Ambulance running towards them now.

'Kian?' The shout made Lucy turn her head towards the stairwell. Spotting the distraught girl running down the steps, she recognised her as the girl from the break-in at the chip shop.

'Kian? Please God, no, don't let it be Kian!' the girl shrieked, as she frantically took in the scene that unfolded in front of her, the paramedics huddled around a body on the floor. She tried to get a look at her brother but all she could see was the outline of a body, a dark splay of blood seeping out all around him.

'No, Kian! God, no!' she screamed, collapsing then.

Lucy put her arm around the girl's shoulders and hugged her tightly as DS Morgan and a couple of other officers joined the crime scene. Lucy nodded to Morgan, pointing over to where Philip sat still huddled in the corner. She'd let Morgan take the boy in. Right now, she was needed here.

'My brother, is he dead? Is my brother dead?' Shannon screeched.

'They're doing everything they can,' Lucy said, shaking her head, not wanting to tell the girl just how critical the situation was.

'He can't die. He can't leave me,' Shannon sobbed as the paramedics placed the body on the stretcher ready to take him on board the Air Ambulance.

Then she saw the look on one of the paramedics' faces and caught the shake of his head to his colleague. He called the time of death.

The next noise that came from Shannon's mouth was deafening. A loud, agony-filled wail like that of a wounded animal. The noise so brutal, so raw that even Officer Murphy felt her chest restrict at the poor girl's visible heartbreak.

'Let's get you home, yeah? I can get a family liaison officer to come and sit with you. Is there anyone else at home? Your mother or father?'

Shannon didn't answer. Instead her eyes were fixed on the stretcher as it was carried past her and out the door.

'Kian's not dead,' Shannon whispered.

'I'm so sorry…' Lucy said, knowing what a shock it must be, and how the girl wouldn't want to believe the truth.

'No. He's not dead. That's not my brother.' This time her tears were those of relief.

'Shan? Shan?'

A voice called out from the crowd that was being pushed back and controlled by police officers.

'Kian? Oh, Thank God!' Shannon said, clambering up from the floor, overcome with emotion.

Turning again to the body on the trolley that was just about to be wheeled to the helicopter, Shannon saw the victim's face. It was Jax.

CHAPTER FORTY-NINE

'Okay everyone, gather round!' DS Morgan said, heading up the debriefing back at CID.

'The murder victim's name is Jax Priestly. Eighteen years old and the leader of the gang the Griffin Boys. We still don't as yet have any leads for who he was working for; however, a significant haul of weapons was seized following the murder that took place in the vicinity of the residence where Jax Priestly was reported to be temporarily residing, in the days leading up to his death, according to the statement made by both Philip Penfold and Kian Winters. Weapons that we managed to recover include a Taser, a cosh, and several knives, as well as a very nasty looking two-foot zombie knife…'

'Sounds delightful,' Lucy said, rolling her eyes disparagingly.

'Or head splitters as they are so fondly nicknamed, for obvious reasons,' DC Holder interrupted. He was back from medical leave, after being diagnosed with concussion following the attack he'd suffered on the Griffin Estate just days before. The recent murder was of no surprise to him. The Griffin Estate was rife with gangs and he'd known it was only a matter of time until something like this happened. 'Appropriately named, I guess, seeing as these "kids" seem to think they are living through some kind of zombie apocalypse, going by the amount of knife attacks happening now on the daily. That's the real head splitter.'

'Philip Penfold, the perpetrator,' DS Morgan continued, and raised his eyebrows at the term now that he knew the full ordeal Philip Penfold suffered. 'Twenty-three years of age and suffering from physical disability and mental illness. He has been detained for Priestley's murder, but I believe once we get word back from the CPS, the attack will be classed as self-defence.'

DS Morgan turned to his team now to reiterate what he had learned so far in the investigation. His team had worked flat out on the case, through the night and for most of the day. 'Philip Penfold gave a very long and detailed interview about how his flat had been used by Jax Priestly and his boys as a cuckoo house. They held Penfold hostage in his home against his will and terrorised him both physically and mentally. This happened repeatedly, over many months. Jax Priestly's mother, Karen Priestly, is Philip's carer, which is how we believe the boys gained access to Penfold in the first place.'

Lucy shook her head sadly, recalling how she'd looked over at Philip when he'd been huddled on the floor at the murder scene and wondered what had gone through his head to make him attack someone like that. The man had been pushed to a brink of no going back. He'd committed the ultimate crime in order to try and free himself from the gang.

'Penfold claims that he was being tormented and manipulated by Priestly. And going on the evidence found on the mobile phones that we confiscated from some of the gang members prior to their arrests this evening too, it's clear he's suffered greatly. We have got several videos documenting acute violence used against the man.'

'Poor sod. He did us a favour, if you ask me. As bad as he might feel, that's another scrote off the streets. It's just a shame there's such a massive paper trail after an incident like this. Such a waste,' Holder added with disdain.

'I'd go as far to say that Jax Priestly is also a victim in all of this, Holder. Of sorts. He would have been recruited just the same by a gang much higher up in the chain than him,' DS Morgan reasoned. 'He would have been forced into recruiting the younger kids so that he could run County Lines networks for his bosses – with far bigger repercussions and reprisals than he would have been used to in the smaller gang on the estate. That's how these operations work. They are always enforced with fear. They are taught to target and recruit children who are intellectually disabled or from problematic home lives, descriptions which Philip and Kian both fit.'

DS Morgan shook his head. He'd seen it time and time again.

'These two lads have been coerced, controlled and threatened into committing crimes against their better understanding or will. Kian Winters will be protected too. I'm almost certain that he won't receive a criminal record.' He made his way to the end of the white boards and pointed to the list he'd made.

'Following the search of the cuckoo house, this is the full list of items seized as evidence. We seized almost five thousand pounds' worth of drugs – Cocaine, MDMA, and cannabis – as well as other drug paraphernalia, including cling film, plastic pouches and weighing scales. There was also almost fifteen thousand pounds in cash and in total six weapons. All in all, an excellent day's work!'

'Congratulations, you survived your first week! Though the same almost couldn't be said for me,' Holder said, pointing to the massive bump on his head, and the nasty scar that was starting from the stitches he'd had to have following the assault from the two boys on the estate. 'Though I suppose I have you to thank for that.'

'No worries,' Lucy grinned. 'Happy to come to your aid. I mean, they were pretty nasty bastards. For two ten-year-old kids…'

'Small details, Murphy! Small details.' Holder rolled his eyes but laughed then, too, taking the officer's humour in jest as it was intended. His colleagues had been ribbing him all morning over being attacked by two kids.

'I take it no one's filled DC Murphy here in on the rules of new recruits on the team surviving their first full week in CID?'

Lucy narrowed her eyes and shook her head dubiously.

'If you make it through your first week on the job in one piece, then you get to join us in the bar. Call it a celebration, if you like…'

'Well, that doesn't sound like such a bad rule to me.' Lucy smiled. 'If anything, getting wasted after the week we've just had sounds like the dream!'

'Wasted! Did you hear that everyone?' Holder grinned. 'We'll all hold you to that. Because the rule of thumb is last one in buys all the drinks tonight.'

Holder winked, grabbing his coat and starting to make a swift exit with the rest of the team. 'We're warming to you, Murphy! We'll save you a seat, yeah!'

'I take it that's the seal of approval, is it, Sarge?' Lucy said after the rest of the team had filtered out of the office, all eager to have a few drinks and let their hair down after a manic week of policing. 'Holder's finally accepting me on the team. Despite my eighteen months' experience and the fact that I'm a girl.' Lucy grinned at her boss.

'Holder can be a royal pain in the arse at times, as I'm sure you've already noticed. But he's a good DC. It's a shame he doesn't realise that it's his quick mouth that's been holding him back, not other officers taking "his" place,' Morgan said, grabbing his jacket and walking Lucy to the door.

'On a serious note, though, well done. A result like this on your first week here is excellent work. Truly.' DS Morgan meant it, too. He'd taken his time going back through Lucy's application and file, along with the cold case file from her mother's murder years ago, and he'd noted how Lucy hadn't mentioned it anywhere on record.

He'd guessed that she hadn't wanted to disclose it, because that would set her up from day one on the force as a victim. And Lucy was anything but that. She was a fighter, a survivor and more than that she was a fantastic officer. And until Lucy wanted to broach the subject with him, DS Morgan would respect her decision, and keep the fact that he'd been an attending officer at the scene to himself.

'I mean it. I have very high hopes for you, Lucy. I think you are going to go far.'

'Thanks, Sarge,' Lucy beamed, glad that her efforts this week hadn't gone unnoticed.

'And as much as Holder loves the sound of his own smug voice, he was right about one thing…' DS Morgan said, pursing his mouth as if he almost didn't want to say it out loud.

'What's that then, Sarge?'

'We take the rule of the newest recruit buying all the drinks very seriously. And let me warn you, that lot can drink.'

Lucy laughed as DS Morgan switched the lights off and he and Lucy went to join the rest of the team in the pub.

'It's a small price to pay to keep you lot sweet, Sarge!'

CHAPTER FIFTY

'Come in, come in!' Benny Lynch said, giving Lucy a welcoming smile as he showed her into his home.

'This is Sarah Buckley, she's the Targeted Youth Support Officer,' Lucy said, introducing the woman to Benny. As soon as Lucy had heard that the officer would be sent out to carry out a Families First Assessment for Shannon and Kian, she had asked her sergeant if she could attend too, wanting an excuse to check on the two children and put her mind at ease that they were both doing all right.

'Your house is gorgeous!' Lucy said, looking around in awe at the immaculately decorated entrance hall of the Victorian terraced house.

'Thank you,' Benny beamed. 'I'd love to take the credit, but the decor is mainly Anita's doing. The place needed a complete renovation when we moved in, and apparently Wandsworth is on the up. Though I'm not sure she's on the money on that one, but don't tell her I said so…' Lucy smiled. 'She's done a blinding job on the chippy too. Thank God the insurance paid up. The place is doing better than ever. Come on through, they're just in the kitchen having some breakfast. Anita's making them pancakes. Though she's cooking for the thousands, and I've never seen so many choices of toppings. Typically, I'm only allowed to look at them. She's made me a nice, healthy omelette instead!' Benny crossed his eyes playfully as he patted his stomach.

Lucy couldn't help but laugh.

'Anita, love! DC Murphy's here and the Youth Support Officer, Sarah Buckley.'

'Hello, DC Murphy. Hi Sarah!' Anita smiled, standing at the cooker and tipping the last of the pancakes from the pan and onto a plate just as the young officer stepped into the kitchen. 'Just in time. I've made far too many probably! Do you fancy joining us?'

'Ahh, I've just eaten. Otherwise I would have loved to. They smell delicious. And please, call me Lucy,' Lucy said, before making her way over to the breakfast bar where Shannon and Kian were sitting and giving them both a friendly hug.

'How are you guys doing?'

'We're doing good, thanks!' Shannon smiled, grateful to Lucy for keeping her word and checking in on them like she'd promised she would. She liked Lucy.

The officer had been so kind to her the night that Jax Priestly had been murdered. Lucy had come and found Shannon and Kian at the station and bought them both some hot chocolate, before sitting with them for hours as they both made their statements. Shannon had found herself opening up to the officer afterwards too, and telling her all about their home life. It was as if the night's events had just brought everything to the surface for Shannon. Just knowing how close her brother had been to being the victim of a fatal stabbing. She'd broken down and Lucy had helped her pick up all the pieces, just by being there and listening. She'd told Shannon that what she'd witnessed that night would affect her more than she could realise and that it was okay to ask for help. She didn't have to do all of this on her own anymore. Shannon had asked Lucy to call Benny and he'd kindly not only offered to pick them both up from the station, but he'd also offered them both a place to stay.

'I'll tell you what, you guys all help yourselves!' Anita said, placing the pancake stack in the middle of the table, before dishing up a couple of plates for her girls. 'Come on, Poppy and Jasmine, let's have ours in front of the telly, shall we, and let Lucy and Sarah have some time alone with Daddy, Shannon and Kian.'

'Can we watch cartoons?' Poppy squealed, as Jasmine jumped for joy at the rare offer of being allowed to eat their food in front of the TV.

'Course we can!' Anita smiled, leading the girls out of the room as Benny shut the door behind them.

'Do you fancy a cuppa, ladies? The kettle's just boiled,' Benny asked the two officers.

'Can I just pop to your loo first, Benny?' Sarah Buckley said, smiling at Lucy to let her know that she had a few minutes to chat with the kids off the record before she began her official assessment.

'Thanks,' Lucy said, appreciating the gesture before nodding at Benny. 'Yeah, I'd love one. Milk and one sugar, please.' She turned her attention back to Shannon and Kian then, while she had the chance.

'So, how's your mum doing? You must be pleased that she agreed to do the programme in the end? Benny said that she'll be in there for twenty-eight days?'

Shannon nodded. 'She agreed to do the full month. She didn't really have much choice in the end, though.' She smiled at Benny then. 'Benny told her if she didn't agree to doing the month's programme, he'd tell the police that she'd stolen my money,' Shannon said, having found out later that night when the police had finally tracked down Michelle Winters to the local pub. Wasted and buying everyone in the bar drinks with her newfound fortune, the woman had been boasting about stealing money from her own daughter. Hearing news of her son Kian's involvement with a murder had sobered the woman up pretty quickly though.

'I mean, Benny wouldn't have grassed on her, but the threat of it alone did the trick. She believed him. Though to be honest, I think Mum actually felt really bad about taking the money from me. She kept crying and telling me how sorry she was. She kept trying to hug Kian, too. I think it was finally the wake-up call she needed.'

'Not only that, but I think your mum realised deep down what a good thing you'd done for her, Shannon, working all that time and saving up your money. Your example was her incentive to start doing right by you both!' Benny said, placing the tea on the table top and giving both the children a hug.

'And I tell you what, I know it's only been a few days, but we've loved having you both here. Anita and the girls do too. Anita is in her element, bless her, running around the place making us all these family feasts!' Benny laughed, making a joke that all the food was even more reason for him wanting the kids to stay as he picked up a pancake and shoved it quickly into his mouth, one eye on the kitchen door to make sure there was no sign of Anita catching him. 'Seriously, though, you are both welcome to stay here, as long as you want, you know that, don't you? Even when your mum comes out, if you want a bit more time here while she finds her feet.'

'Thanks, Benny!' Shannon said, giving the man another huge grin. He and Anita had been a godsend the past week and Shannon would be for ever grateful for all their support. To her, they were family now and always would be.

'What about Philip?' Kian said, looking to Lucy.

Lucy had noticed that the boy's plate of food was still untouched and she wondered if Philip's ordeal was still weighing heavily on Kian's mind.

'What's going to happen to him, do you know anything yet?'

Lucy nodded. 'It was one of the reasons that I wanted to come here today. I wanted to see how you guys were doing, of course. But I promised you I'd keep you up to date with news on Philip… And I'm pleased to say, he is going to be just fine, so please don't worry. The police and the CPS are treating the attack as self-defence,' Lucy said, glad that her boss had been right about the outcome. 'Philip's doing really well now he's got the proper help and support that he needs.'

'Has he gone back to the Griffin Estate?' Kian asked, knowing how much he himself was dreading having to go back there eventually. Staying with Benny and Anita, even though it was just a few streets away from the Griffin Estate, felt worlds apart from their lives there.

Lucy shook her head. 'We've placed him in temporary accommodation for now, but our Social Care team are relocating him to a new home, well away from the estate. We call it safeguarding,' Lucy said, hoping to reassure Kian that the man was safe now. 'And between us, it's a much nicer place for him. It's a special unit for people with physical disabilities or mental illness. He'll have a lot more support around him there, too. He won't feel so isolated or alone.'

Kian nodded, instantly feeling relieved then, because as much as Jax had been the ringleader, he knew there would be repercussions for Philip, from Jax's boys, if he went back there. That was how the estate worked. The man's life would have been made hell.

'I told him that you were asking after him, too, Kian!' Lucy said, knowing how distressed Kian had been on the night of the stabbing. How Philip had been tricked into believing that Kian had been the one to murder his cat. How it had almost been Kian on the end of that frenzied attack.

'He told me to tell you that he's sorry that he chased you. And that he knew that you didn't hurt Mr Bobcat, because you were the only one who was nice to him. He said he'd known that the whole time but Jax had manipulated him. That's why he turned on Jax when he did. Philip just finally saw red, because Jax had been the main instigator and tormentor throughout all of his abuse. Philip didn't mean to kill him, he just wanted it all to stop,' Lucy said sadly, shaking her head at the tragedy of it all before finishing her tea and standing up to leave.

'Oh, and Philip doesn't know this yet, but I spoke to the house manager at the new centre that he's moving in to, and they've given him permission to have a pet. I wanted to ask you, Kian, if you'd fancy helping me pick him out a new kitten? I thought that maybe, if you wanted to, we could both take it to him when he's settled in, as a nice surprise for him?'

'Yeah, I'd love that!' Kian said, finally cracking a smile then and picking up a forkful of food. He wanted to make things up to Philip and show him that he wasn't like Jax and the other boys.

'Right, looks like I'll be back in touch very soon then!' Lucy said, as Sarah Buckley came back into the room. 'I'm going to leave you guys to your assessment. You enjoy all those pancakes.' She gave the kids both another hug before Benny showed her back out again.

'I'm so pleased to see them both doing so well. I can't thank you and Anita enough for that,' Lucy said as she reached the front door.

'Oh, it's nothing at all. They're good kids,' Benny said, blushing at the officer's praise.

Lucy shook her head. 'It's not nothing, trust me. You and your wife are doing more than you can ever realise for those two kids. I wish there were more people out there like you!'

'Well, it's like Anita's always saying. Some people just need a break.'

CHAPTER FIFTY-ONE

'Well I have to say, this place seems really nice, Winnie,' Vivian beamed as she, Lucy and Winnie all sat together in the day room at Treetops Care Home. So far, they were all very impressed with the place, even Winnie, though they all knew that the woman would never actually admit that fact out loud. But the fact that she hadn't complained once since she'd arrived here a few hours ago, spoke volumes.

'It's more like a swanky hotel! Don't you think, Lucy? Going on lovely outings and doing activities, and they have wine and cheese tasting nights and bridge and carpet bowls. I wouldn't mind getting away from my crazy lot at home and staying here for a few days myself, Winnie!' Vivian laughed.

'I'm not staying here for a few days, am I, Lucy? We're going home, aren't we? You said,' Winnie said anxiously, checking once again that that hadn't been a trick to lure her here for the day, and that Lucy wasn't just going to leave her here.

'Of course we're going home, Nan. We're only here for a few hours. And when you come next time you're going to be here for the day, remember? We're going to take this really slowly and make sure you're a hundred per cent happy.'

Winnie nodded. She actually liked this place. It wasn't any-where near as bad as she'd thought it was going to be in her head. And Vivian was right, it was very fancy. Winnie could certainly get used to spending a little bit of time here occasionally. Especially if it meant putting Lucy's mind at ease when she had to work.

'They are going to pick you up in their minibus and bring you home again when I've finished work. It will be lovely for you. You'll make lots of new friends,' Lucy said, watching as her nan took a sip of her tea.

Vivian, as always, had been right. Her nan would benefit greatly from the daycare the centre offered. It was a much better option than trying to introduce her to another home carer.

Here, her nan would receive round the clock care from qualified nurses, trained in dementia care, as well as being able to spend time with any new friends she made. It was the ideal solution before the centre started to introduce her nan to respite care. The nurse had told Lucy that her nan could stay here overnight and for the odd few days here and there, until the place became as familiar as possible, given her condition. So that Winnie would feel at home before she eventually needed full-time residential care. By then, Lucy would be more comfortable with the arrangement too. It was going to be an adjustment for them both.

'The carers seem really nice here, don't they, Nan? They said that you were settling in nicely this morning. I hear when me and Vivian went for a coffee, you had a little go at playing bingo? Did you have fun?'

'Fun? Oh, yes. I only bleeding won it, didn't I? Got a full house and won a little box of chocolates.' Winnie tapped her nose. 'Between us, I think I was one of the youngest ones in there. I'm too quick for them, Lucy. Half of them have got such dodgy eyesight, that by the time they saw the numbers on the paper, I was already done. I'd crossed them off and was out of my chair before anyone else got a chance.'

Lucy smiled then at the bolshiness of her nan.

'Skimped a bit on the prizes though. You only get four little chocolates in a box,' Winnie said, turning her nose up at the prize she'd won. 'And they tasted like that cheap Easter egg chocolate. You know that stuff that burns your throat when you swallow it down. Ever so sickly...'

'Oh, I bet they're not that bad. Did you save us any?' Lucy asked, in her element at times like this when her nan seemed her old self. Full of life and all of her opinions, quick with her wit and her words. And as far as Lucy was concerned that called for a celebration. Chocolates were a good start, except, glancing around the chair where her nan was sitting, Lucy couldn't spot any.

'Oh, they're all gone. I told you, there were only four. I ate them myself.' Winnie flashed a cheeky smile at her granddaughter then. 'That's what happens when you get to my age, Lucy. You can shovel a whole box of choccies down your neck and who's going to stop you? Huh? No one.'

'Oh, without a doubt. Stand between a woman and her chocolates, they wouldn't dare,' Vivian chimed in, pleased to see Winnie on such good form. She'd been worried about the change making her anxious. The woman needed her routine more than ever at the moment.

But Lucy was right, a smooth gradual transition certainly seemed the right way forwards.

'I'm going to have to get off, but thanks for letting me join you guys. It's a lovely place! And when you start doing your daycare, Winnie, I can pop in and have a cup of tea with you still, can't I? If you'll have me?' Vivian said, a rare tinge of emotion in her voice, as she stood up and kissed the older woman on her cheek.

'Of course she'll have you, Vivian. You just try and get rid of us.' Lucy squeezed the woman's hand, reminding herself that

Vivian cared about her nan deeply too. It was a nice feeling. It made Lucy feel as if she wasn't so alone.

'See you all soon!'

Lucy watched as Vivian made her way out of the room, leaving her and her nan alone.

'When am I coming here for the day again?' Winnie asked, which again made Lucy smile as she heard the enthusiasm in the woman's tone. She clearly approved of the place.

'Thursday, Nan. I'm going to see those children from the Griffin Estate. Do you remember the ones I told you about? Shannon and Kian Winters?'

Winnie nodded, vaguely recalling something about two children from the estate, though she couldn't remember exactly what.

'They are both helping me choose a kitten for that man I told you about, Philip Penfold. The poor man whose cat was killed.'

'Ohh, yes. Terrible business all of that. Didn't it get run over?' Winnie said ruefully, shaking her head.

Lucy went to correct her nan, but decided not to bother. Her nan didn't seem to be listening anymore, anyway. She was back to staring ahead of her again, out into space, an expression on her face as if she was lost in her own dark thoughts.

'Nan? Are you okay?' Lucy said gently after a few minutes.

Winnie's next words surprised her.

'That estate was a bad place…' Winnie said quietly, shaking her head as if trying to shake the bad memories out with each movement. Her mind was on the exact place that Lucy had just been thinking of too.

'I see your mum all the time, do you know that? All the time. Every room of the house. Every doorway. I smell her floral perfume and her coconut shampoo. And sometimes I feel as if she's really there. As if I could reach out my hand and physically touch her.'

Lucy bit her lip, worried about whether or not her nan was becoming confused again. Winnie looked over at Lucy then, her watery blue eyes meeting hers.

'I know what you're thinking. That I'm mad as a box of frogs. But I don't mean like that. I mean that I see her. Really see her. Every time that I close my eyes. How she was, you know. Back then. Before.' Winnie gave a small smile at the memory of her beautiful daughter. 'She was like you in a lot of ways, you know. Only she had my temper. God help us, the rows we used to have when she was a teenager! She was always so strong-willed and fiery. You know, she would have been so proud of how you turned out, Lucy. She loved you so much, do you know that?'

Lucy nodded, frightened to speak in case she broke the spell. It had been so long since her nan had spoken about her mum like this. Properly spoken about her; not mumbled confused ramblings but real memories.

'When you were little, Lucy. After *it* happened,' her nan said, still not able to say the words out loud. 'You were so angry. I don't know if you remember because you were so young. But that's when I really saw her in you then. How headstrong you could be, in your own quiet way. You told me once, that when you were bigger you were going to be a police lady and you were going to catch all the bad people. All the bad men.' Winnie laughed at that and shook her head.

'I don't know if you'd even remember. But I thought to myself, back then, how you've got the same fire burning inside of you, just like she had. And then I tried to talk you out of it, of course. I kept harping on at you to be a bleeding hairdresser or something instead. Because I didn't want you to put yourself in anymore danger, mixing with nasty, cruel people. You'd already been through enough. But I should have known that once you made your mind up there'd be no reasoning with you! And look at you now, eh? You did it. You're there. Making a difference, just like you said you would.'

Winnie held out her hand and wrapped her fingers around Lucy's, looking at her granddaughter proudly.

'I guess I thought that you being around that kind of life would make you more vulnerable. I was scared something bad would happen to you, too. And I couldn't bear the thought of anything happening to you, Lucy. Not after your mother…'

Lucy nodded, understanding exactly what her nan was saying. She sometimes felt it, too, herself. The fear of walking into the unknown, of dealing with people and situations that could be so volatile and angry. Seeing all the poverty and depravity of some people's reality, first-hand. It was a hard job and, in time, it could grind you down. Lucy was well aware of that.

Winnie squeezed Lucy's hand tightly then, as she gave the young woman a warm smile. 'But you know what, it takes a special person to do what you do. After everything.'

'Oh Nan…' Lucy said, about to play down the compliment, but Winnie shut her down, shaking her head, and ordering Lucy's silence.

'You need to hear this, Lucy. Please. Because I know I'm not well. And I know sometimes I forget the things that I want to say. But I know what I need to say now,' Winnie said seriously, now staring Lucy dead in the eyes. 'You'll never catch him. You know that, don't you? The man who killed your mother.'

Lucy felt her chest constrict at her nan's only mention in all these years of her mother's killer. Twenty years it had been between them, unspoken. And now, her nan was talking about it. About him, and there was a lump in Lucy's throat so large she was unable to speak.

'He got away with it, Lucy. All those years ago. And no matter how many times you beat yourself up about the details or you try and wrack your brains for some small bit of information, it doesn't matter anymore. It's done. You did this job because of your mum. Not because of *him*. You wanted justice for the victims. You wanted to be a good person and help people when you can. It's not just about catching the bad people anymore.'

Lucy nodded, crying openly now. Her nan always had a way of reading her as if she was an open book. As if all her thoughts had spilled out of her head and were neatly arranged on a page for her nan to see. It had taken all these years for them finally to be able to talk about what had happened. A conversation, that ever since her nan had got ill, Lucy had never thought they'd have.

'I know it's stupid, and I know it will never happen, but sometimes I wonder what would happen if I saw him again. Would I remember what he looks like, if I saw him somewhere? Because I look all the time, Nan. Every time we get called out on a job. Every pub or cafe I go into. Every street I walk down. I'm constantly searching for his face. Only I don't know what his face looked like. I can't remember. It's like my brain just won't allow me to go there!'

Lucy was shaking now at finally admitting to her nan the thoughts that tormented her so greatly.

'Oh, you don't even have to explain how that feels, darling, let me tell you. My brain won't allow me to go bloody anywhere at all,' Winnie chuckled lightly.

'I feel like I let her down, Nan. Because I saw him. I was the only witness, only I couldn't give the police anything. Because I can't remember and in my head all I saw was a monster.'

'Because he *was* a monster, Lucy. And you were just a young child. You were only five years old and you were absolutely terrified. The doctors always said back then that it was a normal response. For you to block it out. In order to function, in order to survive.'

Lucy nodded reluctantly.

'And that's what you did, Lucy. You survived. We both survived. What I'm trying to say, is…' Winnie squeezed Lucy's hand affectionately. 'You can't help her, Lucy. It's done. She's gone. He's gone too. Stop tormenting yourself. You're an excellent police officer and already look at the two kids you've helped. You did that. You! And Christ knows how many more people after them you'll be helping. You are making a difference. This is your calling. But you've got to let your mum go. It's time, darling.'

She wiped her eyes with a tissue, just as the nurse who had been looking after them today came back in the room.

'Right, now, Winnie,' Nurse Hamilton said with a broad smile and a no-nonsense tone. 'I'm sure it's just a little mix-up, but Brenda Crawford said that her bingo prize has gone missing. A little box of chocolates. I'm just doing the rounds and asking everyone. I'm not accusing you, darling, but I have to ask. You haven't seen them by any chance, have you?'

Lucy stared at her nan in disbelief as she put on her best show of innocence. Sitting upright in her chair as if taking great offence to the accusation, Winnie widened her eyes, feigning innocence and shaking her head.

'Chocolates? Oh God, no! I hate chocolate. They give me hives.'

Nurse Hamilton stared back at Winnie, then looked to Lucy who, unlike her nan, wasn't so brazen faced about lying to the carer and diverted her gaze to the floor, confirming the woman's suspicions.

'Well, maybe you could just have a think for us, Winnie?' Nurse Hamilton said lowering her voice. 'Because it might have just been a bit of a mix-up! You might have just been a bit confused, love.'

She winked at Winnie, before looking pointedly down at the floor to where the corner of the chocolate box peeped from under the chair, where Winnie hadn't hidden it as well as she thought she had.

'I'll come back in a bit. Maybe you might have remembered something by then.' Nurse Hamilton raised her eyebrows playfully before leaving the room.

'Nan!' Lucy said, shaking her head in disbelief. 'You said that you won those chocolates!'

Winnie shrugged brazenly. 'Well, I ate them, didn't I? So technically I did win them. Besides, Brenda doesn't need them, trust me. The woman's got more meat on her than the window at the local butcher's. I was doing the old girl a favour, Lucy.'

'Nan, that's stealing!'

Then with a little mischievous wink, Winnie said, 'What are you going to do, girl? Arrest me?'

A LETTER FROM CASEY

Dear reader,

I want to say a huge thank you for choosing to read *No Escape*. If you did enjoy it, and want to keep up to date with all my latest releases, just sign up at the following link. Your email address will never be shared and you can unsubscribe at any time.

www.bookouture.com/casey-kelleher

I loved writing about DC Lucy Murphy and all the interesting characters' paths she crossed at the notorious Griffin Estate. Winnie Murphy was a particular favourite of mine with her sharp wit and her fierce love of her granddaughter.

I hope you loved *No Escape* and, if you did, I would be very grateful if you could write a review. I'd love to hear what you think, and it makes such a difference helping new readers to discover one of my books for the first time.

I love hearing from my readers – your messages and photos of the books always make my day! Please feel free to get in touch on my Facebook page, or through Instagram, Twitter or my website.

Thanks,
Casey Kelleher

OfficialCaseyKelleher

@CaseyKelleher

caseykelleher

www.caseykelleher.co.uk

ACKNOWLEDGEMENTS

Many thanks to my brilliant editor Therese Keating. It's been an absolute pleasure working alongside you! I really appreciate all your advice and loved your feedback on the storyline, particularly your comments about Winnie Murphy, bless her! I'm glad you loved her as much as I did.

Special thanks to Noelle Holten, as always one of the most supportive people in this industry. I am so blessed to have you doing the PR for my books and for your friendship! Thanks also to the rest of the Bookouture team, it really is a pleasure to be published with you. Biggest shout out to the Bookouture authors too, that I've been so lucky to meet along the way. For all the giggles, and for keeping me sane!

Huge thanks also to all of those at the scene of the crime. You guys are the best!

Special mention to the real-life Lucy Murphy, my bestie! Who has always been so super supportive of everything I do. I still think we should have used the photo of you in your leopard print get-up on the front cover ;)

Thank you to David Gaylor, Peter James' real life Roy Grace for all your help and advice when it came to police procedures, as well as Sarah Adams, for allowing me to pick your brains about County Lines. You both were super helpful. Thank you so much!

To all my fantastic readers and book bloggers. Thank you so much for all your kind words about my books. You are the very reason I write; without you, none of this would have been possible. I love receiving your feedback and messages, so please do keep them coming!

As always, I'd like to thank my extremely supportive friends and family for all the encouragement that they give me along the way. The Coopers, the Kellehers, the Ellises. And to all my lovely friends.

Finally, a big thank you to my husband Danny. My rock! Much love to Ben, Danny, and Kyle. And not forgetting our two little fur-babies/writer's assistants, Sassy and Miska.

Made in the USA
Columbia, SC
16 February 2022

56348473R00171